CRUSHES & CHRISTMAS

Crushes & Christmas

K.E. Monteith

A Snowfall Valley Novel

Crushes & Christmas

K.E. Monteith

Also by K.E. Monteith

ISBN: 9798330392032

Cover designed by: K.E. Monteith

For all my queer worryworts. Orgasms and Prozac can help.

Contents

The Playlist

- Last Christmas - Carly Rae Jepsen
- Wanna Be Missed - Hayley Kiyoko
- IDK How To Talk To Girls - Beth McCarthy
- Close To You - Gracie Abrams
- Strawberry Crush - Tanner Adell
- Guilty Pleasure - Chappell Roan
- My Only Wish (This Year) - Tia Kofi, Priyanka
- Girls - Girl In Red
- False God - Taylor Swift
- A Nonsense Christmas - Sabrina Carpenter
- Red Wine Supernova - Chappell Roan
- My Favorite Time Of Year - PeteMasitti
- Lover - Taylor Swift
- You Make It Feel Like Christmas - Gwen Stefani, Blake Shelton
- Snow Angel - Renee Rapp
- Coffee - Chappell Roan
- Kiss Me - Sixpence None The Richer
- Call It What You Want - Taylor Swift
- II Most Wanted - Beyonce, Miley Cyrus

ICYMI

The Snowfall Valley Series is a set of interconnected standalones. You don't have to read them in order if you don't want to. Here's all you need to know for Shea & Margo's story:

- Shea came out to her parents as a lesbian in high school and has not had a relationship with them since
- Shea spent most of her high school days with the Hartley's after coming out, her best friend's family
- Margo is Shea's best friend's little sister
- Margo graduated in the spring with her master's in library science
- Shea often has a flask on

Author's Note

Please note that this book contains sexually explicit content, mentions of homophobic parents, and a brief detailing of an unhealthy relationship to alcohol/borderline alcoholism.

1

SHEA

The last place that really felt like home was my childhood bedroom when I was 11. My sheets were purple, I had a combo TV/DVD player nestled in the corner of my dresser, there were girl band posters taped all over the walls, and the floor was cluttered with everything from clothes to books to stuffed animals. And most importantly, I was completely unaware that I was a raging lesbian.

In comparison, my adult apartment was … different. Nothing was hung up on the walls, all my furniture was cheap and colorless, and there wasn't a single thing out of place. Well, minus the cups that littered the coffee table and kitchen counter. But I looked at that as evidence that this place was lived in and so it didn't count as cluttered.

I hated being here. I needed people, I needed noise. But unfortunately, tonight was one of the rare evenings that everyone in my friend group was busy. So I had no choice but to go back to my apartment, alone.

Kicking my shoes off into the closet, I went about my normal routine. Turned on all the lights in the living room. Turned on the TV and clicked the first suggestion on Netflix. Then preheated the oven for some frozen mac and cheese.

My glamorous adult life.

I'd just plopped back down on the couch when I finally registered what was playing on the TV. Paul Hollywood describing the Christmas baked goods contestants needed to make for this technical challenge.

Right. The holidays were right around the corner. My friends would either be tied up with their partners or families all month. Even Roxie took a break from her hook-up adventures to stay in town with her mom.

Which left me right where I was, alone on my couch surrounded by reality TV reruns and empty cups.

And I couldn't even complain to anyone, not really. The second I say something about being lonely, I'd receive invitations to every single one of my friend's places for Christmas. They'd all be happy to have. Meanwhile, I'd feel like an out-of-place third wheel if I accepted.

I did that shit a lot as a kid. While my parents didn't kick me out or straight out disown me, they made it clear I wasn't welcome. So I hung out at Bailey's place more than I did at my own home. Her folks took care of me as if I was their own kid, throwing me birthday parties, having me over for Christmas, the whole nine yards. But once I graduated, got a job, and did the whole adult thing, I realized just how much they'd done for me and felt ... ashamed they had to.

My phone lit up in my hands and I jumped at the chance of a shot of dopamine or a simple distraction from the oncoming existential doom spiral.

> **Estelle:** Margo is home and we're planning on doing a big brunch for her tomorrow, are you able to join us?

Bailey's mom, speak of the devil.

Despite my conflicting feelings of gratitude and the dread that I could never pay the Hartleys back for what they dud for me, I also could never turn down a straight-up invitation from them. Plus this was a welcome party for Margo being back in town and not an important family event I'd be crashing.

> **Me:** Of course! I'll bring mimosas!

I tossed my phone away and went into the kitchen to grab a bottle of wine, completely giving up on dinner. Dinner and fighting off existential dread.

2

MARGO

I woke up in my childhood bedroom and internally cringed at every aspect of it. The posters, the neon flora comforter, the desk covered in stickers of fandoms I was no longer a part of. My 'adult' belongings were stuffed into a closet filled with graphic and flannel shirts.

I hated being here.

Well, maybe hate is a strong word. I hate the circumstances that brought me here and I hate the fact that everywhere I turned, I was reminded of it.

I guess it's my fault for expecting the New York City Public Library to have enough funding to staff a newly graduated librarian for more than five months.

Now I was back in Snowfall. And back in Bailey's shadow.

"Ba— Margo, you up?"

Right on cue, Mom.

I scrambled out of bed, pulling on some leggings and an oversized sweatshirt before fumbling downstairs.

And there, sitting in the kitchen nook, was Shea.

My older sister's best friend, my parents' surrogate daughter, and the first girl I ever had a crush on. Fuck, she was probably the first real person I had a crush on. The woman was unknowingly responsible for my sexual awakening.

And besides a few quick events, I hadn't really seen her since I graduated high school. And for all of those events, I had several days' notice to get myself together. I certainly wasn't wearing a sweatshirt with a stain on my tits.

"There you are, sweetie," Mom called from the kitchen. "I thought we'd do a nice little brunch for your first Saturday back. And Shea brought mimosas."

At the table, Shea lifted a champagne glass of bubbly liquid, a gentle smile pulling her full lips.

Fuck, I'm gonna be sick.

But it's fine. Shea doesn't look at me like that. She probably doesn't even look at me enough to notice the stain on my sweatshirt. Or how my leggings are covered in Lancelot's hair, which was my fault. I'd forgotten how much our cat liked to lay on anything in his reach. There was nothing to worry about, Shea didn't look twice at her best friend's little —

"Nice socks," Shea said, her smile cracking into a wide grin, hazel eyes sparkling.

Shit.

"Thanks, I stole them from the president," I murmured, shuffling to sit at the table before my mom thought to look down at my socks. My bi-flag socks.

I haven't told my parents yet. Not for any real reason. I mean, they'd be fine with it. Just look at how they took in Shea after her parents ... sort of ignored her once she came out.

My parents were fine. They were woke.

But just picturing coming out to them made me queasy.

"Stole them from the — oh my god!" Shea threw her head back and laughed, one hand on her stomach and the other covering her eyes. Meanwhile, I was turning every shade of pink under the sun.

Why the hell was an old Tumblr joke the first thing I said to Shea in like a year?

"Wave one of brunch incoming," Mom said, stepping into my air of awkwardness to slide a huge fruit tray onto the table.

"Wave one?" I asked. My mother was an amazing over-achiever. I should've expected her to have something planned for my first weekend back. And I should've assumed that when she said brunch, she meant *brunch*.

Mom had gotten really into Pinterest since she retired a couple of years ago.

"That's amazing, thanks, Estelle." Shea plopped a strawberry in her mouth, the socks blessfully forgotten.

"Of course. And with Bill out, we've got the perfect girls' morning." Mom hummed and did a little shimmy as she sat at Dad's usual spot. It was their little bit together. She'd sit in his seat just to see if he'd notice afterward. And he always did.

Mostly because Mom had the worst poker face ever, always raising her brows as soon as Dad sat down.

"So girl talk," Mom sang, poking a fork into a piece of cantaloupe. "Do either of you girls have partners for the holidays?"

"Mom," I sighed, "I already told you there hasn't been anybody since Dustin."

Across the table, Shea's eyebrow, which had that little shaven line because of course she had to have every hot feature available, rose.

"I know, but you could be casually seeing somebody. With the whole job thing, I would understand not wanting to label relationships."

I wish I could go just one day without thinking about my job loss.

"What job thing?" Shea asked.

"Cutbacks," I answered before Mom could give a more detailed description in front of my first and forever crush.

Honestly, it's wild that as a full-grown adult, with sexual experience, at least with men, I was still so swoony over Shea. But after my first trip home after undergrad, when I saw Shea in swim top and tripped over a whole ass child on a tricycle, I'd given up pretending I'd ever fully be over her.

It had to be a first crush thing. Most people's first big crushes were celebrities who did something awful to make them unlikeable. Unfortunately for me, Shea just stayed perfect.

"Shit," she hissed out, leaning back in her chair, chomping on a thick slice of honeydew.

Absolutely perfect.

"And they couldn't transfer you to another branch or something?" Shea asked.

"No. It was a state-wide cut. And since I was the newest employees, I was the first to go. I've been looking online for something, ideally in a big city. But since the holidays are coming up, nobody's hiring." I stab into the honeydew.

"Shit, that sucks."

I hummed in agreement as I chewed, trying to look anywhere but at Shea.

"How about you, Shea? Any special ladies in your life?" Mom asked and I told myself not to listen. I had zero desire to hear Shea describe her latest fling. Better to just tune it all out.

"No, I've been too busy with work and other side projects."

My dumbass nearly choked on my fruit.

"Shea, you should take a step back from some things," Mom tsked. "You always seem to be doing something. You can't be fully booked all the time. That's not good for you."

"Oh, I like staying busy," Shea answered with a shrug, eyes focused on her fruit.

"You're going to burn yourself out like that. You need a girl who can get you to relax some. Let me see if anybody in my book club knows someone your age." Mom instantly pulled out her phone, the taps making artificial key clicks. "What's the youngest you'd go? Janice's daughter, Abigail is a lesbian. She's Margo's age though. Are you two still close?"

The last question was directed to me.

Abigail was one of my best friends in high school. We didn't have a big fallout or anything, she just sucked at answering the phone. Or emails. Or carrier pigeons, probably.

I'm sure as soon as I run into her or track her down after I got bored with my pity party over being fired, we'll pick right back up where we left off.

But that didn't mean I'd be cool seeing her date my forever crush.

"Yeah. But I think she's seeing somebody," I lied.

"Hmm, how about —" Mom started before the oven timer went off. She stood, excitedly mumbling about the quiche recipe for wave two as she rounded the kitchen peninsula.

"Sorry to hear about your job. That really sucks," Shea said, tilting her glass toward me. I hummed in response, still worried she'd notice the stain on my tits or say anything else about my socks.

"Are you looking for work in the meantime? Because my office could use some admin help. Pretty sure some of us have unanswered emails for October."

"Oh, I don't think —"

"That's an excellent idea!" Mom butted in, a pie dish held between two Christmas-themed oven mitts. "You were doin' event organization, I'm sure it's similar."

"It's not —"

"And it'll look good on your resume to have something there instead of a blank space." Mom set the quiche on the table before turning back to the kitchen.

"It was just a suggestion. My feelings won't be hurt if you say no. Just take some time to think about it and text me."

Yup, such an easy thing to do. Texting your crush who might as well be a celebrity for how impossible it is to talk normally around them. Super easy.

"Sure, I'll do that. Thanks."

3

SHEA

I was the first one to get to the diner, which was pretty typical. Rosie was still serving somebody on the other end of the restaurant until one of her brothers could take over. Dennis said that Olivia was holed up at home on a new project and he would try to entice her out of her work haze. Zoey hadn't responded to the group chat, either because she was under a car or Stephen or simply binging Supernatural with him. Ashley was going on four months pregnant, so there was no telling if she'd been feeling well enough to hang out. And Mason was adorably, idiotically overprotective and would probably spend a good amount of time arguing with Ashley to stay home and rest. And Roxie ...

A text flickered up on my phone.

Roxie: My landlord has decided that, on a Saturday evening, with less than an hour's notice, I have to be at home to let the plumber in

Me: Rox, you need to leave this place, this is like the 7th time this year this dude has fucked you over

Roxie: Well the years almost over

Roxie: Plus for as cheap as I'm paying, all the inconveniences probably even out

Roxie: And it's walking distance from my office

Me: I'm sure I could find you some place better

Roxie: It's fine, my lease ends soon enough

Me: How soon?

Roxie: ... August

Me: Rox, that's almost a whole year?!?!

Ashley: Please let me sue this man

Ashley: Also Mason is convinced I'm going to trip and fall on my stomach if I'm on my feet anymore today and won't let me leave

Ashley: This is Mason and that's not true. Her feet are starting to swell and she refused to take today off and won't admit she's in pain

Ashley: He read one parenting book and thinks he knows shit

Rosie: Oh sweetie, get some rest

Rosie: I'm honestly done being on my feet today too. Shea, want to come over to my house? We can get milkshakes to go

I set my head on the diner table and groaned.

Rosie still lived with her family. Her ridiculously large family. They were lovely and caring, but if I felt the internal cringe of all the family holiday things I was missing out during the Hartley brunch, it'll be ten times worse at Rosie's place.

> **Me:** No thanks, I'll just head home. Tell your folks I said hi

I slid out of the booth and out the diner before Rosie had a chance to talk me into either going home with her or taking five to-go boxes because she knows I likely wouldn't eat with no one to eat with.

The struggles of having caring friends.

And the struggle of watching them all find partners or have fulfilling careers or a family they like and not having time for you anymore.

Down Main Street, the storefronts had been turned into a Hallmark movie minus the snow. Garland decorated with bright red ribbons and golden ornaments wrapped every lamppost and lined all the storefronts. Wreaths adorned every door, window, and the backs of all the benches. Twinkle lights filled all the trees and bushes with a soft golden glow barely visible in the late daylight.

Despite it only being the first weekend of December, couples and families were already crowding the street. There was lots of hand-holding, giggles, kisses snuck in between conversations.

Why can't I have any of that?

Turning off of Main Street towards my apartment, I pulled out my phone to call Bailey. When the normal two rings turned to five, I almost hung up and accepted that it'd be another lonely night.

"Shea! Sorry about that!" Bailey answered, her chipper voice already brightening my spirits. I should've known I could count on my best friend.

"No worries. What're you up to?"

"Um, I'm hiding in the dark room." Bailey said this with the same cheer as when she picked up. A lot of people pegged Bailey as flighty or ditsy. But really, the high-pitched thing was a nervous response.

"And you're hiding in the dark room because ..." I trailed off.

"Well, I was asked to provide photographs for the gallery's Christmas event."

"That's amazing, Bales! Congrats!" All Bailey did in response was hum. "Oh come on. You're gonna do it, right?"

"It's a lot of responsibility. And I'd have to stay in town for longer than usual. I'd miss a lot of the Snowfall traditions."

"Some of those traditions I'd happily miss out on."

"Oh come on, don't be like that. The kids' choir is adorable," Bailey chastised, knowing exactly which event made me cringe the most. I liked kids well enough, but having to listen to 20 of them sing Christmas songs out of key was a bit much for me.

"I'm pretty sure last year one of the kids peed their pants."

"That wasn't their fault, they were —" Bailey started.

"Nervous, sure. But when they tried to slip off stage, their mom threw a hissy fit and forced them back up. I hate that shit."

"I know." Bailey's voice was soft, like a hug. And fuck, I needed my best friend back in town. I needed someone who knew all my baggage and how much heavier it gets during the holidays. I needed —

On the other end of the line there was a knock and a barely audible, "Bailey girl?"

"Yeah?" There was some shuffling as Bailey set the phone down and covered her water buckets or whatever it was she did in a the dark room.

"You're doing the Christmas party!" Greg cheered as soon as the door clicked open.

Greg was … a good guy. He was fine. He was gentlemanly. There was nothing wrong with him, not even subtle red flags like Zoey's ex who wound up cheating on her. He was just … a little bland.

"I haven't actually —" Bailey started before her words became muffled in, what I guessed was, a hug.

"It's going to be amazing. Is there anything I can do to help?" Bland, but he clearly cared about and supported Bailey.

"Oh, I — well, one second." There was some more shuffling before Bailey spoke directly into her phone. "Shea? I'll call you back, all right?"

I hated that I clocked that our call only lasted 10 minutes before we were interrupted but reminded myself how nice it was that my best friend found love. Though that did nothing to ease the knot in my stomach over going back home to an empty apartment.

"No problem. Have fun, Bales." I sure wasn't going to.

4

MARGO

"I'm not serving you that," Wendy said, arms crossed, shaking her head so hard the black pigtail through her pink baseball cap swayed into view.

"What do you mean, 'you're not serving me'? It's literally right there?" I pointed to the glass case full of pizza. And more specifically, at the golden, delicious Hawaiian pizza.

"I'm not giving that abomination of a pizza to my friend."

"Aw, we're friends," I teased. Wendy wasn't the type to admit anyone was her friend unless it was forced out of her. So I liked to make a big deal out of it any time she slipped up.

Wendy's eye twitched and I waited for her to throw me out of the shop. Instead, she grumbled something under her breath before moving around to serve me a slice. Pizza on a flimsy paper plate, Wendy slapped it down on the counter by the bar stools. Humming, I moved over to my usual spot and settled in for a delicious meal.

But once I sat down and really looked at the pizza, I noticed something was off.

"Why didn't you want me to have this?" I asked, narrowing my eyes at the slice and leaning back and forth to look at it in different lighting.

"It has pineapple on it."

"Okay? I thought you got over your pineapple on pizza thing back in middle school." Back then, Wendy had ... strong opinions on what should be allowed on pizza and took rather drastic measures to derail her father from stocking it. I remember it involved dominoes and her older brother's T-Rex doll.

"I did."

The simple answer was unsettling. I picked up the slice and tilted my head to look at the bottom. The dough was distinctly redder than normal.

"Okay, who else likes pineapple on their pizza and what did you do to them?" I asked, setting the slice down and pushing the plate away.

"Tristan."

Oh, that made sense. Tristan was, for lack of a better word, Wendy's nemesis. Some people would say he was Wendy's bully since he was a few years older, but Wendy one hundred percent started it and was smarter with her pranks. If anything, Wendy was the bully.

"And where is Tristan now?" I asked.

Wendy shrugged. "Probably on a toilet."

I pushed the plate even further away. So far, that it tilted over the counter and toppled onto the floor.

"I'll take pepperoni then."

Wendy smiled, humming to herself as she went to the hot plates to grab a safe slice of pizza.

"So are you gonna do it?" Wendy asked, slapping the new pizza in front of me before cleaning up the contaminated slice on the floor.

"Do what?" I asked through a bite. Wendy, and her dad before her, made the best fucking pizza. The sauce was rich, the cheese perfectly melted, and every bite was heaven. No other shop compared. Which made free pizza during college ... disappointing.

"The job thing with Shea."

I set down my pizza.

"Pick your pizza back up, bitch. I don't know why you're making such a big deal about this. So what if she was your first crush? It's not like —"

"Shush!" I sprang up, looking around the empty pizzeria as if one of the old lady gossips would pop out and instantly put two and two together, out me to everyone, *and* tell Shea about my forever crush.

"Okay, yeah, sorry." Wendy held up her hands. "Didn't think it'd freak you out to say it in an empty room. Lesson learned."

Wendy was a sarcastic bitch. It was her most well-known personality trait. But her best trait, her strongest trait, was being a loyal friend. I told her I thought I might be bi back in middle school and she hasn't breathed a word to anyone. Not even when she could have stepped in to play wing-man, which was hard for her because she loved any and all opportunities to play mastermind.

"Sorry, I freaked. It's fine. Just ... being in downtown makes me jumpy. She could walk in here at any moment, you know?"

"I guess. But this time of day, I think Shea's down at Denny's shop." I grumbled in response, turning just enough to look out the window and down towards the bike shop. "But what's really the big deal? The coming out part or the old crush part?"

I turned back to Wendy with, what I hoped, was a heady glare. She was unimpressed and merely raised an eyebrow.

"I don't know, coming out just ... won't matter. My parents won't disown me or some shit, but nothing would change either. It's pointless. And as for Shea ..." I looked back over my shoulder at Main Street and shrugged. "Nothing would come of that either. I don't even know if I really like her or if it's just obnoxious nostalgia."

"Then take the job."

"What? I can't do that! Shea definitely clocked my socks and I can't function around her without saying something stupid. I said that bullshit Tumblr line at brunch yesterday. I'm not sure if I can ever look her in the eyes again."

"Yeah, that's bad. Like I'd probably change my name and leave the country if I was you bad." I slammed my head on the counter and Wendy patted my shoulder. "But like you said, it doesn't matter. Your parents don't care, Shea doesn't care, so you can just take the job and make some easy cash while looking for your next gig."

"It's not that —"

"Double dog dare you." Wendy crossed her arms, a dish rag draped over her shoulder and miscellaneous flour patches coating the thighs of her green jumpsuit. She was like a scary mechanic telling you your car needed a new engine. It might be what I needed to hear, but there's no guarantee I can afford it. Or in this case, be physically capable of working alongside Shea without constantly freaking out.

But she double dog dared me. And that was serious business.

"Okay," I said, stretching out the word as I tried to think of an out.

"Now." Wendy nodded to my phone on the counter.

"Now?"

"Now."

"But I don't think —"

"Now."

Grumbling, I picked my phone up and opened a new text with Shea.

After a solid minute and several impatient noises from Wendy, I finally sent something.

> **Me:** I am interested in that position, who would I need to talk to?

"Bland, but acceptable," Wendy remarked, before moving back to the register as a couple of folks stepped into the shop.

> **Shea:** Awesome! I can get everything set up for you. Do you wanna start tomorrow?

"Wendy!" I screeched. She tossed the folks' their card back and ran over to the counter, squinting at my phone that I held out to her.

"Wait, what am I looking at here?"

"She responded so quickly!"

"Okay?"

"And she wants me to start tomorrow."

Wendy's shoulders sank and she left me to fix up the new customers' orders. I sat, staring at my phone, my brain spinning like a draining bathtub.

"Give me that," Wendy said, snapping me out of my tizzy as she snatched my phone away.

"Hey!" I pushed up on the stool and tried to grab my phone back but Wendy was quicker. She stepped back, fully protected by the counter unless I literally climbed over it.

For better or worse, she didn't leave me in suspense for long. After the briefest of taps on my phone, she handed it back to me.

I was almost afraid to look down at what she'd typed.

> **Me:** Perfect!!! See you tomorrow!

"I don't use that many exclamation points," I grumbled, sitting back on my stool.

"Sure, but you would with Shea."

I only half heard her retort, because Shea, once again, responded immediately.

> **Shea:** Perfect! I'll get things set up HR wise, you can just come in around 9 and organize anything at the front desk until I'm in (a little closer to 10). And wear whatever you're comfortable in!

God, this was going to be the fucking worst.

5

SHEA

When I got into the office, at a respectable 10:15, Margo was sitting all prim and proper at the front desk. She had on one of those long pleated skirts and a turtle neck. The kind of look Denny called Olivia's good girl outfits. I'd never understood what he found so attractive about them.

Until I saw Margo, good girl outfit and glasses, being the cutest damn secretary the world will ever know.

Weird.

"Yes, I'll tell Ms. White to call you back during your lunch hours. Thank you," Margo said to whoever was on the phone before hanging up with a heavy sigh.

"Going well already, huh?" I asked, sitting on Margo's desk. She jerked back, going ramrod straight. Guess she hadn't noticed me come in.

"Shea," she squeaked, "Hi. Yes. Um, it's been fine. Phillip was here earlier and got me all set up in the HR system and emails. I've gone through all but last week's. Once I'm through with that, I'll send out a list of what needs to be addressed to each of you."

"Oh wow, fantastic, thanks. Phil show you around and everything?" I felt a little bad for not being here when she got in to show her the ropes, but given how much she got through work already, I guess Phil did a good job of that. Which shouldn't be surprising, he was an up-seller type of realtor, and he did that with a lot of flirting. And since Margo was all dressed up like a cute little secretary, he was probably happy to help.

"Oh, yeah. He did, thanks. I ... uh, I don't wanna keep you from work, so don't mind me."

Margo was always a little awkward as a kid, in the nervous jittery way. I would've thought she'd grown out of it by now. I mean, she was only a couple ... five years younger than me. There wasn't any reason for her to feel awkward around me unless ...

"Oh shit, are you not —" I stopped looking around the office building. Nobody else was in right now, which was pretty common with folks doing showings. But still, I leaned over to whisper in Margo's ear, "Are you not out?"

I was close enough to Margo to smell her perfume, something soft and floral and feminine. Little barely visible hairs stood on her neck and she jerked away, hands on her desk so the chair rolled back. She looked at me, eyes wide and face red.

"Um, that's —"

"Oh shit," I whispered, pulling back. "I totally almost outed you the other day! Shit! I'm *so* sorry."

"No, no. It's okay. I mean, I did wear the socks around the house. If I was *hiding*-hiding, I wouldn't've done that. My parents just ... don't know what the colors mean and it hasn't come up." Margo fiddled with a pen in her lap, nervous energy coming off her in waves. Tsunami level waves.

And shit, seeing her like that brought up a lot of feelings. Coming out was hard and fucking scary. I wanted to reassure her that the Hartleys would be fine with it, that her parents would still love her and not look at her any differently. They damn near took me in after I came out, they would surely keep loving their daughter.

But I knew none of that helped. Anxiety, especially anxiety so intertwined with your life and your identity, didn't listen to logic. And listening to logic only made things worse if you were proven wrong in the end.

"It's all right, Margo. I won't say anything. But if you want any help talking to them or need someone to vent to, I'm here for ya." I stood, knocking my knuckles against her desk. It was sort of nice to hold this secret for her, like I was paying it forward to future generations of queers.

"Oh really?" The hesitancy in her voice popped my bubble.

"Yeah, of course. Why wouldn't I be?"

"Well, it's just ... you're Bailey's friend," Margo said, shrugging.

"Yeah. But we're friends too, right?" Looking back on my post out memories, Margo was in a lot of them. And sure, we didn't have any sort of heart-to-hearts, but we hung out during the Hartley family outings. We might not have been close, but I'd at least say we were friends.

"Oh, okay. I just always thought you thought of me as Bailey's little sister. That's all I really am to anyone in town." Margo looked down at her lap, chewing on her lip.

"No. You're Margo and Bailey's Bailey. Two completely different people. Although, you both do that high-pitched bubbly voice when you're nervous."

"I do not," she said, her voice pitching up. She immediately giggled, burying her head in her hands. "Fine, I guess I do."

"I won't tell anyone that either."

Margo's shoulders softened and she looked up at me with a timid smile. "Thanks."

"Any time. And if you want to dip your toes into the queer scene around here, there's a pub out in Elmville that I go to pretty often. I'd be happy to take you and introduce you to some folks."

"There's a gay pub here?" Margo asked, voice pitching up, this time in excitement, as she twisted in her chair to fully face me.

"Well, I wouldn't say it's a gay pub so much as it's been co-opted to be one. But it's a nice place, real chill. Folks aren't all over you but you can usually find someone to hook up with if that's what you're looking for." Even as I was saying it, I found it hard to picture Margo just hooking up with someone. And the way her face twisted in response reinforced that idea. Good. She shouldn't be hooking up with just anyone.

"No, I don't think ... I'm ready for that. I mean, I went to a bunch of clubs in New York but going somewhere here is —"

The front door crashed open and Margo went quiet, pulling away from me and resituating herself behind her desk. I turned to the door to see Mayor Jeannie, hair frizzy and forehead crinkled with worry.

"Hey Jeannie, how can I help ya?" I asked, stepping in front of Margo.

"Oh, Shea, it's bad," Jeannie drawled. "Everyone needs to come over for an emergency town hall. And if you wouldn't mind spreading the word too."

And then she was off, slipping out of our office and into the one right next door.

"Whelp, let's go, Margo," I said, knocking on her desk again before moving to the door and holding it open, waiting for her to join me. She sat at her desk, eyes flashing from me to her computer.

"Seriously? But what about work?"

"Community before profit. That's our motto."

"But ..." she trailed off, dark brown eyes flickering to her computer screen. I sighed and let go of the door. Walking around her desk, I slid my arms under Margo's and pulled her up to standing.

It'd been a while since I'd hugged Margo or done something silly like try to pick her up. She was a full-grown adult now, that's for sure. And maybe she was right about us not being friends after all, because holding my friends like this never felt so awkward.

So once I got her up and steady, I stepped back and patted her on the shoulder.

"Don't worry about it. The work'll be here when we get back."

6

SHEA

"How are so many people able to take off work at a moment's notice?" Margo muttered behind me as I led us through the crowd to my crew's usual spot. More specifically, I guided our way without touching Margo.

"Do you really not remember living here your whole childhood?"

"Well town halls always felt like adult business, so I didn't pay much attention to them. And I certainly didn't realize people were taking off work just to talk shit."

It was funny to hear Margo curse. Since we'd only ever really been around each other with her parents present, it made sense. There were probably a lot of little things I was going to learn as we worked together.

"Over here," Zoey shouted, just loud enough to be heard over the crowd, standing on a pew and waving her hands. We joined her and most of the crew, exchanging hellos and hugs while Margo hung back.

"Oh, Margo, sweetie! How was your first day of work?" Rosie asked as we all sat down. We nearly filled the pew with all us. Mason at the end, his pregnant wife missing and likely on forced bed rest, Denny and Olivia, Zoey and Stephen, Rosie, me, and Margo.

"Oh, it was fine for an hour," Margo said, her tone stuck halfway between respectful for her elder sister's friends and grumbles.

"She's unfamiliar with what it's like living in Snowfall as an adult," I told Rosie.

"Oh, that makes sense. You'll get used to it before you know it. There'll probably be more than the weekly town halls as we approach Christmas."

"Ms. Taylor tries to outdo herself every year. So we should be in for a good show at least," I told Margo.

Then from the other side of the pew came some vicious stomping and I looked over just in time to see Mason curse under his breath before Ashley came into view and smacked his arm.

"You locked me in my office!" she shouted, smacking his arm again before shoving him so she had a space on the pew.

"I didn't lock you in, sweetheart. I just —"

"You might as well have. You set a nap trap."

"What's a nap trap?" Margo whispered beside me.

"Oh, Ashley's four months pregnant and Mason is a little ... overprotective. He probably gave her some chamomile so she'd get some rest."

"Should we be concerned about that?"

"Nah. Ashley is one hundred percent not resting as much as she should."

"That's kind of sweet. I want someone to fight to take care of me like that," Margo said, voice quiet like she wasn't really talking to me anymore.

"Yeah. Me too."

"Are you really not —" Margo started before she was jostled by Wendy crashing into the open space to Margo's right.

"I'm surprised you're here. I would've thought you'd go into hyper fixation mode reorganizing the whole office," Wendy said before leaning over to wave and say a quick hello to everyone else.

"I was pulled out of my seat," Margo grumbled, nudging me with her elbow in a light, playful jab.

I guess having Wendy around made her feel less awkward. Maybe I should invite her to the queer pub too if she knows about Margo, that might help her get out of her shell a little.

But when Wendy clocked the little poke, her eyes narrowed at Margo, like she was accusing her of something. Wendy raised an eyebrow, eyes flickering from me to Margo. Margo instantly started shaking her head, mouthing something I couldn't catch before scooting closer to Wendy and leaving a distinct space between us.

That was weird. Did Wendy have something against me? I've heard she was one for petty vendettas like her thing with

Tristan Hux, but I thought we were cool. Unless she gets pissed when people who order regularly drop off for a few weeks. I guess it had been a while since I ordered pizza. Maybe I should grab some today before heading home.

"Um, order?" Jeannie said from the podium, only speaking loud enough for the first few rows to be able to hear her. I'd never thought of our Mayor as timid, but without the demanding force of Ms. Taylor behind her, she was clearly struggling.

So I stood up, put my fingers to my lips, and whistled. The sound reverberated in the high ceiling as the chatter died and all focus shifted to the front of the room. I gestured to Jeannie and sat down.

"Thank you, Ms. White." Jeannie nodded to me and I threw her a thumbs up. "I've gathered you all here today to discuss a rather ... sensitive topic. Ms. Taylor has suffered a heart attack and —"

If Jeannie finished that sentence, she couldn't be heard over the cacophony that erupted. A casserole chain was forming in one corner of the room, grocery runs in another. It was chaotic, but Snowfall's best feature as a community.

Meanwhile, at the podium, Jeannie was shuffling through the underside and pulled out a hammer. With three sharp taps, she regained everyone's attention.

"We can discuss community care in a minute, but Ms. Taylor is doing well and expected to make a full recovery so long as she gets enough rest and avoids unnecessary stress." Everyone was quiet for a moment before it all dawned on us at the same and a chorus of distraught ohs sounded. "Right, which means Ms. Taylor is no longer able to manage and organize the December events in Snowfall. So we're looking for volunteers to run point on these events, particularly the children's choir, the holiday craft fair, tree lighting, and the Eve-Eve Fest."

The crowd was suddenly deathly quiet. Like hear a pen drop on the carpet quiet. The idea of someone else filling Ms. Taylor's shoes, especially for the holiday events, was unimaginable. I mean, whoever volunteered would have to have a lot of free time and no plans for the holidays. And with a town as family-focused as Snowfall, that didn't describe anyone except ...

"I'll do it."

7

MARGO

I was being dragged around for the second time today. But this time instead of getting butterflies, I was getting irritated.

"Wendy, cut it out already," I said once she'd dragged me out of the community center's main room and around a corner.

"What's this about being pulled out of your chair? And the touching and the goo-goo eyes?"

"There were no goo-goo eyes," I argued.

"Of course there were goo-goo eyes. You always give Shea goo-goo eyes."

"Then why even bother pointing it out?"

"Because you were touching her!" Wendy threw up her hands, pacing in a circle.

"I don't see how me casually touching her is a big deal. It was just a ... joke nudge. Between friends."

"*That's* the problem. You're supposed to be falling madly in love, not becoming friends. My plan is already off track."

"Plan? What pla— Were you trying to mastermind shit again?" Along with planning elaborate schemes to make Tristan's life miserable, Wendy liked to make even more elaborate plans to "help" her friends. Like breaking into the school at night to get our English essay prompt so Abigail could prepare.

In her defense, Abigail was supposed to be given those prompts beforehand as a part of her IEP. That teacher was just a bitch. Which was how we were able to avoid getting suspended when we were caught.

"Not masterminding, just helping you along," she said, shrugging.

"I thought you told me to take this job to get over my crush?" Wendy shrugged again, not meeting my eyes. I sighed, resting my back against the wall. How was it day one of this new job and I was already so tired of everything to do with Shea? "Wendy, I get what you're doing, but nothing will ever happen between me and —"

I stopped just in time to save myself another helping embarrassment as Shea popped her head around the corner.

"Margo, we're gonna go over to the diner to plan, wanna come?" she asked, head tilting like a cute puppy asking for a treat.

"But what about work?" I managed to ask over the quickly forming lump in my throat. Beside me, Wendy nudged my stomach, muttering something about me getting pulled into the friend zone. I guess her master plan accounted for me never making the first move and if I got put in Shea's friend zone, I'd happily stay there for the rest of my life while my pining likely got worse.

"Oh, it's fine. You got through so many emails before I got in, you could just call it a day." Shea waved a hand around to dismiss my concern. "You can come too, Wendy. If ya want."

Wendy eyed me and I gave her a little nod. If I was going to stand a chance at hanging out with my biggest crush and my sister's other friends, I'd need backup. Otherwise, I'd bail the second I saw the opportunity.

"Ugh, fine. I'll go," Wendy grumbled and Shea flashed us both a friendly, crooked smile before ducking back into the main hall.

"Why didn't you wear a button-down? You were supposed to wear a button-down," Wendy grumbled, kicking at the ground as we moved toward the main door.

"It was cold this morning. What does it matter?" I looked down at my turtleneck to find whatever error Wendy was seeing.

"You were supposed to show off your tits and make Shea see you as a possible sexual partner. Playing your goody two shoes bit is gonna keep you in best friend's kid sister territory."

"Oh my god. How are you the same person I talked to yesterday? Where did all the 'it's not a big deal' go?"

Wendy sighed dramatically, throwing her head back. "I was trying to lull you into a false sense of security so you wouldn't be nervous. Obviously."

"Obviously," I scoffed.

Then the cacophony of Bailey's friends surrounded us. Shea wrapped one arm around my shoulder, the other around Rosie. I reached for Wendy and dug my fingers into her arm to drag her along with me. Like a hoard, we walked down Main Street several conversations happening at once.

I didn't hear a word of it though, because Shea kept shuffling her arm against mine. First she had our arms connected by the crook of our elbows. But as we walked, her arm rubbed against my chest and she jerked her arm lower so that just our forearms were pressed together. The touch hadn't been offending. It was clearly unintentional and could in no way be misconstrued as something sexual.

And yet Shea was so put off by the accident, she had to immediately course correct.

I slipped my arm out from around hers and fell back with Wendy, grabbing on to her for comfort.

"What're you doing?" she whispered. "You were like half way to holding hands."

"She doesn't see me like that. She practically jumped out of her skin just grazing my tit," I grumbled.

"Well, maybe she —"

"No, it's fine. I just ... let's just find a quick out and get back to work."

Wendy opened her mouth to say something else, but for once, remained quiet. Instead of arguing or pushing me out of my comfort zone, she tugged me closer and rested her head on my shoulder as we walked to the diner.

8

SHEA

We crowded into the back booth of the diner. Olivia, Zoey, and Ashley to one side and Rosie, me, Margo, and Wendy squished together on the other. Stephen, Denny, and Mason had peeled off at some point during our walk, either to get back to work or to avoid a loud conversation they had nothing to add to.

"This is perfect," Ashley started, leaning over the counter, hands folded under her chin. "This is step one to taking over for that presumptuous bitch."

The whole table reared back, making various sounds of shock.

"You can't talk about Ms. Taylor like that," Olivia whispered.

"I mean ... she's not wrong. The woman regularly demands everybody's attention in the middle of working hours," Zoey said, shrugging. As Ashley threw out a hand to agree, Olivia nudged Zoey's other side. Beside me, Rosie mumbled something before waving for the attention of someone behind the counter and making a series of hand signs.

"She at least needs to be taken down a peg," Ashley muttered and on the other side of Margo, Wendy nodded in agreement.

"So what're we thinking? Greasing her sidewalk? Planting money for fraud?" Wendy said, leaning forward.

"No, no. We can't do anything that we could be liable for. We need to be more subtle than that." Despite the insane shit Margo's friend had just spouted out, Ashley didn't bat an eye. Though I guess given the things that Ashley had done to her now husband when they were in rival mode, it shouldn't surprise me. It was kinda nice to know Margo had a friend with the same vibes as mine. It might be a little awkward at first, but I think Margo'll get along with everybody if she's stuck in Snowfall for a while.

"The best plan, the one that'll really get under Ms. Taylor's skin, is to do better than her. Make all these events run smoother, make them bigger, gain more traction. All of it." Ashley waved her arms around before turning to Rosie to ask, "Can we get another one of those big sheets like we did for Olivia?"

"Oh sure," Rosie said before standing and whistling for one of her crew's attention. "Paper tablecloth and crayons, please."

"Let's make the yule goat!" Wendy suggested, then adding, "And burn it."

"Wendy," Margo groaned, nudging her friend with her shoulder.

"That sounds pretty fucking cool," Zoey muttered.

"They're made of straw though, right? And they're huge. We can't light that on fire," Olivia rationed.

"That's what makes it cool," Wendy grumbled, slumping down in her seat. Across the table, Zoey nodded, a wistful look in her eye.

Before the two could get too gloomy about their bonfire dreams being rejected, Frankie, one of Rosie's younger brothers, came over with a tray of food and milkshakes in one hand and a roll of paper in the other. Rosie helped him get the paper spread out and then we all grabbed our usuals from the tray.

"How did you know our —" Margo started, looking down at her mint shake.

"Oh we know everyone's usual orders, sweetie. That's what makes us a good restaurant, right, Wendy?"

"Oh, yeah. I know everybody's usual orders," Wendy said, mouth full of chicken tenders.

"Except you don't use that knowledge to make anyone's lives easier," Margo chastised, giving her friend a very pointed look.

"I only make shitty people's lives shittier, so it's fine."

"Perfectly reasonable," Ashley muttered as she started jotting down things. "So what're all the events you're going to need to cover? I've got the tree lighting and the holiday fest, but I know there're a shit ton of things going on that I never bother with."

"Have you really not been to the craft fair?" Olivia asked. "It's so cool."

"Mmm, that's just you, Olivia. It smells ... old," Zoey said, scrunching her nose.

"Oh and it smells so much worse than your mechanic overalls," Olivia scoffed in return.

"And there's the kids' choir," Rosie chimed in. "That's next week, I believe, so it should be mostly set up."

"Oof, this is gonna be a lot more than I thought," I murmured, leaning back to pull a flask from my jacket and tipping a little spiced rum into my chocolate shake. I shuffled to sit up straight and noticed Margo's furrowed eyes on me. I pulled the flask back out and tilted it towards her in offering, confused as to what the look was for. Margo simply shook her head and refocused on the conversation. That focus lasted a whole 10 seconds before she looked back at my glass.

"Are you okay?" she asked, big brown eyes flicking from me to my drink. The check-in caught me off guard.

"Yeah, why?" I asked, laughing a little out of awkwardness. Margo reddened, looking around the table at the others who were completely absorbed in whatever Christmas-time event they were already plotting.

"Oh, nothing. I was just overthinking, I guess."

I was about to ask if my drinking bothered her. For all I knew, she could've had a bad experience with alcohol in college. But Ashley waved a crayon in my face to get my attention.

"You're gonna have to focus to take down Ms. Taylor, all right?" I nodded in agreement, though the whole one-upping Ms. Taylor thing was ridiculous. I just wanted to have something to keep me occupied while all my friends did family things for the holidays. Sure this'll keep my days full, but I don't expect it to be all that stressful.

9

SHEA

Three days later my desk was covered with documentation for the child's choir. A one-night event, an event that lasted no more than three hours. And somehow it still required a million waivers and documentation.

The only bright side was that Rosie was right, since the choir was this Sunday, most everything was filled out, I just had to do the final review and sign on the dotted line.

The bad news was that this was a shit ton of stuff to do for just the finalization of an event, which meant I had my work cut out for me with everything else.

It was enough to make anyone reach for the bottle and spike their coffee.

As I was screwing the cap back on, Margo rounded the corner from the lobby. She eyed the bottle, biting at her lip until her eyes drifted over my desk. Then her eyes went wide as saucers.

"Shea, is this all for the holiday events?" she whispered in horror.

"Oh no, these are just for the choir." I pushed the coffee away and picked up one of the sheets to show Margo. "This is just detailing the stage setup. There's a packet somewhere in this pile about the decor that needs to be pulled from storage. Yadda yadda yadda."

"Has Ms. Taylor sent you any procedural documentation?" Margo asked, sitting down across from me and grabbing a stack of papers.

"No. Her granddaughter sent me some pretty basic notes, but she doesn't want me to talk to Ms. Taylor and stress her out. Which is fair, sure, but you'd think she'd have some sort of instructions. I know Ashley wants me to take down Ms. Taylor as like a bitter revenge thing, but it's not like she's gonna live forever either. She has to train a successor at some point."

"She probably thinks that just by making instructions, she's admitting defeat. She'd rather die with everyone knowing how instrumental she is than keep the community moving forward. Typical selfish behavior," Margo muttered. "Have you tried going to the library or the actual town hall to look up past receipts? That should at least give you an idea of what you need to purchase and who the vendors."

"Oh shit, that's smart. I never would've thought of that." I turned back to my computer and shot off a quick email to Jeannie about past invoices. "You probably just saved me a *ton* of trouble. I haven't had time to look into anything other than the choir yet."

"Really? But isn't the craft fair next weekend? And the tree lighting is right after that. I'm sure a lot has already been done but —"

"It'll be fine. You don't have to worry about it," I assured her, waving a hand over her concerns. "Like you said, a lot has already been done. Plus, everyone knows what their part in these festivities are. I don't think there'll be much for me to do beyond red tape shit."

I took a long sip of my coffee, trying to convince myself of what I'd just said.

Margo stared at the pile of paperwork on my desk for a long, quiet moment, face shifting through several stages of confusion and discontent.

"Um, you probably don't know this, but my library science specialty is community engagement, specifically event programming. These types of city-sponsored events are sort of my wheelhouse, so I can help you out if you want."

"Shit, really?" I sat up in my chair, knocking a handful of papers to the ground. "What kind of stuff did you do?"

"Oh," Margo murmured, pulling back in her chair like she was surprised I asked. She looked down at her lap, one side of her lip sucked in, a canine poking out. "I didn't get a chance to get any of my programs off the ground with the whole layoff thing."

"Well, what did you wanna do?"

Margo let out a long sigh before her shoulders slumped down and she crumbled into the chair.

"Predominantly I wanted to expand our resource center. All the sewing machines were from the 80s, we didn't have a good collection of park or museum passes, and no one was maintaining the instruments. That's the number one issue with most libraries, nobody takes the time to do a proper inventory and maintain everything."

"Wait, libraries have all that shit?"

Margo's eyes met mine in a hard, 'you've got to be kidding me' stare. It was so funny coming from her. Margo, who was always shy as a kid and who even now felt pretty bashful, was practically glaring at me. It made me giggle.

"Ugh, nobody uses their libraries fully. They don't even know all the services provided. And since they don't know, the services aren't used and it looks like a waste of money. But there are *so* many cool things a library can provide for the community." Margo was so cutely enraged, all I could do was keep laughing. "Seriously. Think of how useful a functioning sewing machine that anybody can use is? How many times have you had clothes you threw out because even if it was simple to fix, you didn't have the supplies to fix it? Or how many times have you considered picking up a guitar, but wanted to test it out before investing the money in it? Some libraries even have full studios, including recording equipment,."

"I'm sorry, I'm sorry, that's incredibly cool. I had no idea the library had all that stuff. It's great. You're just so defensive it's cute," I said, still trying to stifle my giggles. Her cheeks flushed red, the color flowing all the way to her ears.

She had a little rose gold cuff on her left ear, which made me smile. Margo had all the dressings of a bi girl in the way that anyone in the community would recognize but outsiders wouldn't. I remembered that stage. How scary and exciting it was.

"Come out with me Friday night. I think getting into the queer scene around here will do you some good. I'm the only one that goes in from Snowfall, so you won't have to worry about outing yourself before you're ready."

"Umm," Margo said, eyes wide as she looked around the empty office. Her hands fiddled with the folds of her skirt before they clutched the fabric and she said, "Sure. Friday's good. I'll … go with you. But … um, first I'm gonna check the library. For um … Christmas event stuff."

Margo skittered out of her chair and through the front door of the office like a sitcom character that just spilled food all over themselves in front of their crush.

Guess I'll have to be prepared to be an extra helpful wingwoman if she finds anybody at the pub she likes.

10

MARGO

"You have to come to the library. Right. Now," I hissed over the phone to Wendy as I stepped through the front doors of the Snowfall library.

Snowfall had two libraries, one in the downtown area behind the high school and the other at the edge of town. The two were ... not treated equally. The one on the outskirts of town, closest to my house, was about the size of shack and had the structural integrity of one too. Their selection of books didn't include anything published after 1998, there was no resource center or community events, and the bathroom never had toilet paper.

Meanwhile the downtown library had a mini Snowfall museum devoted to the town's history, just in case any tourists stopped by. There was a fresh rotation of new releases and front displays that were damn near Instagram worthy. It was still a far cry from what a library could be, but it was clear where the town was putting the meager library budget.

"The nice one or the crappy one?" Wendy asked.

"The one in downtown," I grumbled.

"Oh, you're enemy. Nah, I'm working."

"They're not my enemy. And are you really working or is the shop completely empty and you just don't feel like coming over?"

"Eh, doesn't really matter."

"Wendy," I groaned. "I ran away from work like a fucking cartoon character. I need you."

"Hmm. I'll contend that it's weird for you to run out of work. But since you work with Shea, I don't think this is an emergency."

"She asked me to go to this queer pub with her Friday," I whined, ducking into an empty corner of the library.

"Shit." Wendy was quiet for a long time before finally saying, "I'll be there in a few minutes."

I sat at a back table in the archives section, my knee bouncing so hard the table shook. I pressed a hand over my knee and tried to take a deep breath to stop the anxious buzzing.

Why the hell did I say yes to going out with Shea? It's going to be an absolute disaster. What if she meets someone she wants to hook up with while we're there? What if I meet someone? How was I going to flirt knowing Shea was watching? I wouldn't consider myself the smoothest person in the best conditions, but with her around I was bound to flounder in one way or another.

I rested my head on the counter and considered how I could fake a headache come Friday afternoon so I didn't have to go and face whatever embarrassment I would bring upon myself.

In the back of the archive section was one lonely microfilm reader beside a large cabinet for the microforms. I got up and started scanning the labels, happy to have *anything* else to focus on. And I did say I was here to research things for Shea, so it only made sense to pull out the last few December copies of the Paper.

Most of the December articles were basic fluff pieces. There was a lot of celebrating Ms. Taylor's accomplishments, notes of new traditions, and *so* much gossip about who brought who to Eve-Eve Fest. Apparently, during the fest, they used to have sprigs of mistletoe hidden around downtown, and couples that found and kissed under them had long happy marriages.

Unfortunately for that tradition, Ms. Taylor found her first husband under one of the bundles with another woman and the tradition was nixed.

I took a picture of the article and texted it to Shea.

"So you're still able to text her despite your freak out? Interesting."

I screeched, jumping to turn around and smack whoever snuck up behind me. But of course, it was Wendy and she expertly dodged my wild arm and took my phone.

"Wendy," I groaned, reaching over her to try and get my phone back. Unfortunately, Wendy had always been the shorter of the two of us, of anyone our age really, and she'd learned how to use that to her advantage. She folded herself in two, flicking through my phone upside down while I tried to reach over her back.

"Humph," an old, crackly voice interrupted us and we quickly broke apart, my phone noticeably remaining in Wendy's hands.

"Sorry, Ms. Delaney," we both murmured as the elder librarian glared at us. Ms. Delaney was every bit the stereotypical old librarian. Glasses attached to a chain around her neck. A floral dress hidden under a heavy cardigan. And a stare that made grown men whither.

"Just because you're not loud, doesn't mean you're not disturbing," she tsked, then her sharp gray eyes narrowed in on me. "You've got your library science degree now, don't you?"

"Yes, ma'am," I answered, my back stiffening with nerves. But Ms. Delaney just huffed, murmuring something about picking up the microforms before I left as she meandered back to the front desk.

"That woman has to be friends with death to be living this long," Wendy muttered and I nudged her side with my elbow and snatched my phone back.

"Don't be rude," I grumbled, opening my phone back up to read a new text from Shea.

> **Shea:** Holy shit, Ashley's gonna have a conniption when she hears about this

Shea: But that's actually kinda cute

Shea: Think there's some kind of gay spin we can put on it?

"So you're going to a pub together?" Wendy asked, grabbing my arm to tilt my phone so she could read it.

"We're not going *together*, she's taking me to ... I don't know, introduce me to friends or something. I think she sees me as a baby queer and is trying to help make me more comfortable."

Wendy threw her head back and laughed.

"Does she not realize you've known you're bi for nearly as long as she's been out?" Wendy said quietly, the words bless-fully muffled by her laughter.

"Shut up," I grumbled, knocking into her as I went back to the microfilm to clean up.

"But that means our plan is simple." Wendy leaned against the cabinet, arms crossed.

"*Our* plan?"

"Yeah. So what you're gonna do is hit up the hottest babe in the club or whatever and get them to take you home. Shea'll realize you're not a baby and have experience with women and start seeing you in a new light. Bada-bing, bada-boom." Wendy waved her hands around from side to side like the transition of her plan would be that simple. I had to stop what I was doing to make sure she wasn't going insane.

"Wendy, you are fully aware that I have never gone home with anyone on the first night. And," I pulled her closer to whisper, "And you know I haven't been with a woman all the way yet."

"Yeah, but that's just sorta circumstantial." Wendy waved her hand in a circle. "Dustin just happened to be the first person you met that you vibed with and didn't have anything to hold you back. Like being your sister's best friend."

My heart ached a little at the thought of Dustin. Being the bookworm, library nerd I was, it wasn't surprising that Dustin had been my only serious partner. He was sweet and kind, but also kind of boring and *very* into dinosaurs. It was an amicable breakup, predominantly spurred by a dig excavation he got selected for. But I did miss the reliable intimacy.

"If I end up meeting someone at this pub, that'd be nice, I guess." Wendy's eyebrows shot up. "But it's not going to be to make Shea realize I'm a woman or some other bullshit. The me and Shea together plan won't work."

"Why not?" Wendy persisted. I pushed around her to put away the microfilms and started to the door.

"Because I..." I looked around the empty library and hooked her arm with mine to bring her closer. "Because I've fantasized about getting together with her too many times. I can't match what's in my head. It's better for me to be with someone completely new so those fantasies can't trip me up."

We kept walking out the door, but I could see Wendy gnawing at her lip out of the corner of my eye.

"Ugh, just say it," I grumbled.

"I think you're a coward who needs to up your Prozac," Wendy muttered.

I just pinched her side in reply.

11

SHEA

I wouldn't consider myself a great employee. I mean, I helped folks find their dream shop location and brought in money, but I didn't go out of my way to be useful if I didn't have anything specific to do. And during December, I almost had nothing to do.

Except today, when I found something *very* attention absorbing.

Margo's ass in some skin tight jeans.

I don't know what was wrong with me. I mean, sure I had realized Margo was a cutie over the past few days. But to spend a whole work day ogling her ass any time she got up was insane.

This was Bailey's sister after all, a new, queer version of her sister. But still, friend's siblings were generally off the table. Especially closeted siblings.

"Margo, would you mind grabbing that contract I just sent to the printer?" Phillip called.

"Oh, sure," Margo said, pushing back in her chair.

I stood before she had the chance to get up.

"I'll get it," I told her, glaring at Phillip as I made my way to the printer and back, slapping the contract down on his desk.

"I know what you're doing. Cut it out," I whispered. Phillip just shrugged and leaned back in his chair with his hands behind his head.

"Don't pretend you weren't looking too. At least I have a shot with her."

God, I must've been really bad for Phillip to notice.

I kicked the corner of his desk and returned to mine.

Maybe I should bail on the pub tonight. Margo seemed nervous about it and I did sorta force her into it. She'd probably be glad to have an out.

"Shea, you ready?"

I looked up from my laptop at Margo, her wavy hair tied to one side, her make up touched up, and another tight turtle neck covering too much skin and also not enough. It was probably a body suit with how tight those jeans were.

And fuck, she'd gotten dressed up for this. Her first gay bar outing. She was nervous, but ready. I couldn't bail after she'd spent all day being anxious about this.

"Yup, let's go."

"Go? Where are y'all going?" Phillip asked, immediately getting up to crowd over my desk as I grabbed my things.

"We're meeting up with Bailey at this pub half way between here and Charlotte," I told him, throwing my arm over Margo's shoulder and pulling her towards the door before calling back, "Have a good weekend, Phillip."

"Have a good —" Margo started to say, twisting in my arms, but I pulled her back in place.

"Don't bother. The guy's been ogling your ass all day. He's probably enjoying watching you walk away, no need to wish him a good night too," I grumbled, keeping Margo tucked safely under my arm.

I always considered my height a little inconvenient with other women. Most of the girls I dated were considerably shorter than me. Just enough to make things like having my arm around their shoulder or walking while holding hands uncomfortable.

But Margo fit perfectly beside me.

Wait, that's not something I should be thinking.

I slid my arm off of Margo and pulled my keys out of my pocket, swaying them around my finger, wracking my brain for appropriate small talk.

"Thanks for that by the way. The cover," Margo said, moving away from me to the passenger side of my car.

"Oh yeah." We both got into the car and settled in. "I've got a million excuses just in case."

"Do you need to use them often? I mean, since you're out and all."

"Eh, not really. But sometimes …" I drifted off, not sure how to describe why I kept a stack of excuses handy. A lot of it came from anxiety about my parents showing back up and I didn't want that kind of thinking to spread.

But no matter how long it's been, I always expect to see my mom when I round the corner at the Market. Or my dad when I drive past the park. And those nearly impossible possibilities meant I had to be mentally prepared with comebacks, excuses, outs, covers, and everything else under the sun.

And unfortunately, some of those things came in handy from time to time. That was just a part of being openly queer in the South. Which was another thing I didn't want Margo to have to dwell on when deciding to come out or not.

"Rarely," I finally said. "It's more of a security thing, you know? It makes me feel better to know I've got a backup plan or two."

"And do you have a backup plan for if you find somebody you wanna go home with tonight?" Margo asked, the question ending with a small laugh. I chanced a glance at her from the corner of my eye to see her nervously fiddling with her turtle-neck.

"That's not happening," I assured, maybe a little too force-fully. Her eyes looked up to mine, bright and wide. I snapped my eyes back to the road. "But what about you? Do you want to have a code word or something in case you find somebody you want to leave with?"

Picturing Margo being swept away by some chick made my skin feel tight. This was Margo, Bailey's little sister, she shouldn't be going around having one-night stands. She deserved a little romance, somebody that'll treat her right and not jump right into sex.

Except I definitely enjoyed the occasional one-night stand and always cheered my friends on if they wanted one. Plus I couldn't exactly blame anybody for wanting to hop into bed with Margo. I mean, she probably picked out those jeans specifically for how good they made her ass look. She might be looking for something tonight.

A soft little laugh broke up my thoughts.

"There's no way somebody'll want to take me home," Margo said, turning to face the window.

"What? You can't be serious," I scoffed because that was the most ridiculous thing I'd heard. Margo was going to catch a shit ton of eyes at the bar.

"I've never really been good with flirting. Especially with women," Margo said, shrugging. Then she smooshed her face against the window, murmuring, "They're just ... *so* cool. And gorgeous and funny and brave and kind."

"You talking about someone specific there?" I asked, looking over to catch Margo violently shaking her head. She was still facing the window, but I could see the tips of her ears reddening.

Huh. Maybe she had been with somebody back in New York and is still hung up about them. Just because she hadn't come out to her parents, didn't mean she hadn't been dating women miles away from home.

Shit, it was completely possible she was still with that person and things were just rocky because of the move. But she'd have told me if that was the case, right?

"Well, we're just going to hang. No flirting necessary," I said, ignoring the temptation to ask more.

"Right. No flirting, just here to make friends," Margo said, nodding her head like she was reassuring herself of something.

12

SHEA

Margo was delusional. Like, I kinda wanted to double-check her sanity delusion.

Like I suspected, she caught the eye of several folks when we walked in. We didn't even make it to the bar before some of my friends asked who I'd brought along. And instead of the nervous little tics I'd grown used to, Margo fell into easy conversation with everyone, bright smiles, tiny giggles. It wasn't that she was acting like a completely different person, just more ... her. More comfortable.

Meanwhile, I stood around with a weight on my chest because she hadn't been this comfortable with me.

And for some reason, the way one of the girls, Dana, was looking at her, had me regret introducing Margo as Bailey's sister.

Dana was showing off her bicep, explaining a cultural tattoo that wrapped around the muscle, and Margo was enraptured. I looped a finger through one of her belt loops and pulled to get her attention. When her face turned to mine, a blush started creeping across her cheeks.

I wanted to know if she was embarrassed by me or that she was caught flirting when we'd declared we were just here for friends. But instead, I said, "I'm gonna go grab a drink. Do you want anything?"

"Oh, yeah, can I get ..." she trailed off, the red in her cheeks deepening as her eyes darted around. "Um, the one with mango rum, peach vodka, pineapple, and —"

"You mean a sex on the beach?" Dana asked and when Margo nodded, she laughed. "You're too cute."

I tugged a little harder on Margo's belt loop, making her fumble into me. I furrowed my brows at Dana before I dipped down to whisper in Margo's ear. "I'll get our drinks. Don't get too flirty without me."

I let go of the belt loop and pressed my palm over her waist. Then I slid my hand away and went to the bar.

Drinks ordered, I stayed facing the bar, trying to reroute my thoughts. Because it was stupid to feel so many things over Bailey's sister. For one, we were barely friends. I mean, she didn't even consider me a friend the other day and one shared secret didn't mean anything changed for her. Two, this protective, angry, fizzy feeling was unnecessary. She was a grown adult, she didn't need me looking after her like a big sister. And I certainly didn't feel like she was my sister.

But I did feel like she was mine to protect.

"You all right there, Shea?" Shawan asked, pushing the drinks over the bar. She'd been tending this bar since before it had been unofficially dubbed a queer bar; an older lady who would listen to your shit but never sugar coat her advice. The perfect bartender.

"Ah, I just brought this sorta friend along and I'm starting to … I dunno, feel weird about it." I took my pint, some local IPA, and took a long swig.

"She some situationship thing then?" Shawna asked and I nearly died choking on my beer.

"No, she's Bailey's sister," I said after a minor coughing fit.

"Eh, so what? Bailey seems like the type to eat that shit up. She'd be talking about being sister-in-laws the second you tell her." Shawna, supposedly determining that was all the advice I needed, moved down the bar to take some other folks' orders.

She was right. If Margo came out to Bailey, and hadn't asked it to be a secret, I would immediately get a text about the possibility.

Bailey wasn't the problem.

The problem was that my attraction to Margo was new and uncomfortable. And probably not even mutual.

What was I even thinking about this for? So what if I was a little attracted to Margo? We hadn't gotten all that close yet, there was no reason to read into all these things or even care if she liked me back.

These were just intrusive thoughts that I was better off ignoring.

Drinks in hand, I turned around to see Margo giggling with Dana's hand on her arm.

The sight gave me heartburn.

I went over and held out Margo's brightly colored drink, just far enough away that she had to step away from Dana's touch.

"There ya go, babe," I said once her fingers wrapped around the glass. Margo's eyes darted up to mine, so wide and bright that the twist in my stomach turned into a flip.

Before she could question me, I wrapped an arm over her shoulder and pulled her in place beside me, facing the group.

"So what were y'all talking about?" I asked, trying to casually sip at the remnants of my beer.

Dana raised an eyebrow at me, but just shuffled back a step before answering. "We actually have a friend in common. This dude I went to college with, Henry. He did the whole follow your dreams to New York thing and always talks about going out to queer spaces up there, so I figured Margo might've met him. And lo and behold."

"Yeah, it's wild. A grown adult going out on the town without some sort of chaperone," Margo muttered under her breath before sipping at her drink.

"What?" I asked, because I couldn't have heard her right. There's no way Margo thought of me as a chaperone for this, right?

"Nothing," she murmured. "But yeah, Henry's a good friend. He crashed on my couch for like two months during grad school after he broke up with some dick."

"Oh, Isaac?" Margo nodded her head, still nursing her drink. "Oh, you're Margo-Margo. I've heard so much about you. What a small world."

The stomach twist that turned to a flip was now a complete drop.

13

MARGO

By the time we were walking back to the car, I was beyond frustrated.

Shea had spent the whole evening glued to my side, tense and awkward and butting in to every conversation I tried to have with someone. It was like having the worst possible body-guard, one who didn't care if you got what you came here for or not, just that you didn't get ... I don't even know what Shea thought she was protecting me from. But whatever it was, could *not* have been worth all the awkwardness of the evening.

I felt like the troubled kid who was forced to sit next to the teacher. Like I was a burden she had to carry. It fucking sucked.

"So ..." Shea started as she got settled into the driver's seat, fiddling with her seat belt, "What'd you think?"

"What?" I asked, or nearly shouted, as I twisted to look at her. Shea didn't respond to the incredulity in my voice and remained focused on the road, a small nod the only indication that she even heard me. "What do you mean 'what did I think?' What about *you*? You were horribly uncomfortable the whole time."

"No I wasn't," Shea argued, her shoulders tensing.

"Sure, so you just stuck by my side the whole time for fun and not because you were worried I was going to embarrass you or some shit. I mean, I know I'm just Bailey's little sister and you probably have more memories of me as an awkward teenager than an adult, but I know how to act in public. I'm not a little kid you have to watch every second. And if you felt like that, I would've rather not come."

"What? That's not it at all," Shea argued, voice high-pitched as she shuffled in her seat.

"It's not?" I questioned.

"No. I just ... I didn't want you to feel like I dipped on you or anything, so I just ... stood by you."

"It was more than just standing," I scoffed.

"Well, I — was I making *you* uncomfortable?"

Flickers of heart-ending memories played in my head. Of her pulling on my belt loop, of her breath on my neck, of her arm draped over my shoulder like I was hers to hold.

She didn't make me uncomfortable, she made me want to lean into it. She made me want to act delusional. Which only made everything worse because for her, all those little touches were the equivalent of holding a kid's hand at the mall so they don't get lost.

It was pathetic, *I* was pathetic.

"I wasn't uncomfortable, but you gave everyone the wrong impression," I grumbled, sinking into my seat so I didn't have to see Shea pretend to not be grossed out by the thought that other people thought she was dating her best friend's little sister.

"I mean ..." Shea started. I heard her fingers tap against the steering wheel, but refused to turn to look at her. If I looked at her my tongue would get all heavy and I'd stop arguing and she'd continue treating me like a kid.

"Dana was making you uncomfortable, right? With her flirting?"

"What?" I shot up, nearly choking myself on the seat belt as it locked.

"I just noticed you were acting strange with her is all."

"Acting strange?" I repeated, fuddling with my seat belt to undo and redo it while we were at a stop light.

"Yeah, like you were forcing yourself to be more talkative than normal," Shea said with a shrug, her eyes almost drifting to look at me before focusing back on the road.

The thing is, I wasn't being more talkative with Dana. I wasn't pushing myself out of my comfort zone or anything.

However with Shea, I was extremely shy and out of my comfort zone every second. So of course she thought I was acting weird in comparison.

"You'd said you weren't there to flirt either. And since Dana was flirting, I figured I could, you know, act as a buffer. Make her stop coming on so strong. I mean, she's my age, so that's sorta weird, right? I wouldn't want some old lady creeping on you like that." Shea laughed, the sound shrill and awkward. She shuffled in her seat, tapping on the steering wheel rapidly. "I was just protecting you. Yeah, that's it. I was protecting you. That's what Bailey would want me to do for you. And since she can't play the older sister role 'cause you're not out yet, I should do it."

"So you do just see me as a little sister?" It was an obvious truth, but hearing it aloud stung. Not like I had a chance with her even if she didn't see me as a little sister, but still.

"No, I definitely don't see you as a sister," Shea said, her voice somewhere between a grunt and a laugh. Whatever the fuck that meant.

"Well, fine. But I don't need your protection either way. I'm not a kid."

"I know you're not. But it was your first time there and —"

"I'm not inexperienced either. I mean, not completely. I lived in New York for the past six years for fucks sake. I've probably been to more queer clubs than you." I crossed my arms and turned back to the window, fully aware I was handling this conversation like a bratty teenager. But being treated like a kid was hitting a sore spot I hadn't realized was so sensitive and all I wanted to do crawl into bed and forget about this whole night.

"God, I do *not* want to think about you going around to clubs in New York," Shea groaned, like it was so gross to think of me kissing somebody.

"Fine, don't think about it then," I grumbled. "I'll just go on my own from now on."

"What? I'm not letting you go out on your own, that's —
no, it's not safe to go alone."

"Not safe?" I repeated. "What's not safe about it?"

"Well Dana, for starters."

"What? How is Dana not safe?"

"She was trying to get in your pants."

"She was not. We were just talking about a mutual friend."

"Uh-huh, sure. And she just called you cute like a friend
too."

"That's —"

"And if she wasn't trying to get in your pants, why'd she
back off when I wrapped my arm around you? She just wanted
sex, I saved you from having to turn her down."

"Okay, fine, maybe she was flirting with me. But I don't
need you to 'save' me from that. I'm a grown woman, I know
how to turn somebody down if I want to."

"So you didn't want to turn her down?" Shea asked, her
voice dropping. I chanced a glance over at her to see white
knuckles and her face turned away from me.

"Well I didn't get the chance to decide, did I?" I huffed.
Shea's jaw worked, but for once she remained quiet.

The rest of the ride to my parents' place was silent, no jokes,
no signing along to the radio, nothing.

Maybe this was for the best. I was clearly not over my crush
on her and she was clearly not interested. We weren't ever going to be friends. Better that we got this failure out of the way
now so we can go into the office on Monday and not bother
with small talk.

So when Shea parked in front of my place, I mumbled a quick thanks and bolted out of the car. I was about halfway across the yard when Shea rolled down her window and leaned all the way out, arms braced on the door.

"I'm sorry, I treated you like a kid. I didn't mean to do that."

I bit my lip to keep from arguing and just shrugged. Sorry or not, it didn't really change anything. She'd keep treating me like a kid because that's all she saw me as.

Shea shifted back, resting her chin on her arms. She looked childish like that, eyes shifting side to side like she wasn't sure if she'd get in trouble for what she was about to say.

"Will you still come to the choir on Sunday?"

It was the last thing I expected her to ask. I had to bite down on my lip just to keep my mouth from falling open like a cartoon. But Shea didn't elaborate, just stared up at me with big, pleading eyes that made me answer without thinking.

"Sure."

Shea's face split into a wide grin and I knew I was totally fucked. Because no matter how she'd treated me tonight, intentional or not, I'd still do damn near anything for that smile to be directed at me.

14

SHEA

I have no fucking clue what I was doing with Margo, but whatever it was, I was doing a shit job at it.

I guess the first thing I had to do was admit that I'm attracted to Margo, to Bailey's little sister. Like attracted enough to want to get to know her before introducing her to my toy collection.

It was fucked. And what's worse, I didn't even know what part of it bothered me more, the fact that she's Bailey's sister or that she isn't out yet.

I needed to talk to somebody. But that was just another problem with this whole thing. Even if I described the situation in the vaguest of terms, any of the girls would be able to figure out what was going on and I'd essentially out Margo.

Which meant If I was going to talk to anyone, it had to be Dennis. He hadn't met Margo, probably, and wouldn't be able to put everything together the way the girls would.

So right around his opening time, I went to the last shop on Main Street, Dennis' Steel Wheelz. I'd gotten him the shop a little over a year ago and Dennis had done well for himself. He worked with one of the high school teachers we'd grown up with, Eli, and spent a lot of time helping the kids dirt bike. For as grumpy as Dennis could be, he really took to those kids.

But thankfully none of them were hanging around the shop this early on a Saturday.

"Dennis, how ya doin'?" I asked once I'd stepped into the shop, craning my neck around to make sure no one was hiding behind the bike racks.

"I'm fine. How are *you* doing?" he asked, dropping the magazine he'd been reading to raise an eyebrow at me.

"There's nobody else here, right?" I asked, pushing up on my toes to see over the racks and the storage room in the back.

"Nah, it's just me today. You planing some sort of surprise party or something?"

"Uh … no." I rested my arms on the front desk and leaned in. "I need you to promise not to mention any of what I'm about to say to any of the girls. Including Olivia."

Dennis stared at me for a long moment before sighing and resting back on the stool he kept by the register.

"You don't have to be ashamed if you need help with all holiday shit or even if you need to cut one of the events. It's honestly insane that Ms. Taylor does so many things in one month."

"What? God no, I would never cancel any of the events. Ms. Taylor would me beheaded."

"She can't do that," Dennis said, voice flat. I waved him off. Ms. Taylor might not literally behead me if I fuck up the holiday events, but she'd definitely find a social equivalent.

"Whatever, I'm not worried about the holiday stuff. I've got that handled. What I don't have handled is ..." I stumbled over my words, trying to decide where to start. "You swear not to tell Olivia or the others?"

"Will she be upset if I don't tell her?" he questioned.

"Ugh, maybe. But like, in the 'we're friends and should tell each other everything' way. Not like it'd *really* hurt her feelings. It's just if I tell her or any of the other girls it'll become a bigger deal than it really is."

Dennis crossed his arms and stared at me for a solid minute before nodding. "All right, I won't say anything to anybody."

I let out a long sigh.

"Right, so I met this girl. Or re-met her, I guess. I've seen her around, but we hadn't really talked since she was little."

"Little?" Dennis repeated.

"Little like she's five years younger than me. So when I was in high school, she felt a lot younger, but now she's an adult. Like graduated college and has an ass that ..." I stopped to whistle and Dennis nodded in understanding.

"So the problem is she's straight?"

"No," I cried, knocking my head onto the counter. "She's bi."

"So ..." Dennis said, confusion clear in his tone.

"But she's not out to her family."

"Oh."

"Yeah, *oh.*" I stood up, throwing my hands in the air before pacing around in a circle. "So not only is me being into her awkward 'cause I'm close to her family, but it'd also come with a shit ton of stress to not accidentally out her. Not like it matters because she probably doesn't like me anyways and she definitely doesn't after last night."

"Sounds like you're jumping to conclusions. What happened last night?"

I stopped my pacing and pulled myself up on the counter to sit, cross-legged, in front of Dennis.

"I took her out to the pub in Elmville to get her acquainted with the queer community here." I shrugged, trying to think of a way to explain my behavior last night without coming off as a jealous prick.

"Did she not know that's where you were taking her?" Dennis asked.

"No. She knew."

"So the problem was ..." Dennis said, waving his hand at me to continue.

"Well, before we got there, we confirmed that neither of us intended on going home with anybody. So when some chick started hitting on Mar— hitting on them, I ... got in the way."

"What do you mean you 'got in the way'?"

"I may have put my arm around her shoulder and called her babe," I murmured.

"So you did the lesbian equivalent of a cock block? Well if she didn't realize you were into her before, she probably does now."

I buried my face in my hands and screamed.

"What? Is it that bad that she knows?"

"I don't think she does. On the way home she was irritated with me, saying I didn't need to protect her like a little kid and that I was acting like an older sister. And I think she's pissed I messed up her chances with that other chick."

"Yikes. Sounds like you're not even in the friend zone," Dennis said, whistling.

"That's all I was aiming for," I groaned. "But then I saw her acting all chipper with that other woman and blushing and shit, the caveman part of my brain said I needed to protect her from that."

"No. The caveman part of your brain said, 'she's mine, I saw her first.'" Dennis shoved at my knees. "Is this just an attraction thing or do you actually like her?"

I wanted to lay on the floor.

"I don't know. I'm *definitely* attracted to her, but I get the impression she isn't into casual sex and that's kinda all I've been into recently."

"Is that because you haven't found anybody you're interested in having a relationship with or because you don't want one?"

I spun around on the counter so my legs hung off the customer end and I wasn't facing Denny. It wasn't that I didn't want a relationship, it was that searching for one had led to so much disappointment. And I'd had enough disappointment for a lifetime. It was best to keep things casual.

And there's no way Margo could do casual. Not with how close I am with her family, not with how hard it'd be to keep things from Bailey, and certainly not with my inability to stand by while she's hit on.

"You're right. It's not an issue. I'm just freaking out because it's weird that she's hot now. That's all. I need to focus on tomorrow's choir anyway. Any chance you wanna do some cool bike tricks as an opener?" I hopped off the counter and faced Dennis with a conspiratorial smile.

"Do bike tricks? In the community center? Not only is there not enough space, I have negative desire to do that."

"Whelp, can't blame a girl for asking. I'm still trying to think of a way to top Ms. Taylor, if only to keep on Ashley's good side."

"Right, then get out of here and get to it."

15

MARGO

"You're being an idiot," Wendy said, throwing a pillow at my face. I'd decided that after a whole day with my mom asking about how I'm getting along with Shea and if I enjoyed working at the realtor's office, that I needed to spend the night with my friends.

Next to me, Abigail took the pillow and stuffed it behind her back, probably so Wendy didn't snatch it up for another shot.

Unfortunately, there was another pillow on the ground and Wendy immediately grabbed it and tossed it at my face.

"Wendy!" I groaned, throwing the pillow right back at her. "It's not stupid to not want to be treated like a little kid."

"No, she was —" Wendy started, arm up to toss the pillow again when Abigail stood between us. She snatched the pillow from Wendy and then went around collecting the other remaining pillows scattered about Wendy's apartment. Once collected, Abigail tossed them down the hall and sat back down next to me.

"No more pillow fights," was all she said once she'd settled down. Wendy collapsed back, groaning dramatically.

"What do you think Shea was thinking, Abigail?"

Abigail's face was blank as she thought. "Are you asking me as your friend or as a lesbian?"

"As a friend," I said just as Wendy said, "Lesbian."

Abigail nodded and chewed at her lip as she thought and thought. Wendy and I waited with bated breath, leaning ever so closer to her.

"I think both options are equally possible." Wendy and I collapsed back. "Well, you asked my opinion."

"Sure, but we were hoping you'd at least side with one of us," Wendy grumbled.

"Why can't you just ask Shea out on a date?" Abigail asked. That very thought made all the blood rush to my face.

"There's no way I could do that!"

"Why not?" she asked, the words flat as if she truly thought it was truly that simple. Though knowing Abigail, she probably did think it was that easy.

"Because I have social anxiety! What happens when she says no? I'd have to quit and that would *not* look good on my resume."

"What if she says yes?" Abigail countered.

"You two would go out, have amazing sex, then tell Bailey, and then she'd start planning your wedding," Wendy said.

"Bailey wouldn't plan a wedding just like that," I countered, only to be met with equally confused looks from Abigail and Wendy.

"Have you met your sister?" Wendy asked.

"Yeah, she is definitely not the type to be upset that any two people are in love. I'm sure she'd be ecstatic to call Shea her sister-in-law."

"Ecstatic is too small of a word for how Bailey would react."

"Sure, she'd be happy to be related to Shea, but as soon as she realizes that means that me and Shea are sleeping together she'd get all grossed out and ..." It was stupid and self-centered, but what I remembered clearest on the day Shea came out to her parents was that she'd come over for a sleepover with Bailey. I'd walked by her room and just sort of hung around as they talked. And when they got to the part where Shea described how she knew she liked girls, everything just clicked for me. But then Bailey caught me in the doorway and threw a stuffed unicorn at my face, yelling at me for staring at Shea like she was any different from before. "Bailey's really protective of Shea. I don't think that would change just because I'm her sister."

The others were silent for a long while. They knew about my relationship with Bailey. Or maybe it was better described as a lack of a relationship. A five-year age gap was a big deal for kids. For a long while, she tried to include me in stuff with her friends, but eventually I realized how much of a tag-along that made me and bailed. Nobody wanted to hang out with *me*, they just wanted Bailey around. And once I got into middle school, she was all I heard about. *You're not as artistic as Bailey. All you do is read, Bailey was much more involved in class.* And on and on.

"When was the last time you and Bailey hung out? Like actually hung out, not some family event," Wendy asked.

"Ummm. Maybe on one of her summer breaks while she was in college," I said, not anywhere near confident that was true.

"So about nine years?" Abigail asked, humming when I nodded my head.

"I think I'd go insane if I didn't hang out with my siblings for that long. I mean, they're all turds for leaving me to take care of Dad's dream, but I still love them."

"I mean, I'm not on *bad* terms with Bailey. We just ... don't talk."

"How about the last time you texted her?"

I pulled out my phone and searched for the last text from Bailey. I had to scroll so far to find something not a part of a family group chat, that I gave up and searched her name.

"It was ... back in June. She asked for restaurant recommendations for when they visited for my graduation."

"She didn't even text you when you lost your job?" Wendy exclaimed.

"You said to not include family events! That was in the family chat," I argued.

"I suppose that's reasonable," Abigail murmured while Wendy shot towards my phone.

"Stop trying to steal my phone." I cradled my phone to my chest before crawling over Abigail and using her as a shield.

"This is mildly uncomfortable," Abigail murmured.

"Just let me text her for you."

"Text what?"

"Something like, 'Hey, Shea's pretty cute, let's bond about how we both love her'."

"No!"

"It's not the worst thing to bond over," Abigail countered before slipping out from under my arms. Without her support, I almost went flying over the couch arm when Wendy made another move for my phone.

"Just let me text her," Wendy grumbled, sitting back on her feet, eyes narrowed as she tried to think of a way to grab my phone.

"No, I'm not letting you text my sister about how I have the hots for her best friend!"

"But you're not getting anywhere on your own."

"I don't think I'm ever gonna get anywhere. I should just accept that."

"What if you just text Bailey that you got in a fight with Shea and ask her for advice on making up?" Abigail offered, now seated on the coffee table. "All that really implies is that you want to have a non-antagonistic relationship with Shea. And you wouldn't even need to lie about why you're upset at her."

I sat with the idea, letting my shoulders sink. Monday was going to be awkward as hell, especially if I skipped out on the choir like I was inclined to do. Talking to Bailey was the best chance I had to avoid another excruciatingly awkward conversation.

"Fine. I'll text Bailey."

Abigail made a small 'whew' while Wendy just grumbled about it being better than nothing.

> Me: Hey, I got in a little spat with Shea for treating me like a kid. Do you have any advice for making up with her so things won't get awkward at work?

"I think you cushioned that too much," Wendy commented over my shoulder. I nudged her with my elbow.

> Bailey: Oh no! What happened?

"'She was acting possessive and it's confusing my bi little heart.'" This time I got off the couch and sat on the table next to Abigail.

> Me: She was just over my shoulder while I was working and I got irritated and told her off. She told me she was just trying to help me out, but it felt like she didn't trust me to do my job

I looked over to Abigail, waiting for a comment. She blessedly didn't have any.

> Bailey: That's reasonable. She was probably just trying to look out for you but went a little over board. And her go to when things get awkward is to joke and laugh it off, which can definitely make things more frustrating

> Bailey: She should be easier to talk to Monday with that knee jerk reaction out of her system and you can tell her you need space while working.

"Great, super helpful, sis," I grumbled before another message popped up.

Bailey: And if you really wanna get on her good side, or make her feel guilty for being a bit of a prick in the first place, get her a bag of Tootsie Rolls

16

SHEA

Maybe I should have taken the choir more seriously. Or at the very least done what Margo had mentioned when talking about her library program and taken inventory of the setup to make sure everything was in working order.

Because of course, the stage was missing a pin and there weren't enough Santa hats or harmonicas for all the kids. So instead of being at the community center a couple of hours before kids were scheduled to show up, I was running around town trying to collect all the necessary items, only to get a text from somebody from the PTA about something else they needed.

By the time I finally got back to the community center, I was met with several parents glaring at me and a parade of screaming children.

"Shea," Jackie greeted sharply. I think she was the head of the PTA or maybe just the bitchiest mom in the pack. "Are we finally ready to get setup?"

"Yes, ma'am," I said as chipperly as possible. "I need to set up the stage, but you're all good to get settled in the makeshift green rooms."

The adults huffed, stomping into the church-turned-community center and heading straight to the rooms that used to be daycare centers. The kids however all crowded around me, shouting about their part in the choir, asking how my hair got so red, and requesting specific colors for their harmonicas. Blue was very popular apparently.

Once the kids all had their hats and harmonicas and disappeared into the green room, I ducked into the main area to fix the stage. I'd say it took me a good 30 minutes to get it set up and all the pins in place. It was only a three-tier step thing, but doing it on my own was difficult.

Why didn't I ask any of the girls to help with this?

Oh yeah, because I wanted so much on my plate I didn't think about how miserable Christmas made me or my recent attraction to a woman five years younger than me and related to my best friend.

"Shea, we need you to step in and watch the second graders while we get the others lined up," Jackie said, disappearing before I could question what any of the other PTA members were doing and why they couldn't watch the kids.

As quickly as I could, I finished up with the stage, hopping on the steps to make sure it didn't crumble under my weight, then made my way to the green room. Except when I reached the door, there wasn't any noise. Pretty weird for second graders hyped to perform to be so quiet.

So when I opened the door, I was braced for some kind of prank, like a chalkboard eraser at the top of the door. Though none of them were tall enough for that specific prank.

I opened the door to an empty room. Not a single kid in sight.

Fuck, fuck, fuck.

Wait, no, can't panic yet. Maybe it was still a prank and they were hiding in the room somewhere.

Except they weren't under the tables. Or in the cabinets. Or behind the curtains.

"Fuck," I hissed before running into the hallway and smack dab into somebody. For a moment I prayed it was a small child I'd knocked over and my panic could quickly be eased.

But it wasn't one of the choir kids. It was Margo.

Margo on her hands and knees picking up some candy she'd been holding when I knocked into her.

"Oh shit, sorry." I joined her on the floor to help scoop up the candy, shoving them into a pile in front of her while I kept my head on a swivel for the missing second graders. When it was clear the kids weren't anywhere in the hallway, I looked down at the candy and finally noticed what it was. "Oh shit, Tootsie Rolls. Can I have one?"

"Oh," Margo said, sitting back on her feet. "They're actually for you."

A crowd had started congregating outside the main room, which meant I had less than an hour to find these kids before they were supposed to go on stage.

"Shit, sorry, Margo. I can't talk right now. Some of the kids went missing and I've got to find them before the show starts. But I'm sure they're fine. Just playing a prank on me or something."

"Shea," Margo said, her voice sharp and reminiscent of a school teacher. "This is not the kind of situation you can make light of. How old is this group and when did you notice they were missing?"

Now was a bad time to consider if I was a switch, right?

I shook my head clear before looking around and dragging Margo up and into the green room.

"I was getting the stage setup when Jackie told me to come watch the second graders in this room. I still had to check if it could hold weight, so I did that before coming here. Unless Jackie and the other PTA folks had left before that, they couldn't have been alone for more than 10 minutes."

"Why would Jackie ask you to watch the kids when you were in the middle — doesn't matter. How many of them were there?"

"Um ... not more than ten."

Margo hummed, looking around the room. The kids had left their jackets and bags strewn about the place.

"They probably just got bored and wandered off, right?" I asked, getting nervous over how intensely Margo was looking at everything. If this was some buddy cop show, she'd definitely be the hard-ass cop.

"I mean, they might have. But kids their age aren't usually quiet, even if they're trying to be sneaky. So it's odd you didn't hear them from just down the hall." Margo started to the door and I dutifully followed. "I'll check the rooms on this side, you check that side. Text me if you find them, okay?"

"Rodger that," I said, saluting her. Margo narrowed her eyes but walked off without saying anything.

I'd never thought the community center was that large of a building, but then again I only ever came here for town halls and the occasional seasonal event. Apparently, this place was fucking huge. There was a dedicated room for every religion, a full locker room, a half-court gym, and a restaurant-sized kitchen. And that was only on my half of the building and didn't include the second floor, which as far as I knew was always locked up during events.

The one thing I didn't find was the kids. Not even a stray Santa hat.

> **Me:** Any luck on your end?

> **Margo:** No. I've looped back to the front and a bunch of folks have asked where you're at.

> **Me:** Shit

> **Margo:** I told them you took the kids back for a bathroom break, so hopefully that'll buy you some time

> **Me:** What do we think the possibility is that they went outside?

> **Margo:** There were folks meandering outside when I got here, so I don't think so

> **Margo:** But I'll do a lap around the front and check the garden. Have you checked the upstairs yet?

> **Me:** No, they keep it locked up whenever there're events. I think that's where they store the wine

> **Margo:** Well check the doors just in case

> **Me:** Yes, ma'am

I bit my lip and considered texting her something more ... flirtatious. It wasn't a smart thing to do considering I'd just lost a bunch of kids and I hadn't even really apologized for the whole Dana thing yet.

But impulse control was never my strong suit.

> **Me:** If I find any wine, wanna split it with me afterwards?

The dots came and went away about five times before I got a response.

> **Margo:** Maybe

Well, that was better than an outright no, so I'd take it.

I rounded back to the other end of the church, ducking my head in every room and supply closet I passed, and then went up the stairs. As far as I knew, there was only one staircase to the second floor, tucked across the hall from the backside of the main room. It was narrow and dark and the steps squealed under my weight. But despite the creepy vibes, I made it to the top and lo and behold the door actually was unlocked.

The sounds of children's laughter was immediate. Like I think the priests or whoever used to live up here before the church was refitted into a community center were into some kinky shit. I mean, what other reason would they have to soundproof this floor *that* well?

I followed the sound of the kids to one of the further rooms and when I opened the cracked door, they all hopped up and shouted.

"Santa came!"

"It wasn't Santa, it was Mrs. Clause."

"She gave us candy!"

"And we got stickers!"

"She helped us practice too!"

"Woah, woah, woah, kids. That's all crazy exciting, but let's take a quick breath and remember to save our voices for singing, yeah?" I said, eyes whipping around the room to do a head count. All the kids were here but there wasn't any sign of this mysterious Mrs. Clause.

"Ms. Shea is it time for us to go down now?" one kid asked, pulling at my pant leg.

"Yeah, bud. But … did Mrs. Clause say why she brought you up here?" I asked, dipping down to the kid's levels.

"So that we wouldn't get in the way," one girl answered.

"And 'cause the candy was up here," another boy said, holding out his half-eaten lollipop.

"She said somebody'd come to get us when it was time for the show and to stay here and be quiet," the first kid added.

"Right. Well, you guys did a great job staying in place. Are y'all ready to sing now?" A choir of yes's went off from the kids and I told them to do a search around the room to make sure everything was cleaned up before we went downstairs. With them occupied, I pulled out my phone.

> **Me:** Children secured.

> **Me:** Apparently somebody dressed as Mrs. Clause told them to come up here for candy

> **Me:** Oh shit, I just noticed the time

"All right, kids. Let's line up and go back downstairs. It's time for the show." And by time, I mean we were definitely late and there was no way somebody hadn't noticed that we were missing. I was, at the bare minimum, looking at a harsh phone call with Ms. Taylor.

So I grabbed a bottle from a random wine rack on the way back.

Once we were all downstairs, I led the kids to the back area of the main room and was strangely met by … nothing. The few parents and adults that were in the back were all silently standing around the door to the stage. When the kids all ran up, the adults motioned for them to be quiet before ushering them out the door. Curious, I followed the kids.

I don't know what I expected to walk into. Maybe the other grades signing or someone playing the equivalent of hold music while parents chatted in the pews.

Instead of singing, all the kids were seated on the floor in front of the stage. And sitting on the stage, was Margo. She had a stack of books to her left and one in hand that she was reading from. And she was wearing one of the Santa hats.

"A wink of his eye and a twist of his head," Margo read, looking up from the book to give the kids a wink. Several of them winked back, giggling. "Soon gave me to know I had nothing to dread."

Margo continued reading from the storybook, pausing to mimic the poem or make hand gestures. Her voice was so gentle and engaging, she had all the kids giggling and smiling like it was Christmas day.

Then as she approached the last line, she leaned forward to wink at the kids. They all nodded their heads and Margo continued reading.

"But I heard him exclaim, ere he drove out of sight," Margo started.

"Merry Christmas to all and to all a good night!" the kids shouted in unison, throwing up their Santa hats and giggling. In the pews, parents laughed and applauded their kids.

"Thank you for joining me for story time," Margo said to the kids, before gesturing to the door behind the stage. "Now, let's get ready to sign, yeah?"

The kids all cheered before rushing to the door where I was standing. I barely managed to step back in time before they stampeded in. And once they cleared, Margo followed.

"Hey," I said, having a hard time finding the right words to thank her. I mean, I don't think anyone's covered my ass in front of a whole crowd like that. "Thank you for —"

"Shea, can you *please* go into the office and print the music sheets for the pianist? Someone didn't get a chance to before the event started," Jackie said, her voice edging into a sneer as she looked over her shoulder at one of the dads.

"Sure, just a second, I —"

"Go ahead," Margo said. "I'll help with the kids here and we can talk after."

"After. Sure."

17

MARGO

It was another hour after everyone left that we got everything cleaned up and put away. And despite working up a sweat and being just generally exhausted, when Shea turned to me with a mischievous smile and asked if I wanted to stay for wine, I couldn't help but say yes.

Plus I still had to give her the Tootsie Rolls.

"All right, now where should we enjoy our spoils?" Shea asked, holding up the wine bottle.

"How about the baptismal pool?" I jerked my head to where the pool was behind the stage.

"Huh. Sure, but I have no clue how to get up there. Is there a ladder hiding somewhere?" Shea started to walk to the stage, so I grabbed her hand and led us to the back.

"I forget that your group didn't do the summer program here."

"That 'not' Bible camp thing?"

"Yeah," I laughed. "They really didn't teach us any religious stuff. It was more like a park and recs summer program. And since there's no rec center in Snowfall, this worked just as well."

"Oh, the gym and locker rooms make a lot more sense now."

"Did you really not know they were there?" I asked, stopping to give her a raised eyebrow look.

"Nah, I've never been past the main room. I didn't even realize the building stretched this far back."

I laughed and continued dragging her upstairs.

"Well, during summer camp, Abigail found most of the activities overstimulating and I didn't have any interest in being outside in 100-degree heat, so Wendy took it upon herself to scout out a place where we could just chill all day. The counselors used the upstairs as their break room, so they always left the door unlocked."

I brought us around the corner to the pool door and let go of Shea's hand to shove it open. I went down the steps and settled into a corner of the empty pool while Shea looked around in wonder.

"Shit, this must have been a cool hideout," she whispered before settling down next to me. She pulled out her keys from her jacket, which of course included a wine opener, and opened the bottle. After one long swig, she handed it over to me.

It took me an embarrassingly long time to take a sip because knowing our lips touched the same bottle made my head fuzzy.

"So," Shea and I said at the same time and laughed.

"You go first," I murmured passing the bottle back to her.

"Sure, I ..." Shea trailed off and took another sip of wine. She set the bottle down on the concrete floor and spun it around her finger.

It was weird to see Shea act nervous. For my whole life, she was the casual, always cracking a joke, knew what to do in any situation kind of person. She was comfortable in her skin and had nothing to feel awkward about. Both of those ideas were being broken right in front of me.

Or maybe not broken. More like dissolved.

Shea wasn't a person I used to have a crush on. She was a person I was just getting to know.

"I'm sorry for treating you like a kid the other day. That was *definitely* not was I going for. But I did take a choice away from you and that wasn't cool. So I'll be better about making assumptions about what you want or what's best for you. And if you want me to, I'll track down Dana and explain that we're not together."

No, I definitely still had a crush if the twisting in my gut was any indication.

"No, that's not — that won't be necessary. I wasn't ... upset about that. I was upset about ..." I paused and decided what the hell. "Sometimes being the youngest in a small town sucks."

"What do you mean?" Shea asked, the bottle still in her hands.

"I'm always Bailey's sister, the little kid. No matter how old I am, everybody sees me as this kid that needs to get taken care of. You did, my parents are constantly over my shoulder, and any time I go and get something from the bookstore that old man always comes over to get a book off the high shelf for me like I can't just get a stool. And if they're not babying me, they're comparing me to her. I don't have a career, I'm not good at the things she's good at, I failed at moving out of town, I'm not as outgoing as she is. It's so stupid. And anytime I want to correct it, I feel like a jerk because everyone means well. And … you hit a nerve, I guess. and I'm sorry for yelling at you."

I rummaged through my coat's pockets and pulled out a handful of Tootsie Rolls, holding them out to Shea as a peace offering.

"For me?" she asked and when I nodded, grabbed the whole lot of them. She unwrapped two at a time and stuck one in her mouth, holding the other right in front of my lips. Heat burning my cheeks, I opened my mouth and let her slip the candy in.

"I'm sorry shit's been like that for you. And I'm sorry I contributed to it," Shea said between chews. "I'd never really thought about the side effects of having a sibling. The comparison shit. But for the record, I think that old man at the bookstore does that to everyone so he can feel useful, so you're not alone there."

I snorted so hard I had to cover my face for fear of spit or snot or candy shooting out my nose. When I chanced a glance at Shea to see if she caught me being absolutely ridiculous, she was smiling at me, head rested on her knees.

"Dana was right. You really are cute."

I had to look away or else my face would explode.

"You know calling me cute just feeds into the little kid thing," I grumbled, pulling up my knees so I could hide my face.

"Would you rather I call you sexy instead?" Shea teased. I wanted to look up, I wanted to see her face and gauge how genuine she was being. But I simply couldn't.

"Maybe," was as brave of an answer as I could manage.

"I can work with that," Shea said with a laugh. I dug my fingers into my jeans till I could feel the bite of my nails. "But Margo, you and Bailey are incomparable, no matter what people say. Anybody who can't see that isn't looking, therefore their opinion doesn't matter. As for the treating you like a kid thing, just give people a look like they're doing the most insane shit ever and they'll back off."

I threw my head back and laughed. Well, snorted. And once my laughter calmed, I couldn't help but look at Shea. She had the softest smile pulling her lips up, soft pink coloring her cheeks.

"You've got a sexy laugh," she said, the smile tipping into something more mischievous.

"Sexy?" I repeated. Shea took another sip of wine and hummed. "Shea, I literally snorted. How is that sexy?"

"Well, I'm not allowed to call you cute, so, you know."

I leaned my whole body into Shea's, knocking her shoulder, and we both giggled.

"But in all seriousness, I don't think folks'll compare you to Bailey as much after tonight."

"What'd'ya mean?"

"Your little story time save. That was amazing! You had the kids eating out of the palm of your hand and all the adults were charmed by you too. You shouldn't be surprised if folks assume you're doing that every year now."

"Yeah right. I'm sure none of them will notice if I'm not here next year."

"I will," Shea said quietly, staring off. The bottle was at her lips again and she pushed away from me to stand. "But anyways. I owe you big time for saving my ass today."

Shea leaned down with a hand out and I took it so she could pull me up. Then her hand snuck into my coat pocket with all the Tootsie Rolls. But instead of just stealing the candy, her finger trailed along the waist of my jeans through the pocket. As she toyed with me, her eyes landed on my lips and she sucked in a deep breath. My body was screaming to close my eyes and tilt my head, but my mind wasn't able to rationalize that sort of action. Or maybe it'd be more accurate to say, I didn't have enough proof Shea wanted to kiss me to assuage my anxiety.

"Margo, I need you to do something for me, okay?"

My heart was either in my throat or in my stomach. Or maybe lower.

"Sure," I squeaked, cursing how the nerves affected my voice.

"I need ..." Shea paused, licking her lips before her eyes finally met mine. She blinked a few times before stepping back, her hand falling out of my pocket. "I need your help with these holiday things. Obviously. You've clearly got a better idea of how to plan big things like this, while I ... don't."

I am not *disappointed.*

"Don't be to hard on yourself. You're a forest person, I'm a tree person. Every project needs both."

"So you'll help with the rest of them?" Shea asked, eyes brightening.

"Yeah. I mean, I'm your office's assistant, so that sorta makes me *your* assistant too." I shrugged, busying myself by looking around the pool to make sure nothing got left behind.

"Fuck," Shea hissed and I turned back to face her. Her head was tilted up to the ceiling with one hand covering her eyes. She rubbed her hand over her face moaning something unintelligible.

"You okay there? Too much wine?" I asked, stepping up to take the bottle. It wasn't a huge glass, but we had managed to drink half of it.

"Sorry, no. Just … tired. You need a ride home?" Shea asked, already walking over to the exit.

"No, I drove." I followed behind, but once I'd said no, Shea's steps sped up.

"Right. Drive safe then. See you tomorrow." And then she practically sprinted away, leaving me with a half a bottle of wine and a lot of confusion.

18

SHEA

I had four days left until the craft show at the high school and I was already feeling a hundred times more prepared than I was for the choir. And it was all thanks to Margo.

On the downside, I was barely getting any sleep. Also because of Margo.

A good three hours after I'd left the community center, she sent a detailed list of things I needed to do for the craft show, broken down into a timeline. The list included everything from confirming supplies available at the school to what needed to be rented and from whom. And it even covered what vendors were scheduled to show up and who still needed to be followed up with. It was incredibly detailed and exactly what I needed to stay on track.

The thing is, every time Margo texted me about some holiday event thing, I felt the need to ask her something personal. Not invading, just ... something to get to know her better.

I'd thought a lot about what she said about being in Bailey's shadow all her life. And I could see it. Bailey was amazing and bright and kind. And Margo was those things too, just in a different way. Different, *not* wrong, no matter what anyone else said. And I had a lot of experience with being different and thinking I was wrong.

Margo: T-minus 4 days checklist attached

Me: Oh it's getting smaller

Margo: I like to front load things. Either the big tasks need more time and I've got it or I've got less to do and can relax

Me: Smart and sexy

Her chat bubbles popped up five times before I got a reply.

> **Margo:** Are you ever going to let that go?

> **Me:** Maybe, you'll have to stick around to find out

Another series of bubbles.

It was a shame her desk was facing away from me. I'd loved to watch her chew at her lips as she figured out what to say.

On second thought, it was best that I couldn't see her. After our little chat in the baptismal pool, I realized my sexual attraction was getting to the point where one little comment, like her being my secretary, had me ready to pant at her feet.

And yet here I was, flirting with her digitally.

So to keep it light, I texted her again before she could respond to my flirting.

> **Me:** How many types of library sciences are there and how'd you decide on yours?

> **Margo:** I don't know if there's a set number. There're the basics and the specialized concentrations to study. I picked community engagement because it was what interested me the most. I mean, Snowfall has its town halls

> **Margo:** and Ms. Taylor, but other places don't. The library is a perfect place to start building a sense of community. And the best way to do that is by providing things people actually need.

Me: Like a sewing machine?

Margo: Don't underestimate the usefulness of readily available machinery

Margo: My library back in NY even had a 3D printer

Me: They had a 3D printer but they didn't update their sewing machines?

Margo: ... well, yeah, priorities were a little skewed. The printer was cool, but not super useful for most people

Margo: But there's tons of shit you can print with them that help with accessibility!

Margo: [link]

Me: Imma be honest, Margo, I have no idea what I'm looking at

Margo: A lot of those are for folks that have poor hand strength. But there are some 3D printers that can make prosthetics.

Me: You're cute when you're dorking out about community accessibility

Another series of dots.

Margo: You're cute when you're pretending to do work

Can you be frozen and burning up at the same time? Was Margo being cheeky with me or was this how she flirted? I was too scared to look up at her desk and check.

What if she *was* flirting with me? What would I do with that? What did I *want* to do with that? If she was just some random chick, I'd have brought her home already. Fuck, given my recent relationships, she would've dumped me already because I didn't spend enough time with her or always wanted to be out or whatever other bullshit reasons I'd been dumped for.

It could be worth it though.

I crashed my head into my desk.

"You all right there?" Phillip asked and I flipped him off.

Maybe I should just call up an old fuck buddy so at least the sexual attraction will subside. That's the smart thing to do here, move on before it's even an issue.

I chanced a glance up at Margo and caught her looking at me, head tilted in concern. She'd chosen to wear her hair up today, a small little ponytail that was just enough to grab.

I waved away Margo's concern and pulled out my phone, because I had to do something, and that something definitely wasn't going to be Margo. No matter how much I wanted it to be.

19

MARGO

Being back in my high school was weird. Being back at night on a Friday with my childhood crush made it even weirder. I'd spent so many hours here, literally years ago, and it somehow felt like just the other day I was hiding out in the library during study hall so I didn't have to listen to people gossip.

Overall, not much had changed. The hall that led to the commons was covered in posters advertising clubs and plays and various odd jobs around town. The benches that filled up the open space were the same old wooden seats that wobbled and creaked if someone so much as breathed near them.

But there were some things that were eerily unfamiliar. The names along the offices and banners. The designs filling the school store. And the bathroom doors, which had finally been painted to cover the graffiti.

"Is this the first time you've been back since graduating?" Shea asked, coming up from behind me, pushing a cart of the tables that we needed to set up.

"Yeah. Is it always this weird?"

"The first few times, sure. But there're enough town events hosted here that you get over it quick. There's only so many times you can pass by your old locker and think of your first girlfriend, you know?"

"No, I can't really relate to that," I said, laughing at the idea of getting with anyone in high school, let alone a girl.

Shea was quiet for a minute as she pulled one table off the cart and started carrying it to the tape on the floor that marked the layout. Then she paused and straightened. "Oh yeah. Cause you hadn't realized you were bi yet. Duh. Sorry."

I grabbed a table to set up and debating telling her the truth. Since the whole choir fiasco and subsequent … weirdness in the baptismal pool, we'd been getting to know each other. Through 3 a.m. texts talking about the best milkshake flavor combos and forcing each other to watch niche YouTube series from nearly a decade ago. I could open up to her a little bit more. As a friend.

"Actually, I did know."

A table crashed down and I turned to see Shea gawking at me.

"Wait, seriously? I thought you figured it out in college?"

I couldn't help but snort at the assumption before turning back to set up my table. "No, I knew way before college."

"Really? When'd you figure it out? Like your label realization."

"Um, when I was eleven or twelve I think." *Please don't do the math, please don't do the math.*

"So like around the time I came out?"

Fuck.

"Yup." I popped the P, trying to keep my focus on the table and control the heat in my cheeks.

"Aw, did I inspire you?" Shea teased, her steps echoing as she came up behind me. She put her hands on my waist, tickling me. I jerked, twisting around to smack her away. But Shea didn't move like I expected. She kept a light hold on my waist so her hands skated over my shirt. And then we were face to face, pelvis to pelvis. If I pushed up on my toes, I could kiss her.

"So what is it? Did I make you queer or what?" Shea cocked an eyebrow, clearly just trying to tease me. But my brain was taking me to a different kind of teasing. And the heat of our bodies pressed together and the placement of her hands was not helping to keep my thoughts PG.

"I guess when you came out, I realized liking girls was an option," I stammered quietly, wanting to look away but couldn't. No queer woman should be allowed to have such pretty eyes, it's unfair. They sparkled like a fairy forest, even under the harsh fluorescent lights of the school.

"Do you remember much about when I came out?" Shea asked, her voice softening.

"Most of what happened. I think. Or at least a summary of it." At some point afterwards, my parents sat me down and explained what Shea coming out meant and gave me a brief summary of how her parents reacted. They hadn't kicked her out, but they made it clear they had no intention of supporting Shea after she turned 18. For me, as a little kid, all that meant was that Shea was over at our place a couple of times a week.

"So you know your parents pretty much adopted me, right?" I could only nod in response. "So why haven't you told them yet?"

"Well, I ... I think they'll ... or more like because it doesn't ... it doesn't ..." I stammered. It was so stupid that this was so hard to explain, especially to Shea. I mean, she got the dreaded outcome, the one so many people are afraid of. My fear was so much simpler than that and it still got me teary eyed.

"Woah, woah, woah. Sorry, I should've known better than to ask you outright like that. I mean, that's like a post a couple of bottles of wine kind of conversation," Shea joked, moving her hands from my waist to my back as she pulled me into her arms. She squeezed me tight before continuing, half rambling, half laughing. "Forget I asked. Seriously. Here." She spun me around, my back against her chest, and pointed over my shoulder to a corner of the commons. "That's where I had my technical first and only kiss with a dude. He was a nice guy, but dear lord, he should've known I was gay based on the way his tongue kept glossing over my lips and I didn't open up. He texted me within an hour of me being out to ask if he turned me. Turned me were the exact words he used too. Like I'd become some vampire or something. What're your opinions of *Twilight* by the way? Specifically the movies. I think Alice is queer."

Shea let go of me and started back over to the tables. I kind of hated the way she diverted into jokes any time something serious, or even just awkward, came up. I know she was just trying to lighten the mood but it was starting to feel like she was sweeping things under the rug, like she was asking these big questions without caring about the answer.

So I decided to give her the answer anyways.

"I'm afraid they won't care."

Shea turned back around, a flask halfway to her mouth. I stomped over and snatched the bottle from her, taking a long swig. The burn of cinnamon was almost enough for me to question Shea's choice of beverages. On school grounds no less. But I needed to say this before I chickened out.

"I'm afraid that me coming out won't matter to anyone. Because why should it matter? I'm bi, so what? My parents raised me so that I knew I could tell them I was bi or queer or trans and they would still love and support me like they always have. Nothing would change. *Nothing would change.* And if nothing changes, why should I even bother telling them? If I know they won't make a big deal out if it and just say it doesn't change anything, what's the point? My parents love me, they'll always love me, but I can't see them *not* care about something this important to me."

I couldn't really see Shea in front of me anymore. My eyes were blurry and full of tears. And there was probably an amount of snot happening. But that was definitely because the school never invested in a heater that could handle things when it was less than 50 degrees outside.

And since I couldn't see, I didn't notice Shea coming until her arms were wrapped around me. The flask dropped out of my hands and the too strong smell of cinnamon filled the air. But as strong as it was, and let's be real it was *fucking* strong, I was distracted by the almost equally overwhelming smell of Shea. She smelled like a Girl Scout cookie, though Shea was exactly the kind of person to buy cookie-scented shampoo.

"It does matter, because *you* matter," Shea whispered, squeezing me tighter. "Your parents, your friends, anybody you choose to share yourself with should be happy to learn more about you, that you'd trust them with something so personal. Just because it doesn't change things literally, just because your parents have already said the words that they support you, doesn't mean you don't deserve to come out and be celebrated."

I was fully crying into my crush's breast and there was absolutely nothing I could do to stop or hide it.

God, Shea was so fucking nice. How did she know exactly what I needed to hear?

Because she needed to hear it herself at some point.

I squeezed Shea tighter. It wasn't fair that she wasn't celebrated for coming out to her parents. It wasn't fair that they made her feel so alienated that she moved out at 17. It wasn't fair that she went through all that and I was complaining about

—

"You know what? I didn't really celebrate you either. Let's fix that," Shea said, shaking me in her arms before letting go. "We'll have a sleepover. How's that sound?"

Shea held out her arms and twirled around.

"Wait, here?"

"Yeah, here. Weren't you always curious about what the school was like after dark? Now's the perfect chance to find out." Shea skipped over to the cart where all her things were and riffled through her bag for her keys.

"Shea, we can't just stay in the school," I tried to argue despite the giggles I was fighting off. I couldn't help it, Shea's enthusiasm was contagious.

"We most certainly can. Because, one, somebody put in our email to the school that we would need access to the building *all* night. So nobody will get pissed at us or anything. And two, I've got everything we need for a sleepover in my car." Shea threw a thumb over her shoulder and I raised an eyebrow.

"Everything?" I questioned.

"Well, you know. Never know when you might need to crash somewhere. Or spill coffee all over yourself on the way to a showing." Shea shrugged, her face turning the softest shade of pink. "I've got some toiletries, blankets, clothes. Enough for us to share."

"Share?" I repeated.

"Yeah. If you don't mind, that is." Shea shrugged again, fiddling with her keys and not making eye contact.

My brain was TV static. A cacophony of questions looping around my head so many times, it wasn't even words.

"Sure. That's fine."

"Sweet. I'll be right back." Shea swung her keys around her finger, and then headed for the door.

20

SHEA

After getting all the tables set up, because we did have to get our job done before the fun, we built a fort.

Our fort consisted of the tablecloths that were supposed to go over tables 27 to 30, chip clips, a few benches, and all the cushions from the couches in the front office. It wasn't the most aesthetically pleasing fort, especially considering the blanket from my car was still coated in fur from when I cat-sat for a neighbor. And the fact that I was wearing sweats with paint stains because I wanted Margo to have the nicer pair. But it was also cute for all its messiness.

"The gates to the cafeteria are down and locked, so I couldn't get to the vending machines. But I did manage to find Ms. Henderson's snack stash. So we've got mystery Pop-Tarts, Ring Pops, and popcorn. Saying all that out loud makes me realize these might be leftovers from a themed party. What do you think? Did someone pop the questions or are they gonna pop out a baby?"

Margo crawled into our fort with one arm cradling a basket of pop-themed snacks. She set them down on our makeshift bed, then got up on her knees to look around the fort. I would have loved to say I saw a sparkle in her eye or a soft smile of appreciation. But I was incapable of seeing anything beyond Margo in my clothes.

It's a good thing the craft show wasn't held in the community center because if we ended up having a sleepover in the church, I'd burn all the way to hell. Not even thoughts of my grandma could calm the way my fingers itched to slide under that shirt, to take all my clothes back, and to keep her warm some other way.

"Shea?" Margo said and I shook my head. Margo needed to feel cared about and celebrated, not leered at.

"Sorry. I'd guess pregnancy. I feel like offices don't really celebrate engagements like that."

Margo paused for a second before nodding and settled down beside me.

God, she smelled like a thunderstorm. Or soap that was called thunderstorm, as if anybody knew what the actual scents of a thunderstorm were.

"So," Margo said, dragging out the word as she knocked her knee into mine. "What sleepover activities are we doing?"

"Spin the bottle," I said instinctively, hopefully maybe. Then immediately panicked and added, "Is out of the question. No suspense when there's only two of us." I cringed at my awkward laughter and racked my brain for literally *anything* else. Then I remembered Olivia and Denny's shed moment and practically shouted, "Truth or dare."

"Oh, sure. Who's first?"

I chanced a glance at Margo. She'd brought her legs up and wrapped her arms around them, head resting on her knees, looking at me. Her eyes were still red from crying earlier and her hair was frizzy from all our work moving tables. It was a look that I could easily imagine being caused by different circumstances.

"You go. I'll — just let me put on some background music first." Quiet led to thoughts I didn't need or want. It was just a different brand of unwanted thoughts with Margo around.

"Background music?" Margo repeated, her voice hitched up.

"Yeah, just so it's not too quiet, you know?" I pulled up my favorites playlist on my phone, hit play, and set it between Margo and me. It was a small barrier, but it would do.

"Oh." Margo sounded disappointed, but whatever the reason was, she shook it off. "Sure. I guess I pick truth."

I think I forgot how truth or dare worked and how it required a lot of talking and vulnerability. Honestly, I'm pretty sure Margo in my shirt, definitely not wearing a bra, knocked out my ability to have clear and coherent thoughts.

What did Bailey and I talk about during sleepovers? What were our truth or dares like?

"Who are you crushing on right now?" That's a normal question to ask, right? And I definitely wasn't asking because of some personal interest.

"Oh." The noise was so small, I finally stopped staring at the floor to look at Margo. She laid down, shuffling around to get comfortable on her side, facing me, then pulled a blanket up to her shoulder. "I'm still crushing on the same person I always have. But they're never gonna see me like that."

Oh. It was like a stab to the gut. And I didn't have any drinks left to ease the pain because my dumbass literally couldn't *not* hug Margo when she was crying.

Was it pathetic that I couldn't remember the last time I cared about a partner or potential partner more than I did the comfort of a drink? Then again none of my past partners would have jumped to my rescue the way Margo did at the choir. And none of them would have organized a mess I got myself into the way Margo has either.

"It's fine. I accepted it a *long* time ago." It was on the tip of my tongue to ask who this long-time crush was. If it was a friend, if the reason they'd never be a thing was because the other person wasn't attracted to women, if it was her best friend Wendy. But it wasn't my place to ask those questions and frankly I didn't want to hear the answer. Plus this was supposed to be a celebration sleepover, so I shouldn't bring the mood down by asking follow-up questions about something neither of us wanted to dwell on.

"Your turn, truth or dare?"

"Dare." No way in hell could I answer any question honestly without a drink. Maybe I should run out and grab something. That'd make this game more fun and silly, right?

"Uh, I dare you to ..." Margo rolled onto her back, staring at the blanket ceiling as she thought. "I dare you to show me your Hinge profile."

"Seriously?" I laughed. "What? Are you gonna judge my profile?"

"Obviously," Margo answered deadpan, a smile fighting at the corner of her lips.

Still laughing, I grabbed my phone and opened up the app before handing it over to Margo. She immediately started scrolling through my profile, eyes greedily racing across the screen.

"Wow, you've got your location set out far," she said, whistling.

"Well, there's not too many folks available unless my range goes out to Charlotte."

"Charlotte, huh." She clicked her tongue and kept scrolling. Then something she saw made her smirk and I had to bite my lip to keep from asking what it was. "How long did it take you to settle on your favorite Taylor Swift song?"

Margo turned the screen to show a favorite song prompt which I'd answered '*Call It What You Want* by Taylor Swift. Obviously'.

"Oh no, that was an easy answer. It's my all time favorite song, hands down."

"So you want the necklace thing?"

"Yeah. Who doesn't?" I tried to laugh as I spoke to cover how silly the wish was. I mean, it was silly. A necklace with your person's initial didn't prove they knew you better than anyone else. Anyone who didn't care about Taylor would think it's a territorial thing. And sure, it was kind of like claiming someone. But it was a claim of knowing somebody at their worst and still wanting them to be yours.

"Duly noted," Margo said before clearing her throat and adding, "I'll let your next partner know."

Lord knows when my next partner would come along. I'd be happy to just have someone to fuck as a distraction. Meaningless sex is what I did well, might as well keep at it.

"Oh," Margo murmured. But this wasn't the soft oh of confusion or disappointment. This was a strangled, surprised oh. Like maybe she saw something that —

"Shit," I murmured. I couldn't even bring myself to try and snatch my phone back, the damage was already done. Margo had seen my thirst trap photo. The only thing I could do now was curl up in a ball of shame.

It wasn't that the picture was bad or even *that* risque. But the pictures you put on your profile when you're looking for a fling and when you're looking for a partner are very different. And sure, I had some of both because I couldn't quite give up on the idea that someday *somebody* wouldn't get tired of my quirks after a month, but I did leave one picture that was very … well it gave the impression I was down to fuck.

The picture in question was from a pride event in Charlotte last year. Bailey, in all her hippie ways, suggested I wear the strap parts of my strap on under my shorts. The straps made a very suggestive line to follow. Plus the halter I wore gave my tits a nice squeeze for the cut out of cleavage. I think I'd been eye fucking some blonde across the street when Bailey snapped the pic.

I looked hot as fuck, but I didn't want Margo to think I was some sort of sex fiend. I mean, I did like sex and I was *very* interested in sex with Margo. But it was also Margo, Bailey's little sister. It was Margo, who answered my late night texts with something so well thought out that I knew she'd actually thought about her response. It was Margo, who read to little kids so well that I was pretty sure they all imprinted on her from that one story.

Margo wasn't a quick fuck.

"All right. That's enough gawking, everybody has horny pics on their profile. You can't judge me for —" I turned to Margo, hand reached out for her to give me back my phone. But Margo wasn't cringing at my picture or dramatically covering her eyes. No, she was flushed. Flushed and had her fingers pinched over the screen to zoom in at something.

"You see something you like there?" I chuckled. Margo squeaked, turning a bright shade of red, and tossed my phone across the fort.

"You threw my phone." I threw my head back and laughed. Margo twisted around the blankets, her shirt hiking up as she scrambled to crawl to where my phone had landed. Which meant I had a nice view of her lower back and a full view of her ample ass.

That ass was going to get me in trouble.

Margo's hand wrapped around my phone at the same time my hands wrapped around the dip of her bare waist.

"Nah-uh. You can't erase the evidence, I wanna see what you were looking at so closely." I twisted us around so we were lying on our sides and wrapped one arm around Margo, pinning her to me so I could reach for my phone. But Margo squirmed further up so my hold was on her ass, almost dragging the sweatpants down, and my phone out of reach.

"I wasn't looking at anything," Margo grumbled as she started poking at my phone, making a guess at my passkey.

"Mm-hmm. If you weren't looking at anything, why are you keeping my phone from me?"

"Because I —" As Margo faltered to come up with an answer, I slid my hands back up and started tickling her sides. Margo squealed and tried to roll away, but I followed, tightening my grip as I landed on top of her. Margo stared up at me, eyes fluttering.

"Wendy tries to steal my phone a lot, so I have practice at keep-away," Margo said, her hand with my phone slipping under her back, hips arching ever so slightly against me.

Wendy was probably the crush that would never like her back. And having her brought up now, when I was on top of Margo, cracked something inside me.

"Oh yeah? But is Wendy willing to play dirty?"

"Ye—" Margo started to say before my hands slid from her waist, going up and up. My thumbs grazed over soft stomach to ribs till just the tip of my fingers hit the swell of her breasts. Margo arched into my touch, her breaths shallow under my palms. The hand holding my phone slid out from under her, though I had a hard time remembering why I needed to take it back in the first place. She could stare at pictures of me all day if she wanted, especially if that meant she wound up under me. Hot and fluttery. Looking up at me with dark and hazey eyes, licking her lips like she was curious about what I tasted like. Or maybe I was projecting, because I sure as fuck wondered what Margo tasted like.

I don't know who leaned in first. Maybe neither of us did and gravity and my nonexistent workout routine did all the work. But either way, the space between us vanished and our lips were together for the softest, tenderest kiss I'd had in a long ass time. Tender in a way that suited how I was starting to see Margo, sweet and kind and making me feel supported and —

Margo pushed up, hands digging into my hair, one still holding my phone so that the rapid pulse of my heart was drowned out by *False God*. Appropriate. Tilting her head, Margo deepened the kiss, alternating between teasing the corner of my lip with the tip of her tongue and pressing her full lips to mine, the kiss wet and just forceful enough to drive me insane.

My hands were still under her shirt, so I slid them up her back and pulled her closer. I landed on my ass and Margo followed my movement, settling over one of my thighs and lowering just enough for me to feel the heat between her legs. I took my hands out of her shirt to grab her waist and grind her against my thighs. Margo gasped and I took my chance to taste her, really fucking taste her. She tasted like Fireball and brown sugar Pop-Tarts. She tasted like a cozy night, curled up by a fire while we talked about stupid shit.

In Margo's hand, my phone flashed to life with, probably, a text. I had no interest in looking when Margo shifted so her knee rubbed against my cunt. But then it flashed again and

Margo pulled back, holding the phone to the side so we could both see.

For a moment, I didn't look. I was busy memorizing Margo. Her lips were swollen and wet. Her cheeks were a light shade of red that made the beauty mark under her eye stand out. And the brown of her eyes had been swallowed up by hunger.

But then Margo started shifting away from me and I gripped her tighter, finally turning to look at my phone.

> **Nina:** Sorry for the late reply 🫣

> **Nina:** Still wanna hook up?

Fuck. I'd texted Nina earlier in the week and she never responded so I forgot about it. Where I kept my phone on me at all times, Nina was the exact opposite and it annoyed the fuck out of me. Honestly, the way she talked did too, but she was attentive in bed and very good at doing what she was told. I'd needed a distraction from the very person in my lap, but now that she was in my lap, I wanted Nina to lose my number.

A picture of Nina's thighs popped up, a new tattoo added to the garden over her skin, and bubbles danced under the image.

Nina: I got a new tattoo and can't wait to see what it looks like around your head

No, no, no. There was no explaining that away. Fucking Nina. Why did she text now?

Margo crawled off my lap and I didn't fight it. I didn't have the right to. She shuffled over to her side of the fort, reaching for where she'd dumped everything from her pockets, including her keys.

"No, don't go." I started panicking, head racing for ideas to save this night. "I made things awkward, I'm sorry. But stay. We're celebrating your queerness, so you have to stay. I'll make it right. Let's just ..." I wracked my brain for a sleepover activity that wouldn't tempt me into kissing her again. "*Twilight.* Yeah. Let's watch *Twilight* but with it muted and we can make up our own dialogue and soundtrack. Except for *Supermassive Black Hole*, we can't change that, obviously. But it'll be fun."

I didn't chance looking at Margo and focused on pulling my laptop from my bag and getting the movie set up. I also deleted Nina's text. She couldn't have known and I was the one to reach out first, but it all left a bad taste in my mouth. Plus she wouldn't be bothered by my lack of response anyway. And then, just in case any other stupid past mistakes wanted to crop up, I put my phone on do not disturb mode for the first time in like forever.

"You really just wanna watch a movie after that?" Margo questioned. I turned to see her kneeling on her blankets, keys in hand, looking at me with an unreadable expression.

"Yeah. Please?" I hated the hitch in my voice, but not as much as I hated myself for kissing Margo like that, for letting some dumb, desperate need for a hook-up ruin that kiss, and for what I know I would have done if we'd not been interrupted.

Margo chewed at her lip, looking back down at her keys.

Please, please, please don't leave me, don't make me watch you walk away.

"Okay. But I wanna do all of Charlie's lines. He's my favorite."

Every molecule of oxygen I had in me rushed out. The relief hit me that hard. Which was great, she was staying and that was great.

But also that rush of relief reminded me of another reason I had stopped looking for a real partner. The anxiety I felt whenever I thought they'd give up on me, leave me in the dust, was just too much to handle. And if I was feeling like this with Margo before we even went on one date, I was in real fucking trouble.

21

SHEA

Bailey: Has anyone heard from Shea? She hasn't responded to any of my texts tonight

Olivia: No, I think her and Margo were setting up for the craft show tonight, maybe she got home and crashed?

Zoey: Shea and sleep? Pretty sure those two don't go together

Roxie: Yeah, there's no way she's just asleep

Roxie: I bet she's binging something

Roxie: Shea, if we guess what you're binging, you owe us a round at Cal's

Olivia: Hmm, has the new Great British Bake Off come out yet?

Bailey: I don't know, but it's probably something story focused for her to not answer texts

Rosie: Have you tried texting Margo? Shea might've said something to her

Bailey: Yeah, she's not answering either. But she gets crazy grumpy if her sleep is disturbed, so she's got a set bed time mode and everything

Roxie: Focus up guys, we need Shea to pay for Cal's

Ashley: God, I would kill for some nachos. Mason, make me nachos and I'll suck you off

Ashley: ... sorry, I used speech to text and thought I sent before saying the rest

Rosie: Are the cravings getting bad?

Ashley: SO FUCKING BAD

Ashley: If you don't get me nachos, I am going to chop you up and feed you to Clive

Ashley: God fucking damn it

Zoey: Maybe Shea's finally jumping on the Supernatural train

Zoey: Don't feed Mason to Clive, it'll upset his stomach

Roxie: Are you *still* watching it?

Zoey: There are 15 seasons, of course I'm still watching it

Olivia: Is it even still good after running that long?

Zoey: We'll find out

Zoey: Shit, Stephen just asked if anyone ever dressed Clive up as Rudolph and we have to make that a thing

Roxie: I feel like that'd be extremely difficult

Ashley: Make Mason do it, he loves acting like a cowboy. Make me do what? Shut up!

Roxie: Hon, you're gonna have to stop the voice to text

Ashley: But everything's swollen and achey

Rosie: Aw, poor thing. I think my grandma had some homemade remedy for body aches. I'll see if I can find it for you

Ashley: I love you

Bailey: I'll just try calling Shea in a couple hours

Roxie: Anything pressing you need to talk about?

Bailey: Not really pressing, I just wanted to bounce some ideas off of her for the Christmas photos I need. I'm running a little behind and Greg wants me to go to his folks' cabin for New Year's, so I'm stressing about that too

Rosie: Aw, that's so sweet!

Roxie: Meeting the parents already? Our boy Greg is trying to rush you to the aisle

Bailey: Oh no, we haven't talked about that at all. We're just getting started. But his family does mean a lot to him, so he wants me to go

Bailey: But that doesn't make me any less nervous with everything else I've got going on

Bailey: I'll be fine though, thank y'all 🖤

22

MARGO

I was woken up by loud metal clanging. Half my brain was running through a list of things the sound could be while the other half was happy to stay in bed snuggled against something warm and soft. If anybody needed me, they could knock on my door.

My pillow did smell oddly sweet though. I must've grabbed some Tootsie Rolls on my way to bed. I'd gotten another bag to give Shea as a little treat for getting through my overly thorough checklist. But I forgot them in the car and then I was distracted by —

Sudden and blinding light hit my eyelids and I cried out in discontent, burying my face into my pillow.

The problem was, my pillow was grumbling too. My pillow was also moving. And had a hand under my sweats, resting on my ass.

"Oh shit, sorry," somebody vaguely familiar said in the direction of the light. Their voice was followed by a click and them saying, "Woah, absolutely not. Give me that."

"You can't take my phone," a grating man's voice said

"Well, I'm a teacher at this school, so half my job is confiscating phones." The voices kept going, fading into the distance.

My pillow — Shea sat up, her arm still curled around me so I went with her. I looked up at Shea and my brain went fuzzy. She had this lazy smirk, like waking up with me on top of her was a pleasant surprise. And her hair was all mussed up from sleep. I wanted to smooth it out. I wanted to swing my leg over to straddle her lap and run my fingers through her hair before messing it up again.

And *holy fucking shit* I'd kissed Shea last night. I'd kissed Shea and then she got some sort of booty call and decided that the kiss, the hottest thing that'd ever happened to me, was a mistake. Like she accidentally stepped on my toe kind of mistake and all she needed to do to move on was say one little sorry.

And after that, we watched *Twilight* and *New Moon* until we passed out. The kiss completely forgotten.

I was gonna throw up.

"Hey, cuddle bug. How'd you sleep?" Shea asked, still looking down at me with that beautiful, sleepy smirk.

I practically flung myself off Shea's lap and towards my side of our fort, where I should have woken up in the first place.

Fishing my phone out of the pile of blankets, I found several texts and even a couple of missed calls from Bailey and my mom. And even worse, we only had an hour before vendors started showing up.

"Shea, it's 9:00!" I sent quick texts to my family that I'd crashed at Wendy's place and started piling everything together. Arms full, I scrambled out of the fort and nearly ran right into two dudes' knees.

"It's my right as part of the press to take pictures," one of the men argued. The new guy on the Paper, I think.

"No, it isn't. You had no right taking this picture. You shouldn't even be in the school to begin with," Eli argued, waving around the other man's phone. I didn't really know Eli since he was in Bailey's year and not one of her crew, but given that small snippet of conversation, he seemed like a good guy.

Eli, noticing me on all fours near his feet, held out the other man's phone to me. "Here, Margo. You can make sure all the photos are deleted while I escort Mr. Murphy here off school property."

"But my phone!" Mr. Murphy screeched, taking a trepidatious step forward.

"You can retrieve it at the office when the school is open to the public." Eli was using that stern teacher voice that said he was tired of your bullshit and if you kept going you'd face real consequences. And despite all of us being full-grown adults who couldn't be sent to the principal's office, the tone was effective at making both me and Mr. Murphy freeze.

"I'd listen to him, *Abe*," Shea said, crawling out of the fort from behind me. "Eli is one of those Clark Kent-type of nerds. He'll kick your ass if you try any funny business."

"I wasn't doing anything funny," Mr. Murphy gasped, which made Eli cross his arms and take a step closer.

"I'd call taking pictures of two sleeping women funny business," Eli gritted out. Okay, I'm solidly on team Eli. I hope he gets whatever sort of happiness he desires.

Mr. Murphy shrank down and started towards the main door, grumbling something about how he'd be back.

Beside me, Shea stood and hugged Eli.

"Thanks, man. That guy gives me the creeps. He was all over Ashley and Mason when they were opening the Mayberry shop."

"I heard. It also sounds like whoever he was freelancing for over there got sick of him, so now he's working with the Paper."

"Gross," Shea said, sticking out her tongue and making a face. "What're you doing here by the way?"

"Oh, I noticed the gate was down on my morning run and saw your car still in the lot. When'd you realize you'd gotten locked in?" Eli threw his thumb over his shoulder to the front door where the exterior gate was only half pulled up.

Shit. Shea and I exchanged wide-eyed looks.

"Um, sometime after we finished setting up the tables," Shea said and I nodded along, maybe a little too forcefully.

Shea and Eli continued talking about who could have locked us in while I finally looked at Mr. Murphy's phone and the picture he'd taken. The photo was a little dark, but you could clearly see Shea's hand in my pants and my face smothered against her tits. My face was mostly obscured by wild hair and, again, Shea's tits, but Shea was clear as day with her bright hair. It'd be an incriminating photo on the front of the newspaper.

But if it were posted on Instagram, it'd be a cute soft launch.

With my face as red as a tomato, I quickly texted myself a copy of the photo and deleted the text and photo from Mr. Murphy's phone *and* cloud app.

"Margo?" Shea said, leaning over to look in my face. "Eli's gonna help me get this all cleaned up. You can go home and change and then meet me back here?"

Shea said the last part as a question. As if she thought I might bail on her after last night. And sure, spending my Saturday working with a woman who kissed me and grinded me over her thigh, then pretended like it was just a little slip wasn't my idea of a good time. But I'd never just bail on somebody because things were awkward. At least not when there was work to do.

"Yeah. I'll be ... I'll be right back I guess. Thanks. Do you need me to grab clothes from your place?"

"Nah, I'll have Zoey swing by for me. It's on her way."

I was *not* hurt by that. It'd be ridiculous to be hurt by Shea choosing to have one of her closest friends go to her place instead of me. It was a logical decision. I was probably pushing it going home to change anyways. If I stopped by Shea's place, I'd be late.

Pushing out the silly, jealous thoughts, I stood and handed the phone over to Shea so I could get going. Shea flipped through the phone for a second before making a small noise.

"What's up?"

"You deleted it already," was all she said before turning back to Eli to start talking about what needed to get done. I took that as close to a goodbye as I was going to get and booked it.

But instead of getting into my car and going home, I walked straight through the parking lot, down Main Street, right to the back door that led to Wendy's apartment.

It took a solid five minutes of alternating between knocking, throwing pebbles at her window, and calling for her to answer the door.

"Are you fucking dying? Because that's the only good reason to wake me up in single digits," Wendy shouted once she'd flung open the door. Instead of answering, I took her by the arm and ran us upstairs and to the kitchen. Sitting Wendy down at the table, I went about fixing her coffee.

With the coffee prepared and in front of Wendy, I pulled out my phone and opened the picture. I waited until she was a few sips in to slide my phone across the table. Wendy looked down at the photo and blinked furiously. Then she squeezed her eyes shut and threw back the rest of her coffee.

"What the hell is this?" she finally shouted, setting her cup down to pick up my phone and assess the picture. "Where did you get this?"

"That new guy on the Paper took it, Murphy."

"So it's not doctored? That's really Shea's hand on your ass? *Shea touched your ass?*" Wendy slammed her hands down and leaned across the table, eyes narrowed. "And whose clothes are those?"

I looked down at the shirt Shea had given me. It was a Clemson shirt, probably from when she'd gone to visit Bailey at school. The orange was faded and it was just a tad too big on me, but it was comfortable. I should probably wash and return it soon, even if I'd rather keep it.

"Shea's."

Wendy just started screaming nonsense. The only thing I could make out was the tail end, where she said, "How did this happen?"

"Settle down and I'll tell you."

Wendy sat, arms crossed and eyes narrowed. I needed to make this explanation quick, otherwise, she'd start throwing shit.

"We had like a queer heart to hear about why I hadn't come out to my parents. I cried. Shea kind of panicked and suggested we have a sleepover in the school to cheer me up and celebrate me coming out or whatever. The clothes are from her go bag, which I *really* don't wanna think about why she has that. Whatever.

"So we made a fort and were playing truth or dare. I dared her to show me her Hinge profile because I couldn't really think of anything else to say. And there was this one photo where she had ... the straps showing and she was giving eyes at someone and it was ... it was just hot. Really fucking hot. And she called me out for staring, so I panicked and threw her phone across the room. Then we both tried to grab the phone and started wrestling, sort of. But she was playing dirty and put her hands under my shirt and then we just sorta ended up making out. Like she guided me to grind on her thigh type of making out.

"But I was still holding on to her phone and it lit up with a text from some fuck buddy or maybe a ex or something. And Shea just sort said my bad, let's watch a movie instead. Which is a such a wild reaction, but she ... I dunno, when she asked if I'd stay for a movie she got all ... not desperate but maybe self blame-y. So I stayed, we watched *Twilight*, and woke up like *that* because Eli and Murphy came in after they saw that the gates were closed and our cars were still there. Because of course on top of all that, we'd been locked in the school and hadn't notice. So someone is definitely trying to sabotage the holiday events, so ... you know, there's that to worry about."

Wendy continued to glare at me as she got up and fixed herself another cup of coffee, deliberately taking her time to say anything to punish me for not texting her last night. When she finally sat back down, I was on the edge of my seat.

"Have we considered that Shea is an anxious, dumbass too?"

"Wendy!"

"What? That's the simplest explanation. You guys have a little weirdness around what people will think, so everything's more awkward than it normally would be. Once you both get over that, you'll just be together. So with the whole get Shea to see you as a possible partner thing solved. I'm ready to move on to this saboteur thing. What're all the details from the choir?"

"Wendy!" I shouted again. "You can't just brush off my thing with Shea because you're more interested in a saboteur."

"But you're thing with Shea is solved," she argued

"No, it's not! Shea's clearly got somebody on the side she wants."

"If she really wanted that person, she would've let you bail and gone to them. But she asked you to stay for a movie. She doesn't care about that chick, she cares about you."

"No, she — I mean, she doesn't care like *that*. I think."

"You said she grinded you on her thigh! That's pretty concert evidence right there."

"Of sexual attraction, sure. But there's no way I could have sex with Shea and just move on with my life."

"Oh my god," Wendy groaned. "You're so dense sometimes. It's obviously not going to be a *just* sex thing. She likes you enough to do some silly fort sleepover, which means she likes you enough to date you."

"But what if she just did that as Bailey's friend? What if she's just trying to be a good friend to Bailey by taking care of me the way Bailey would if she knew I was bi?"

"Oh my god," Wendy groaned. "Why are people such idiots when it comes to their crushes? Shea wouldn't have kissed you if she was just watching out for her friend's little sister. Did she even bring Bailey up at all last night?"

I ran through everything we'd talked about last night and beyond a brief mention of something she'd did with Bailey, my sister didn't really come up at all.

"No, but that —"

"But nothing. It's clear you both like each other, so now all you have left to do is the boring internal work, which doesn't interest me because you can't mastermind your way out of it. Now." Wendy stood and walked over to the dishwasher, putting her coffee cup away. "Unless you need anything else, I'm gonna go back to sleep."

For the briefest of moments, I considered arguing with her. There was definitely more to whatever was happening with Shea than facing some internal struggles. But honestly, this was the most civil conversation I could expect when waking Wendy up three hours earlier than normal. There was one other thing I needed though.

"Actually, can I use your shower and borrow some clothes?"

23

SHEA

"So ..." Eli started as he folded the last of the blankets that made up Margo and my fort. "You and Margo?"

"Got locked in the school and made the best of it," I said. I stacked up the couch cushions I'd stolen from the office and made my way to put them back. Eli jogged ahead of me and held open the office door. I really couldn't be mad at the guy. Without him, Margo and I would've been awoken by angry vendors and at risk of far more exposure than one little picture.

"Margo and I are ... friends right now."

"Friends?" Eli repeated. I dramatically dropped the cushions onto the floor and we both started putting them back in place. "So you've snuggled Bailey like that?"

"Obviously not." I tossed a couch pillow at his head. "But, and I'm only saying this because I know you can keep a secret and could already put this much together, she's not out yet. So even if something were to happen between us, it'd need to be quiet."

Eli was quiet for a long moment before hissing, "Shit."

"Yeah. Not the greatest situation. But you absolutely saved our assed, so thank you. I owe you one."

"No problem. That Abraham guy gives me the creeps. I shouldn't have let him follow me in here in the first place. I just didn't have the energy to fight him over what I thought'd be nothing."

"Don't worry about it, there's no way you could've known I had my hand in my best friend's little sister's pants." Couch cushions back in place, I sank down onto them and groaned, "God, she's got such a nice ass."

"Who's got a nice ass?" Zoey asked as she burst into the office, Stephen followed closely behind her with a duffle bag from my place.

"Just some girl I'm talking to on Hinge. Thank you *so* much for getting me clothes." I hopped off the couch and pulled Zoey into a hug. Despite it starting to get cold out and Zoey absolutely hating the cold, she smelled like she'd spent the morning out in her garage working on the vintage of the month.

"No problem. But how'd you and Margo get locked in?" Zoey asked.

"What?" I stammered, because in my text I didn't actually say what happened, just that I needed clothes.

"That icky Abraham guy set up a newsletter thing for the Paper."

"Newsletter is too complimentary of a word for it," Stephen muttered.

"I mean, it wasn't fancy, sure. But that stuff has to be crazy complicated to set up, right?" Zoey asked, turning to Stephen. Her boyfriend raised his eyebrows, probably trying to determine just how ignorant Zoey was in terms of newsletter formatting. Despite no longer working for Zoey, I'm pretty sure Olivia managed all the website and emails for Zoey's auto shop because Zoey was quite literally helpless when it came to anything other than cars.

Instead of answering Zoey's question, Stephen pulled out his phone and showed me the email.

When Zoey said it wasn't fancy, I expected basic formatting with little to no images. It was worse than that. There was zero formatting unless you counted centering things formatting. It was literally just an email, like one you'd send to a friend or parents who hadn't caught up to texting. And all it contained was every detail of Abe walking into the school and seeing me and Margo snuggling.

It wasn't a newsletter, it was a gossip blast.

The only blessing was that he hadn't caught Margo's name in the incident and didn't notice my hands were in her pants.

But he did embellish the hell out of it, making it seem like a scandalous affair. If you weren't reading carefully, you'd think he'd walked into an orgy.

"God fucking damn it," I muttered, handing back the phone to Stephen and running a hand through my hair. This was bad. Real fucking bad. Anyone who knew Margo was helping me with the holiday shit would know she was the one I was sleeping — cuddling with. Which was pretty much everyone in town.

"You look like a ghost. Don't worry, nobody really believes you're shaking up with Bailey's sister. She's just a kid," Zoey said, patting my back. I shrugged her hand off.

"She's not a kid. She's not even *that* much younger than us."

"Oh," was all Zoey said, backing off to join Stephen and Eli's conversation. Before I had a chance to trip over myself to explain that my defense of Margo didn't mean anything, Ashley crashed into the office.

Well, the door crashed open and Ashley waddled in.

"I'm going to murder that man. He is enemy number one and I'm sending him to hell in a hand basket."

"Aw, she's picking up some Southern sayings," I crooned, wrapping Ashley in my arms, glad to have her determined anger present and distracting everyone from my fumbling feelings for Margo.

"A hand basket is too nice for that man," she grumbled, patting my arm. "He's disgusting. And breaking several laws about newsletter subscriptions."

"Ashley," Mason grunted from the doorway, gripping at the frame, out of breath.

"What?" was all Ashley said in response, casually ignoring her husband's clear distress. Given the way they argued and pranked each other the two years before they got married, you'd think them being together would calm things down. It didn't. At five months pregnant, Ashley was running her poor husband ragged and seemingly enjoying it.

"You can't just run out like that," Mason grunted.

"Why not? It's not like you let me do anything anyways. I'm pregnant, Mason, not on my deathbed. Most women work until the month of their due date, sometimes the week of it."

Mason stepped up to Ashley and pulled her out of my hug.

"You're not most women, you're *my wife*. And if I can make any part of this easier for you, you damn well know that's what I'm gonna do."

Ashley's cheeks reddened and she abruptly turned back to me without answering Mason.

"Anyways, besides Abe being an absolute menace, you have another problem. Somebody is trying to fuck up operation 'Retire Ms. Taylor'."

"Since when are we calling it that?" Zoey asked, popping up from behind me.

"We're not doing this to take over from Ms. Taylor," I reminded them.

"We'll see about that," Ashley huffed. "But either way, you definitely have some saboteur."

"Are we talking about the saboteur?" Margo said, stepping into the office in different clothes that definitely weren't hers and damp hair.

"Yes," Ashley answered, not missing a beat to turn to Margo and ask, "Do you have any theories?"

"No, I'm sure Wendy will once she's fully awake. She's not exactly a morning person."

Zoey nodded in agreement while Mason was ever so subtly manhandling Ashley towards the couch.

"So those are Wendy's clothes?" I whispered to Margo, looking down at the tie-dye and anime character with green hair.

We'd talked about some of the shows and anime Margo was into, but she didn't really strike me as the graphic tee kind of person.

"Oh, yeah. I didn't want to leave you hanging and it was quicker to get to her place than my parents'. Guess I should've picked something a little more presentable but she didn't have much in the way of clean clothes." Margo held out the hem of her shirt and murmured, "Maybe I should grab a school hoodie."

"Did you walk there and back?"

"Yeah, why?" Margo raised an eyebrow at me and I knew I should drop it, but there was some disconnect between my brain and my mouth.

"You shouldn't've gone out with your hair like that, you'll catch a cold."

"I thought you said she wasn't a kid anymore. Why're you babying her?" Zoey poked, completely oblivious to how hard that hit. Margo didn't still think I was babying her, right? After last night, she had to know that wasn't the case. *Right?*

"You guys are so dramatic. It's barely even chilly," Ashley said, rolling her eyes.

"Not all of us are used to New York winters," Zoey said, pulling her three layers closer. While most of us were Southerners, Zoey was the … babiest about the cold.

"I am though," Margo said.

"Oh yeah, you did all your schooling up there, right? Where'd you live?" Ashley asked, leaning forward to talk to Margo. As they started talking about their favorite delis, Zoey elbowed me and I braced myself for some heavy questioning.

"Stephen has revoked his no illegal activity rule if this saboteur is a homophobe, so we can cut brakes if you figure out what their looks like car."

"I said you can do something illegal, pretty girl. Not commit murder," Stephen muttered, fighting a smile. I wish I could feel a little more happy and a little less jealous that my friend found somebody who could bring her back from the heartbreak her cheating ex caused. Zoey was more herself than she'd been in years with Stephen around and I wanted that comfortable love.

My eyes fell on Margo, now seated on the couch to talk with Ashley. The warmth I got from looking at her was pretty damn close to comfort.

"That's all right, Zo. I think it's just somebody pissed they didn't get chosen to do shit even though it was a volunteer thing. I think if it was a hate crime they'd be after me and not the events themselves."

"If you say so. But if you get any weird vibes, just say the word." Zoey pulled me in for a tight side hug before turning to Eli. "Eli, are there security cameras around the school?"

I tensed, worried about what would show up on the cameras, but Eli just laughed.

"Zoey, you are severely overestimating this school's budget. My textbooks end at the Y2K crisis."

"Yikes," we all murmured in unison.

"Yeah. So no cameras."

"Well, we have to be on guard during the event," Ashley said, holding up a stern finger. "If their motive is to have the events go poorly under Shea's watch, then they'll probably try something else during the craft show. Eli, where's the main breaker?"

"Down in the basement. Why?"

"Because if I wanted to cause trouble with the littlest chance of getting caught, I'd cut the power."

24

MARGO

At Ashley's insistence, we swept the entire school building including the boiler room and auditorium. The closest thing we found to suspicious was a notebook with lots of hearts on it that Eli immediately shoved into his desk.

But we remained ever vigilant as the craft show began in full swing. Between all of Shea's friends, we had every door covered. And my door doubled as a hot chocolate stand. It was a good enough place to keep an eye on who was coming and going, but it also put in me on the front lines of folks' opinions on Mr. Murphy's newsletter blast.

Some folks got a giggle out of it, two kids got locked in the school and they made a blanket fort. Classic. Others simply complained about being sent an email they didn't sign up for.

And a couple of people gave me dirty looks, clearly falling for Mr. Murphy's scandalization of what he saw.

"Margo, there you are, sweetie," my mom called, pushing her way through the crowd to get to my table. Despite my booth being right near the entrance, she'd already filled two tote bags with Christmas decor.

"Hey, Mom." I waved, trying not to cringe at how awkward I sounded. But I knew what was coming and I would much rather she not say anything.

But that wasn't my mom, so of course she did.

"Why'd you lie about where you were last night?"

The adjustment to moving back with my parents after having lived on my own was severe. And sure I wasn't technically alone in New York, but my roommates didn't ask me where I was going every time I left the apartment and they definitely didn't send follow-up texts if I was out late.

"Sorry. I didn't want to worry you with the whole locked-in thing."

"Why didn't you call when you realized you were locked in?"

"My phone died," I lied, shrugging.

"Well, what about the office phone?"

I faltered. There was no good explanation for why we didn't try to call for help. Even the dead phone was barely believable. But how was I going to explain to my mom that I hadn't actually realized we'd been locked in because I was more preoccupied with Shea?

"Hey, Estelle, how're you doing?" Shea asked, popping up to Mom's left and scooping her into a hug.

"Oh Shea! I'm good, but what's this about you getting locked in? Why didn't you call for help?" Mom tsked at Shea, an equal amount of concern and chastising.

"That's my bad. I forgot to include somebody on an email about us being in the school late. So when they happened by and the front gate was still open, they locked us in. We were setting up the tables, so we hadn't heard them. And when we noticed, I sorta panicked, ya know? But I didn't want Margo to panic because I was panicking, so I made a big deal of doing a super fun sleepover. I successfully distracted us, but we sorta forgot that there were phones in the office." Shea laughed, the sound hearty and more genuine than anything I'd managed in my conversation with Mom so far.

"Oh, Shea." Mom laughed, resting a hand on Shea's arm. "You do always try to find the silver lining in things. Thank you for taking care of my girl."

At this, Shea pulled back a bit, face turning red.

"Yeah, of course, Estelle. Always," Shea said through a slightly awkward laugh. "But we're both all right and nothing really came of the incident."

Nothing except the hottest kiss of my life that I guess we're just writing off.

A few folks came up for hot chocolate and while I served them, Mom and Shea exchanged a few words of small talk before Mom returned to her craft shopping spree. She'd have a whole new set of Christmas decorations up by the time I got home.

But while Mom went off, Shea hung around, hovering behind me as I finished handing out drinks.

"So ..." she dragged out the word, focusing on straightening the paper cups. The action reminded me of what Wendy had said. Maybe Shea was just an anxious, dumbass like me. Everything about our maybe relationship/friendship that made me anxious was the same for her, my closetedness and her being Bailey's best friend. And that was on top of the general awkwardness of trying to figure out if somebody likes you as a friend or more. Just because Shea was older than me, didn't mean that awkwardness was less for her.

Though I still wasn't convinced she actually liked me like that to begin with.

Either way, I could at least keep things light.

"What do you think the chances of me finding a roommate in Snowfall is? Ideally as soon as possible."

Shea's head shot up, face pale.

"What do you mean? Is everything okay with your parents? Do they —" Shea paused, leaning closer. "Did they find out about you? Or what happened last night?"

"Shit," I hissed. I needed to get better at avoiding her triggers. I couldn't even be a good friend without managing that. "No, nothing like that. I'm sorry. I didn't mean to scare you. Living with my parents just means they wanna know where I am at all times and I got used to not having to tell anybody where I was going. That's all."

"Oh." Shea let out a long breath, shoulders relaxing. "Sorry, you looked tense with your mom, so I thought maybe she was putting two and two together from that stupid newsletter."

"No, she just didn't understand why we didn't use the office phones to call somebody. Plus, I sorta answered her 'where are you texts' right as we woke up and told her I'd spent the night at Wendy's before we found out about being locked in."

"Why don't you just live with Wendy? Those apartments have a couple of bedrooms, so she probably has the room."

I threw my head back and laughed.

"Not the reaction I expected," Shea murmured with a little laugh.

"I guess it wouldn't be for anyone who doesn't know Wendy. But she is ... not good with change. Her parents' and siblings' rooms are all still the same as they were when they moved out."

"Wait, so does that mean she's not in the main room?"

"Yup. Abigail and I tried to get her to at least take the second-biggest room, but she adamantly refused. She also didn't make either of our favorite pizzas for a whole month. I had to settle with pineapple-less pizza for so long."

"You like pineapple on your pizza?" Shea asked, an eyebrow raised, her voice teasing.

"Yes, I do." I held my head up high, daring her to challenge me like so many others had before. She nudged me with her elbow and laughed.

"Don't worry, I do too. Next movie night we'll have to grab some."

Before I could fully process the word next, Shea was called away by one of the vendors and I was left with an internal scream that dogs could hear.

25

SHEA

All that anxiety and hypervigilance ended up being for nothing.

Beyond the general chaos of event management, spilled drinks, missing merchandise, and Karens bitching about vendors' prices, the craft show passed by smoothly. And while I was bone tired, I couldn't relax. If I relaxed, I'd dwell on the two holiday mishaps that could have very well fucked everything up. I'd dwell on how if things had gone wrong, folks might stop coming to me to sell or buy property. How it could be some homophobic asshole behind this whole. How they might fuck with the tree lighting on Friday. How I kissed Margo and wanted to do that some more. How different my holidays looked from when I was a kid with parents who loved me conditionally to now.

Nope. No thoughts. Thoughts sucked.

"That's everything," Margo said, stacking the last of the tables onto the cart and clapping her hands together. "Well, for the craft show, at least. I'll compile the to-do list for the tree lighting tonight. The tree should be delivered Monday, so at least you get one day to rest."

I didn't want an hour to rest, let alone a whole day.

"Why don't you come over to my place and we work on the list together?" I offered.

Margo froze, her eyes flashing like she was blinking something in mores code.

Right. I nearly sucked her face off last night and have been actively avoiding talking about it. Of course, she didn't wanna hang out with me again. Though it's not like she's tried to bring it up either.

"Just a suggestion, Margo. I mean, we've got more *Twilight* movies to dub." I shrugged, trying to play it cool. "But I get if you just wanna go home and crash."

Margo looked down at her feet, shuffling around. I didn't want to pressure her, so I took out my phone like I was just checking my notifications. I had a shit ton of messages from Bailey. Guess if Margo didn't want to hang out, I'd at least have Bailey to keep me company.

"Sure."

I fumbled my phone, sending it flying to the ground. Playing it *real* cool.

"Great, great. Do you wanna ..." I fumbled my words, bending over to pick up my phone. "Do you wanna ride over with me or drive separately?"

God, was making it sound like a date.

"Well, I need to go home and grab my laptop if we're going to work on holiday planning. Plus it'd be nice to be in my own clothes." Margo looked down at the holiday sweater she'd gotten from one of the vendors to cover the anime shirt. It was wool and smelled like it came straight from a barn.

"Oh, for sure. Just come by my place whenever you're good. No rush." I turned, grabbing onto the cart of tables so I could have something to occupy my hands instead of hugging Margo.

"Shea," she called, my name surrounded by laughter. I looked over my shoulder at Margo, her usual shy smile turning to something more teasing. Suddenly the idea of us being alone at my place sounded like a *very* bad idea. Maybe.

"I don't know where you live."

"Oh, right." Of course, she didn't know where I lived, she'd never been over. Which reminded me of a whole list of things I needed to tidy up before she got there. I pulled out my phone and texted her my address. "There ya go."

"Cool. I'll let you know when I'm headed over."

"Cool," I repeated.

"Cool," Margo repeated, the corner of her mouth tilting up, like she was playing with me.

I was totally fucked.

26

MARGO

Wendy was right. Shea was an incredibly anxious dumb-ass.

And once I got over the shock of her inviting me to her place after our mess of a sleepover, I realized if she was just as anxious as I was, there was no reason to be anxious. Or maybe it was the final thing to make me see Shea as a whole person and not just the person I had a crush on for so long.

And maybe this awkward Shea liked me, maybe she wasn't sure yet. Either way, I didn't need to worry about looking like an idiot because she was busy doing that for herself. It was like that thing where if you were nervous to ask for something, you couldn't do it, but if your friend was nervous, you could.

I parked outside of Shea's apartment complex, grabbed my phone and bag, and started to her door.

Shea: Don't come in yet

Me: Why not?

Shea: I'm still cleaning

I stopped in front of Shea's door and took a deep breath. If it was Shea coming over to my apartment, or my old apartment, with less than an hour's notice, I would have a panic attack. I'd spend that whole hour speed-cleaning everything and hiding anything I deemed embarrassing in a closet.

So I just opened up Shea's apartment door, after taking a brief second to appreciate the doormat that said 'if you're queer, you're family'.

"Shea!" I shouted over the music as I entered.

"Margo!" She whined my name, head popping out from around the corner of the hall. "I told you not to come in yet."

"You don't have to clean when it's just the two of us hanging out." Without waiting for her to reply, I made my way into the living room, setting my bags down and getting comfortable.

Shea's living room was … not what I expected. Shea was bright and outspoken, she wore clothes that figuratively and sometimes literally said she was gay. Her hair was the brightest shade of red they made. And yet her living room was so bland.

The couch was gray, the coffee table black, the carpet beige, and not one spec of decoration. There were no colorful throw pillows, no blankets with expletives stitched on to them, and nothings decorating the walls. Not even a pride flag.

"Your place is … already clean enough," I told Shea, even though I did need to push aside several cups in order to make space for my laptop on the coffee table. Shea came out and stacked up the cups, mumbling something about me lying before heading back to the kitchen.

Resisting the urge to be nosy and look around at more of Shea's things, I opened up my laptop and pulled up the doc I'd made for the tree lighting. Compared to the other holiday events, the tree lighting was pretty simple. We only needed to coordinate with the tree farm and the decorator, both of whom had been booked by Ms. Taylor before her incident. Really all we had to do was call both parties to confirm delivery time and the style of this year's tree.

"Shea, do you have a color scheme you wanna use for the tree?" I shouted, not sure where she'd gone.

"Yeah, my phone should be on the coffee table. Code's 9891. Pinterest is in the camera emoji folder," Shea shouted back. I picked up her phone and opened up Pinterest, letting my eyes go out of focus as notifications popped up once the phone was unlocked.

On Shea's board was one saved folder, titled with three Christmas tree emojis. Inside there was one very clear style, but it was so *not* what I expected. There wasn't bright ornaments and outlandish colors. There wasn't glitter or a pink tree or ornaments based on Taylor Swift songs. All the trees and decor on her board were homey. Classic red and gold bulbs, cheese tourist ornaments and stick reindeer made by children. And there were popcorn garlands in damn near every picture.

Shea didn't get this type of Christmas after she came out.

I couldn't remember what Shea's parents were like before, but it wasn't hard to picture them putting up decorations like this, creating this type of Christmas for the little girl they loved under very specific conditions.

My wheels started turning. It couldn't be that hard to set up a craft station in the library that ran all week long for folks to make ornaments for the town tree. The elementary school teachers could probably do something too. And some folks might be willing to donate things. Lord knows my mom has plenty we could borrow.

Just as I was about to put Shea's phone down and start a list of what we'd need to do to make this happen, Bailey's name flashed on the screen.

"Shea, Bailey's calling!" I yelled and I heard the clambering of dishes. Phone in hand, I went into the kitchen to see Shea bent over, resting her head on the counter, a toppled over pile of cups in the drying rack.

"You need some help?" I offered but Shea just shook her head and straightened.

"Just put it on speaker," she grumbled, gesturing to the phone before reaching back into the sink to wash another cup. How the hell did she have *more* cups to wash?

"Hi, Bailey," I said, answering the phone before putting it on speaker and setting it a safe distance from the sink.

"Margo?" Bailey asked, confused.

"I'm here too," Shea said. "Margo's over so we can plan the tree lighting stuff. But I'm washing dishes, so you're on speaker."

"Oh, so you're *finally* washing those cups you have all over your apartment?" Bailey teased. "And Margo, I have a bone to pick with you."

"Huh?"

"Why'd you lie about where you were last night?"

"Oh." I'd totally forgotten I'd told Bailey I'd been at Wendy's place too. "I just didn't want to worry you."

"Why would I be worried? I mean, sure, it's wild that someone is trying to sabotage Shea's holiday events. But at least you guys were together. Staying the night in the school alone would've kill Shea. All that quiet and —"

"I think Margo's embarrassed to share a friend with her sister," Shea interrupted.

"Am not," I shouted, smacking at Shea's forearm.

"Aw, so you are friends! *That* I was worried about."

"Really, why?" Shea asked.

"Well, Margo asked me how to smooth things over after your spat, so I wasn't sure if y'all were getting along or not."

Shea turned to look at me, an eyebrow raised. I immediately looked away, assessing the magnets on Shea's fridge like I'd be quizzed on them later. She had a few touristy New York ones, which I assumed Bailey got for her during my graduation. But otherwise, they were mostly magnets advertising take-out places

"We're all good now," Shea finally said. "But you're calling about your art show, right?"

"Ugh, yes. I just ... I don't know. The gallery wants something high-end, something that you can barely tell it's for the holidays. And they've strongly hinted that they want pieces that are just one medium. I don't think the selection committee actually looked at my portfolio at all. They just heard I was dating Greg and wanted to be in his good graces. Or his family's good graces."

While I can't say I got all of Bailey's art, I did know she didn't stick to one medium. That was too contained for my free-spirited sister. Instead, she took photographs of all manner of things, had them printed on canvas, and then did something else on top of it. Most of the time she painted, sometimes she did a paper mache like thing, and one time she even made a neon light outline. Her art was really cool, but not what I would describe as vague or high-end. Or at least in the way rich people considered art as high-end.

"Do whatever the fuck you want, Bales. They picked you, if they only picked you because of who you're dating and didn't look at your art, that's their problem," Shea said, finishing the last dish and pulling out a wine bottle from a cabinet. She poured two pint glasses full and handed one to me.

"Sure, but if they hate it, they'll never invite me back *and* it could ruin my chances of getting into another gallery. Greg thinks I should do whatever I want too, but that's a pretty big risk."

Shea's mouth twisted and she mouthed at me, "What do you think of Greg?"

I could only shrug. They'd been dating for almost a year but I hadn't seen much of Bailey, let alone the dude she was dating.

He'd come up for my graduation in the spring with her and the impression I got was he was rich, bland, and nuts about my sister. But beyond him fawning over Bailey, there didn't seem to be much going on there. Like he was perfect on paper but one-dimensional.

"What kind of work would you want to do? If you didn't have to worry about your next showcase," I asked, following Shea as she grabbed the phone and walked back to the living room.

"I want to do a dreamy version of the Nutcracker. There's a dance studio close by that I've worked with before and they're about to start full dress rehearsals for their next show. Without the pictures yet, I don't have a full idea, but lots of glitter and cotton and neons. A trippy dream. Stark bright colors amidst the drab."

"All right, what if instead of trippy dreamy, you do ... I dunno, soft dreamy? Like *A Midsummer's Night Dream?* Soft colors, pastels, night sky vibes. And instead of doing your art on the photograph, you use the atmosphere. Twinkle lights, sheer curtains, a fog machine. It's a compromise, sure, but you'd at least get to keep some aspects of your vision." We settled down on the couch and Shea squeezed my knee, smiling at me.

"Margo!" Bailey stretched out my name excitedly. "That's a perfect balance, thank you! When'd you get so smart?"

"I'm sure you would've thought of that eventually," I said, shrugging off the compliment.

"Shut up, Margo." Shea's squeeze turned to a light slap. "You did all the work for your degree, don't brush it off. It's crazy the things she's come up with for these holiday events. Especially in terms of organization."

"Well being more organized than you isn't all that hard," Bailey said.

"Ouch." Shea held a hand to her heart, collapsing into the couch. "I'll have you know there are zero dirty cups in the apartment, minus the ones we're currently drinking from."

"Didn't you say you were washing dishes when you answered? You just washed up because you didn't want Margo to see what a slob you are yet. Just wait until you've been friends for a couple of months, then you'll realize she can barely keep her head on straight, let alone keep up a calendar."

"Hey! This isn't attack Shea hour. And like you're one to talk. How many dirty brush water cups do you have lying around your place?"

"Not that many," Bailey said before she started quietly counting. By the time she got to seven, Shea's phone flashed with an incoming call from Luckett's Family Farm.

"They're probably calling to confirm the delivery," I said, nudging Shea.

"Ugh, yeah. Sorry, Bales. Gotta answer another call."

"Boo. But fine. Love y'all!"

"Love you too," Shea and I said in unison. Shea paused, thumb hovering over the screen as her face reddened. I'm pretty sure my face was just as red. Maybe redder. How many times had I whispered those words into a pillow as a preteen thinking about Shea?

Shea shook her head and answered the call.

"Hi, Shea White speaking."

"Evenin', Ms. White. This Sandy from Lucket'st Farm, calling about your reserved tree."

"Reserved?" Shea repeated. "What do you mean reserved? We're scheduled for a delivery this week, right?"

"No. You've got a 30-foot tree reserved for pickup. The window for that ended today, which is why I'm calling. I know things got moved around last minute. I think we got the call switching to pick-up just a week ago. So we're willing to keep the tree on hold for you if you can get here in the next couple of days."

"Shit," Shea hissed to herself, rubbing her hands over her face. "And I'm guessing there's no way we could switch to delivery?"

"No. We've got our drivers booked for the week."

Shea tapped the mute button and screamed. Then, just as quickly, she picked the phone back up. "That makes sense. I'll … try to figure something out. Thanks for calling."

Shea hung up, threw her phone across the room, and screamed again.

"What're we gonna do?" she groaned, hands over her face.

"Don't panic yet. We've still got a couple of options," I said. I pulled my laptop closer and started searching for Christmas trees in the area.

"What options are those? Getting the Charlie Brown tree for the town?" Shea sat up and downed her glass of wine. "I need something stronger."

While Shea got up to fix herself another drink, I focused on my search. There were plenty of places that sold trees but nothing over 10 feet. Which wasn't even half the height we ordered. And the farms that did sell taller trees were either just as far away as Luckett's or were already sold out.

"All right, Margo. What's that super brain got churning?" Shea asked, rounding the couch to collapse next to me, her drink halfway finished.

"We're gonna have to drive up and get it. There's no other option."

Shea sank down, her back fully on the couch cushion, head awkwardly angled on the back, drink resting on her collar bones.

"No," she whined. "You've always got a creative solution. There's gotta be one for this too."

I didn't bother pointing out that I really only had a creative solution for Bailey's thing and, at best, a good distraction for the choir. Instead, I was looking up directions to Luckett's.

"We'll need to get a truck, but the drive is only ten hours round trip."

"I can't be alone in my head for ten whole hours. I'll go insane."

"Alone?" I repeated. It hadn't even occurred to me to have Shea go on her own. "No, you're not going alone. I'm coming too."

Shea shot up, somehow managing to slam her drink on the coffee table without spilling a drop and grabbed at my arm.

"You'll seriously spend ten hours trapped in a car with me?"

"Yeah. I mean, Bailey would, so why wouldn't I?"

"Well, Bailey's my friend." Shea shrugged and let go of my arm.

"What am I then?" I was torn between hurt that she didn't think we were friends and curious to see how she classified me if we weren't. I mean, it wasn't that long ago that she called me a friend when I would've said we were just acquaintances.

"You're a ..." Shea's eyes met mine, flecks of gold shining as she looked at me, face flushed. I held my breath as I waited for Shea to answer, reminding myself over and over that what Wendy said was probably true. We both liked each other and we just had to get over that awkward bump. It was just as likely as her not having any feelings to for me.

"A new friend."

A new friend could become something more. Is that what she was saying or is that what I just wanted her words to imply?

"Well, this friend is going to find us a truck and drive us up the mountains." Shea straightened, mouth opened to argue. "No, I'm driving because I know how to drive in the snow and I distinctly remember a story about you and Bailey trying to rent a cabin in Vermont in January and getting stuck."

Shea's grin spread wide and she nudged me with an elbow.

"All right, chauffeur. When are we leaving?"

I thought of all the things I needed to do to make this little trip happen. About the homemade ornament idea and the other prep work we needed to get done for the tree lighting. None of which could get done before we had a tree.

"Tomorrow morning?"

"Tomorrow morning."

27

MARGO

Me: Can you give me all your friends numbers? I need their help with something

Bailey: Sure, what's up?

Me: The tree that was supposed to be delivered was switched to pick up. So we're gonna drive up and get it tomorrow, but there're a couple of event errands that I need help with and I wanna keep it a surprise for Shea

Bailey: Seriously? Someone is really out to get Shea 😠

Bailey: I'll set up a group chat but do you think I should come? I don't like the idea of Shea being alone while someone is clearly running around trying to ruin things for her

Me: It's all right, I've got her back

Bailey: 🖤 🖤 🖤

You've been added to a group chat with Bailey, Olivia, Rosie, Ro...

Bailey: Hey guys, Margo's got a favor to ask since someone messed up the tree delivery

Olivia: What happened with the tree?

Zoey: Did they send us a Charlie Brown tree?

Ashley: Make them send you a new one, expedited and free of charge

Me: Hey guys. The tree was supposed to be delivered this week but we just got a call that it was switched to pickup for last week. They're holding it for us, but we still have to go and get it

Ashley: Two questions. One, this is up in the mountains right? Does it snow up there and does Shea know how to drive in the snow? Two, do you need a truck? Mason will lend you his

Me: I'm gonna drive, so we good on that front

Ashley: Smart

Me: But if Mason wouldn't mind lending us his truck, that'd be great

Zoey: You'll probably need something longer than that, right? Once you pick up the truck, come over to my place and I can give you a trailer. You can probably just stow it in the bed on your way their, so I'll show you how to hook it up too

Me: Perfect, thank you!

Rosie: And what about this surprise? I love surprises

Zoey: Unless they're for you

Rosie: Shush

Me: So Shea showed me her ideas for the tree design and it was all homey decor. Lots of red and gold and handmade ornaments. So I wanted to talk to the school to see if the teachers could get the kids to make ornaments

Me: Then I wanted to open it up to the town to see if anyone wanted to donate decorations

Rosie: Oh my god, that's precious! Yes, of course we'll help!

Olivia: I'll talk to Eli and see who he knows at the elementary school to set things up

Rosie: And I'll print up some fliers to put in the diner and spread around asking for donations

Zoey: And I'll see if I can get Clive to wear a red nose

Olivia: Zoey. No.

28

SHEA

Good things about Margo driving: I could sleep, snack, and drink to my heart's content. She'd also managed to get her hands on Mason's truck and some extender thing from Zoey, so I didn't even have to worry about the tree fitting when we got there.

Bad things about Margo driving: I didn't have the act of driving to keep me from looking at her.

Despite picking me up at 5:00 a.m., Margo was wide awake, chipperly singing along to some musical she'd put on. She was dressed more casually than normal. Leggings instead of jeans and an oversized sweatshirt that said 'mood reader' on the front. It made me wonder what the switch of outfits meant. Was she becoming more comfortable and didn't feel like she needed to be put together around me? Or did she not feel the need to put special effort into her looks because whatever happened with that kiss meant nothing to her?

Or maybe since we were gonna be in the car for a solid ten hours, she just wanted to be comfortable.

It was wild how ridiculous my crush on Margo was becoming. I'd fully grappled with the fact that I was attracted to Bailey's little sister, honestly that was the easiest thing to get over. I've even come to terms with the fact that not only was Margo hot and cute and I wanted to press her up against a wall, but she was also funny and patient and had that calm critical thinking that was exactly what I needed when I put too much on my plate. Which meant Margo wouldn't be a casual fling. I'd almost certainly fall in love with her.

Except she wasn't out. She wasn't even living in Snowfall permanently. She could be gone by next month for all I knew. And I would much rather not start anything than face her leaving me behind.

I just had to remind myself of that possibility every time Margo did something that made my heart skip a beat, made me see a possible future with her.

Margo's voice cracked as she sang but she didn't quiet or stammer to cover the sound, just kept singing about walking to hell to save Eurydice.

"Any luck on the job hunt?" I asked abruptly. Margo's shoulders stiffened as she stopped singing to chew at her lip. Then she reached over to turn down the volume before speaking.

"I haven't really been looking. I figure with the holidays, there won't be many job postings, so there's no point."

"Makes sense," I murmured. "Do you have an ideal location or anything? Maybe I can help you with apartment hunting."

Margo shuffled around in her seat. When she finally stopped squirming, she shrugged. "Not particularly. I'll probably have better luck looking for something in a bigger metropolitan area."

"No more small-town life for you, huh?" I said with a lifeless laugh. I could feel Margo's gaze drift to me, but I kept my eyes straight ahead.

"Why are *you* still living the small-town life? I would've figured you'd want to live in a big city, somewhere with a bigger queer scene."

It was my turn to shuffle around. It's not that I was uncomfortable telling Margo my reasonings for staying in Snowfall. It's that I *was* comfortable. I knew she'd understand and not label me as petty or stubborn. She'd be empathetic and supportive and validate my decisions and I'd have to come up with something else to talk about that would solidify why we shouldn't start anything.

"Because I won by not moving. I proved I belong here when they thought I didn't. The town was on my side. Well, most of the town. The people that matter to me at least. And while they ostracized me, the town ostracized *them*. I don't need to go out and find a community where I belong, I've already got it here in Snowfall."

Margo was quiet, the only sound in the car was my anxious heartbeat and the barely audible noise of Orpheus. Once the silence stretched into the next song, I looked over at Margo, anxious to get a read on her reaction to what I said. She was biting her lip, fingers drumming against the steering wheel. When she noticed I was watching her, her fingers stilled.

"You're right. Snowfall is your home, they can't take that away from you. They don't have the right to. You held on to something important, even when it got hard. You should be proud of that."

Something lodged in my throat. I'd had this discussion over the years with several girlfriends and none of them understood it. They said that just because my parents left town, doesn't mean the sad memories went with them. They were convinced I was repressing my feelings and afraid to move out of the only home I'd ever known. That I'd feel better if I just ripped the band-aid off and left town. They didn't get the reclaiming of it.

"Yeah," I said, voice scratchy. "I am proud."

Margo hummed but didn't say anything else. She probably didn't know what else *to* say. I couldn't blame her. Here I was trauma dumping on her like she was my fucking girlfriend when all she asked was why I hadn't moved.

I started shuffling for my bag, looking for the flask of whiskey tucked in there somewhere. I was more fun when I was tipsy and not spilling my problems out like a ...

"Do you celebrate that win?" Margo asked, just as my fingers wrapped around the lid of my flask.

"What?" I sat back up, drink left in the bag.

"Well, you wanted to celebrate me coming out. So I thought maybe you celebrate all milestones like that."

"Oh, no. I ... I never really thought to."

"I guess it does seem a little petty to celebrate the day your parents admitted defeat and moved out. But fuck them. You should rent out the gazebo and get Ashley to bake you a cake with 'Snowfall's mine' on it. Hell, you could even make it a whole town festival. Pride in … when was it that they moved?"

"September. Just a couple days after I turned 18."

Margo mumbled something under her breath that sounded a lot like mother fucker.

"Then Fall with Pride. Or Fall in Love with Pride. Something like that. Everybody has to wear their flag or rainbows. And there'll be funfetti cake."

Margo kept going, describing this Pride/birthday event for me with the whole town's participation. She drew the line at floats, but said I could have some carnival-esque booths if I wanted.

"Sounds like you've got it all planned. But you'd have to be here to make it happen." I don't know why I said it. It was unfair. But I liked how Margo responded to my hurt way too much. And if she wasn't going to be in Snowfall that long, I needed to put those breaks on.

"Well … you never know what could happen in nine months."

"You never know," I repeated, stomach in knots. I needed to pull so far back, *all* the way back.

29

MARGO

I don't know how I could have handled what Shea said and went through better. In my head, I tried to comfort her in the way she comforted me, with words of affirmation and a celebration.

And it seemed like it worked at first. There was this softness to her voice, a vulnerability that made me think I was on the right track.

But I guess talking about cheesy shit like funfetti cake was a bit too far. Though she had us watch *Twilight*, so I don't know how colorful cake would cross the line.

Now the car atmosphere felt stuffy. After Shea pointed out I might not be living in Snowfall by the time her birthday rolled around, she pulled out some headphones and was glued to her phone for the rest of our drive. The only time she looked up was when I had to stop for gas. She jumped out of the car and spent the whole stop in the store. And sure, call me paranoid, but I caught her walking past the door multiple times to see if I was finished pumping gas or not.

I wracked my brain trying to figure out what I'd done wrong. Shea wasn't the type to let things settle. I heard her call out Phillip on a regular basis for something as small as chewing too loudly. And I know from hanging around with Bailey, she did the same with her friends. Plus the last time things got awkward with Shea, she filled the silence with babbling. In fact, I was pretty sure she was allergic to not talking for longer than a minute. So her whole sitting here in silence thing was abnormal.

By the time we pulled up to the tree farm, I was at my limit. I couldn't spend another five hours driving with Shea while she clearly was trying to forget I existed.

"Shea, can we —" I started as I put the truck in park. But Shea's hand was already on the handle, pulling it open as soon as the locks clicked. She practically threw herself out the car, taking a quick beat to look around the area before sprinting to the front office.

"Shea!" I shouted, scrambling to follow her.

The office set up at the front of the tree farm was ... old. Like the only heating they had was the fireplace in the front and everything smelled like old wood. It was an amazing smell, especially accompanied by some snickerdoodles on the front counter, but it did bring to mind uncomfortable living arrangements, squeaky floors, and rattling pipes.

"Hello, welcome to Luckett's Farm. How can I help you?" a cheery woman said as she rounded the corner from a room behind the desk. As if to confirm my suspicions of poor heating in the building, she had on a green down coat and mittens.

"Hi," Shea said, a cheer in her voice that I'd come to learn was false and held a pitch of stress. "I'm Shea White. We're here to pick up the tree for Snowfall."

"Ah, Ms. White. Lovely to meet you. Did y'all have a safe drive up?" the woman asked, hands flittering over a keyboard. Shea leaned against the counter, toes tapping, and hummed in response. Apparently, she wasn't in the mood for polite small talk with anyone else either.

"It was a nice ride up. A bit long, but the mountains are breathtaking."

"They are, aren't they? I love this season. The little dusting of snow makes it feel more like Christmas than anywhere else I've lived in North Carolina."

"Well, you obviously haven't been to Snowfall's winter fest. It's like a Hallmark movie." The woman and I laughed, exchanging a little more small talk as she pulled up whatever she needed on her computer. Meanwhile, Shea moved away from the counter, pacing around the lobby impatiently.

"Here we go," the woman cheered, she turned and started pulling out some papers from a stand next to her computer. She set a map in front of me and circled one of the areas. "You can pick out any trees in this lot."

"Oh, we get to pick our own? That's so cool. Right, Shea?" I turned around to look at Shea, a little brightened by the idea of picking out the tree for ourselves. But just like the car ride, Shea was focused on her phone.

"And once you picked the one you want," the woman paused, pulling out a bright red ribbon from under the counter. "You'll tie this around it and our staff will handle the rest. What sort of setup do you have for transportation?"

The woman rounded the counter, hands full with the map and ribbon, and started outside. I followed behind her and Shea trudged along after me. I showed the employee the truck and tow carriage we'd brought along and she made a few notes for whoever was going to tie down our tree. Then she handed over the map and ribbon and pointed us in the direction of one of the furthermost lots.

As soon as the woman was out of eyesight, I smacked Shea with the ribbon. Shea gasped dramatically and held a hand to where I'd hit her.

"You hit me," she gasped.

"What is your problem?" I asked, smacking the ribbon against her hand.

"What do you mean?" she grumbled. Before I had a chance to respond, Shea put her hands in her pockets and started towards the lot.

"What do *you* mean what do I mean? What's with your whole —" I paused, stomping after her as I waved my hands around. "Your stoic, grumpy, silent treatment?"

"I'm not giving you the silent treatment," she mumbled.

"You barely said a word on the drive or talked to the woman working here."

"I'm tired, it was a long drive and —"

"Bullshit," I shouted and Shea jerked. Even during our little spat about her treating me like a kid, I didn't raise my voice. Honestly, I barely ever raised my voice out of anger, even with Wendy and she stole my phone a lot. But I was so frustrated with Shea. With the weird ups and downs of how she treated me, with the way my crush had evolved from a memory of a person to something more solid for the complicated woman in front of me.

"You are as friendly as a fucking golden retriever and you'd happily make small talk with anyone you meet. And the silence?" I threw up my hands, trying to dissipate the feeling of needing to wring something. "You hate silence! You would rather listen to Phillip rant about his fantasy football league than sit in a quiet office."

"You act like you know me so well," she grumbled before pulling her phone out of her pocket. I snatched it from her hands.

"I know you well enough to know when something's wrong."

Shea finally turned to look at me, her eyes glazed over like she was trying to not see me. I waited for a beat, expecting her to say something, to explain why she was acting weird. But she just shrugged and kept on toward the tree lot.

I didn't follow.

30

SHEA

Trudging along to the back tree lot, alone, was miserable. Having nothing but my internal screams and howling wind as my soundtrack made it all the worse.

Margo was right. I fucking hated the silence. It reminded me of my parents' place after I came out. Suffocating silence that made my skin itch like I was breaking out in hives. Suffocating silence that made me want to literally run to the nearest crowd for relief. Suffocating silence that would have me seeking out any company, no matter how obnoxious.

I guess I should be thankful this silence wasn't like that. I wasn't itching to get out of my skin, I was itching to get under Margo. She clearly didn't understand what she was doing to me. She didn't understand the way she puffed her cheeks before she was about to go on a rant made me want to kiss her complaints away. She didn't understand that the way she gave space for my baggage and organized it made me want to carry her around in my pocket.

And maybe things wouldn't feel so intense if I could just ask her out on a date. But I couldn't. There was no world where I could take her out and *not* tell Bailey. And there's no world where I would out Margo before she's ready. Which meant nothing, not even one little date, could happen.

I stopped in the middle of rows and rows of pine trees and looked around. There was no one in sight, so I threw my head back and screamed.

It wasn't fair icing Margo out. It wasn't fair that I was acting like an immature brat because I couldn't get what I wanted. I was supposed to be the mature one. I'm pretty sure I'd told her mom I'd take care of her, when this whole time, Margo's been caring for me.

I shouted at the sky again before turning around to head back to the office and look for Margo.

When I walked through the door, Margo was leaning against the counter, talking to the employee. The woman had a soft face, giggling while they spoke. It reminded me of Dana talking to Margo and me immediately acting like a territorial shit. At least back then my biggest issue was just dealing with the fact that grown up Margo was hot. Now I was dealing with the fact that she was hot, I could get real fucking feelings for her, and we have to spend another five hours stuck in the car together.

Today sucked.

"Did you find a tree ya like?" the woman at the counter asked, smiling brightly. I hated it.

"No. Margo took the ribbon," I grumbled, stomping over to snatch the ribbon from where Margo had set it down on the counter. And since I was trying to be more mature, I turned right back around to go pick out my tree and get on the road as soon as possible.

Behind me, Margo huffed.

"Well take you're time. We're not getting out of here any-time soon."

I immediately turned on my heel to face her. Margo's eyes narrowed to assess me. Likely trying to figure out why I was acting so wishy washy. Or maybe she was done trying to figure me out and was just pissed. And maybe I was pissed too. I mean, that kiss hadn't been one sided. It was ambiguous as to who started it, but she took it further. She kept going. She grinded on my thigh and left an impression of heat that I wouldn't forget anytime soon.

I didn't want to. I needed to, but I couldn't.

"There was a rock slide on the road that leads up to the farm," the receptionist chimed in, either trying to ignore the tension between us or divert it. "We had a bit of a slush mix overnight, which can cause some of the rocks to shift and tumble as the sun heats them up. That part of the road is private property, so we've gotta wait for somebody on our staff to clear it."

"And how long will that take?" I asked the woman, turning to her simply so I didn't have to look at Margo any more.

"Well," the woman cringed. "Most everybody that has the license to manage those machines is out on delivery. No one's scheduled to get back for another few hours and by the time they get everything cleared, it'll be dark."

"Shit," I hissed, throwing my head back. What did that mean for us? We're we gonna have to camp out in the truck? Could I last another night in close quarters with Margo?

"Don't worry, they're gonna let us stay here," Margo said, her voice a little curt as she pointed upwards.

"Yes. This building used to be cottage for some of the farmhands. Most of it's been repurposed for storage, but we keep one room ready for instances like this."

"One room?" I repeated. "With one bed?"

"Mhmm." The woman looked between me and Margo and asked, "Is that a problem?"

"No," Margo and I said at the same time, though where she sounded unbothered, I was just a mumbling mess.

"Are you sure? We might be able to find a cot or something around here." The woman clutched at her collar bone like she was wearing pearls, looking around the room like she was re-viewing an internal list of what was in their storage.

"No, no. It's fine really. I just … didn't pack a go bag and I'm worried about … morning breath," I grumbled. I was starting to feel bad about how I treated this woman. And I *really* should have asked her name when we first got here. It's not her fault I was crushing on my best friend's little sister who was still in the closet.

Though it'd be pretty impressive if that was her fault some-how.

"Oh, I'm sure we can scrounge up a spare toothbrush. The main house is a bit of a hike, but we should have everything you need for an overnight stay. And we'll have you over for dinner too, of course."

Yaaaaayyyyyy.

31

MARGO

It turns out Isabel, the receptionist, was one of the elder daughters of the family farm. She ran the commercial side of things while her parents and siblings ran the manual labor.

And all *ten* of them surrounded us at the family dining table. Eight kids and the two parents. It was a madhouse. And here I'd been hoping they'd let me crash on their couch instead of in the poorly heated room with Shea.

"So are you two professional event planners?" Gina, the mom of the family, asked.

Shea laughed, the sound hearty and warm and more comfortable than she had been all day. But then she reached for her glass of wine, her second of the evening, and downed it. I was vaguely aware that Shea drank a lot from Bailey's stories and being around her these last few weeks. But I was starting to see a correlation between her drinking and her attitude.

"No. Well, not Shea. I used to work as a librarian in New York, which required a lot of event planning. But we're both working in a realtor's office now."

"Ah, so you're just volunteering for the town holiday events?" Gina asked before glancing at Shea, her company smile faltering. Shea's attitude had slightly improved and she was her usual friendly self through most of the dinner, but as we were finishing up she started to sour.

"Yeah, basically. The woman who normally organizes everything had a little bit of a health scare," I explained but as Gina's face paled, I quickly added, "She's fine! Just not ready for the stress of organizing all the holiday events."

"Oh, good. Y'all from Snowfall, yes? I hear your events are quite impressive." The younger of the kids at the table started gathering their plates, clearly bored of the small talk. I couldn't blame them.

"Yes, Ms. Taylor puts a lot of work into them. It's going to be hard getting through the events without her." I looked over at Shea, hoping she'd be the one to broach the subject of us leaving. She of course refused to look at me.

How many fake yawns will it take to get us out of this?

"Ma, I think it's time we let them go back down and get settled for the night," Isabel cut in and I sent a prayer up to god or whoever to bless her for the rest of her life.

"Isabel," her mother groaned, but Isabel ignored her and stood, gathering our plates. I followed after to help. While we were in the kitchen, I could faintly hear Shea come back to life without me present and start engaging in small talk.

"Are you and your girlfriend fighting or something?" Isabel asked once we were out of earshot in. I nearly dropped the plates I was carrying.

"Girlfriend?" I repeated, my eyes bugging.

"Oh, are you two not? I got a vibe."

"No, we're not — we just —I don't think she —"

"Okay. Sorry. Didn't mean to break you there," Isabel said, laughing.

"No. We just — it's been awkward lately. But I don't think she wants me like that." I started rinsing the dishes to have something to do with my hands. Isabel gently pulled them out of my grip and put them in the dishwasher.

"Well maybe all the snuggling you'll need to do to keep warm in that cottage will change things," she joked, resting a gentle hand on my shoulder. I was glad her customer service front was gone, but I did *not* need the anxiety of what could happen tonight in the name of keeping warm.

Isabel looped her arm around mine and guided me back into the dining room where Shea was thanking the Lucketts for the wine they just forked over. *Great.*

Shea looked over at me and Isabel, eyes narrowing at our linked arms. She met my gaze and I looked pointedly at the wine bottle in her hand. Shea turned back to the Lucketts and thanked them for the evening and the place to stay.

"Good luck," Isabel whispered, squeezing my arm before letting go.

And then we were off, following a graveled path down the hill to the cottage and not saying a word to each other.

At least the view was pretty. Back in New York, stars felt like a foreign concept. My first thought when I saw a speck of light in the sky was a plane, not a star. I'd almost forgotten how nice it was to look up at a sky full of them. At home, the sky was full and vibrant. Low buildings and the backdrop of mountains made for an amazing view.

But up here in the mountains, it was breathtaking. We were high enough to see across the vast landscape of North Carolina. Specs of light below from small towns and above a blanket of stars, different universes or worlds so far away they could already be gone.

"It's beautiful, isn't it?" I said stopping at a part of the trail that had a clear view of the landscape. Shea didn't say anything, so I turned to look at her to make sure she hadn't kept walking.

She hadn't. She was looking at me, her eyes softened, and my breath caught. Shea was so damn pretty, I forgot all about the stars. She was always so busy, never stopping, always talking, always going. But for right now, she was quiet, at ease hopefully. There wasn't music or a show distracting her, I had her whole and undivided attention. And I didn't know what to do with it.

"Yeah. Really beautiful," Shea said, her jaw working like the words were difficult to get out. Then she took a long swig from the wine bottle and turned away.

As she walked down the path, I stood there, blinking. I turned those words over and over in my head, the way her lips moved to shape them, the concentrated look in her eyes.

She wasn't talking about the sky. And I was tired of being in the stupid anxious part of whatever was happening between us.

"Shea!" I shouted, chasing after her down the path. Instead of slowing down so I could catch up, she started speed walking.

"Shea, stop being so fucking childish," I grumbled, slowing down so I didn't trip over stray roots or rocks.

"I'll do whatever I want," she shouted. "Watch out, there's this huge ass rock in the middle of the path like ten feet ahead of you. It's the size of a baby's head."

"Why're you that far ahead of me?"

"Because ..." Shea paused, the only sound our heavy footsteps as we half jogged back to the cabin. "It's cold and I want to get inside."

"I'd have thought all the wine had warmed you up," I noted. We finally made it to where the path let out to the parking lot. Shea stopped, already halfway to the door, and turned to face me.

"What's that supposed to mean?" Shea asked.

"Well, you haven't *not* had a drink in your hand for the last few hours."

Shea chuckled, the sound a lot lower than I anticipated. Low in a way that made my insides heat and my lungs freeze. She took a few long steps across the lot towards me until she was close enough to knock the wine bottle against my arm,

"That's because if I don't have a drink in my hands, I'm gonna need something else to hold. If I let go of this bottle, I'm going to reach for *you*. So it's better for the both us that I keep a hold on this." She lifted up the wine bottle and without thinking, I smacked it out of her hand. The bottle crashed to the floor, sending glass and wine everywhere. But neither Shea nor I looked down at the mess. We were looking at each other, both of us waiting for the other to make the first move.

Shea inched closer, our chests nearly touching. This close, I had to tilt my head up to look at her. Her lip was sucked in, teeth gnawing at the the skin. She tilted her head and her hands gripped at my coat collar, pulling until we were pressed against each other.

"Are you sure?" she asked, the words a rough whisper, her eyes barring into mine with a hard intensity.

"I'm sure."

Shea stared at me, eyes searching. I knew what she'd find. Frustration, confusion, desire. And frustration won out.

I grabbed Shea's face with both hands and crashed her lips to mine.

There was a moment of stillness where I thought Shea would push me away. Where she would say this was a mistake or that if we went further it'd only be for tonight.

"Fuck," she groaned and I braced myself to be rejected.

Instead, her fingers tangled into my hair and her mouth parted.

32

SHEA

This was going to fucking hurt but I was utterly incapable of pushing Margo away.

I mean, it's not like I had much of a choice when the choices were to keep acting like a little bitch because I couldn't fuck Margo or fuck Margo. Honestly, with the heat of her head in my palms, I was struggling to remember why I was bothering to fight this in the first place. I mean, we were two consenting adults, we had the hots for each other, and being her dirty little secret will probably be hot for the amount of time she'll be in town. And given that Bailey has been distracted with her new man and art project, it won't be all that hard to keep this secret.

Letting go of her hair, I slid my hands down Margo's back to grab at her ass. I moaned into her mouth as my fingers dug into the plumb flesh. I squeezed hard enough to leave marks and Margo gasped. Taking the opportunity, I slid my tongue into her mouth. She sighed, hands digging into my hair to tilt me in a way that encouraged me to devour her.

She tasted like warm dark chocolate, sweet with a hint of bitterness. And just like chocolate, she melted in my arms, her weight sinking into me, trusting me to hold her up.

"Margo, if I don't feel you come on my thigh, my fingers, or my lips in the next five minutes, we're gonna have a problem," I growled.

"That's a little cocky," Margo said, her soft laugh tickling my lips.

"No, I left all my cocks at home. I'm just confident." In truth, it wasn't so much confidence as it was the fact that I was so desperate to fuck her, there was no way I'd have the restraint to take things slow. We could go slow on orgasm three. Maybe four.

Tightening my grip on her ass, I hefted Margo up, guiding her legs to wrap around my waist. Margo wrapped her hands around my neck and pulled herself closer, grinding against my stomach. The heat emanating between her between her legs had me panting. Something deep in my core knew that as soon as I got her undressed, Margo would be drenched for me. And that knowledge, that proof that she wanted me and wanted me badly, made me feral.

Trailing my lips away from hers, I made my way down her neck, sucking at the skin just above her collarbone. As I marked her, I walked us to the cottage, kicking in the door. The building was old and not locked, so the door opened way with no damage and I kicked it close before heading to the bedroom.

"Shea," Margo gasped, her hips still rocking into me, head tilted to give me what I wanted.

"Hmm?" I kept my mouth on her skin, relishing the way she shook in response.

"I — we're about to have sex, right?"

I nipped at her skin and pulled back so I could look her in the eyes.

"That was my intention when I said I wanted to feel you come."

"Cool, cool, cool, cool."

I had always viewed Margo as anxious, but in recent days the little stutters and shiftiness had eased significantly. I figured us getting closer had eased her nerves and I didn't like how they were popping back up now.

"What is it?" I asked, gripping her ass even tighter as a way to keep myself from kissing her some more. Margo fiddled with the hair at the nape of my neck and my body heated at the touch. It didn't make things any easier that Margo was biting her lips, eyes trailing down and over my collarbone.

"I haven't been all the way with a woman yet. That's all," Margo answered, her voice soft.

God, I really am going to hell because that should slow me down. I should give her space and time to decide if she really wanted my pussy to be the first she eats. I should be the mature one and take this slow, I shouldn't let her make this decision rashly.

But fuck if I didn't want to be the first woman to get her off.

"Are you saying that as a warning you might stumble or a reason to stop?" I took a deep breath and loosened my hold on her ass, stopping at the bottom of the stairs. If she wanted to stop, I was gonna need a minute outside to cool down. Then I'd need to find something to make a makeshift sleeping bag.

"A warning," Margo said, the words rushed out in a blur.

"You sure?" I asked, even as I started up the stairs. Margo's arms around me tightened, pulling so she was all I could see, all I could breathe.

"Yes. Don't stop."

Fuck.

I practically ran us into the bedroom. There, I dropped Margo onto the bed and started tearing off her clothes. Hat, winter jacket, sweatshirt, shirt, there were so many goddamn layers. And while I was working to get her naked, she was doing the same to me. Our limbs clashed, frantic and shaky, as clothes flew over our heads and shoes were kicked off and our lips were glued together as often as possible.

Down to our underwear, I shoved at Margo's shoulder so she was laid out on the bed, the wood creaking with her weight. Thank god no one else was in this house because I was planning on that being the quietest sound in the room tonight.

Climbing over Margo, I let my eyes wander over her body. Her underwear was a basic black set, the color dark against her pale skin. Though that paleness was gaining more and more color as I looked at her.

Margo was a full woman, curves that filled my hands, softness that could be gripped and offer comfort. My hands traveled up her sides and I paused to kiss a freckle at the bottom of her rib cage. I kissed up, keeping my hands on her side until my fingers hit the edge of her bra. Tilting my head up, I met

Margo's eyes, looking for permission before I stripped the last remnants of her clothes off.

Margo sucked in a breath before nodding. I immediately tore the fabric off, tangling it around Margo's limbs before getting it off and tossed into the corner of the room. Resituating my stance, I propped myself up on my knees, one thigh between Margo's leg. She immediately lifted her hips, grinding against me so I could feel the damp, warm spot on her panties.

"So you want to come on my thigh first?" I teased, bracing one hand next to her head so I could capture her lips again. My other hand went to her breast to knead the heavy flesh before running my fingers over her nipples until they hardened.

"W-wait," Margo stuttered through sighs. I held still but didn't move away. "Why do I get to come first?"

"Because I said so." It felt as simple as that. My body burned to watch her come undone, to taste her release. There was no way I could relax into my own climax without having her first. I was too tense, too anxious this would all fall apart before I got her, to do anything but see her go first.

"But I'm excited to make you come too."

God, this woman. I was one thread away from tearing off her underwear and the knowledge that that would mean she'd have to go commando on our car ride home did nothing to temper me.

Pressing my thigh against her cunt, I let go of her breast to grab her hip and guide her to grind on me.

"You want to play with me, Margo?" I whispered before dragging my teeth over the edge of her ear. She didn't have her cuff on today, but she had three studs trailing up her ear. My tongue traced around each of them.

"Yes," she sighed. "Please. I wanna learn what you like."

I chuckled against her skin because that was just *so* Margo. She liked to learn new things, always got so bright to find out some unconventional use for something, always the first to spit out a fun fact. It wasn't hard to imagine she was a good student in school, I mean she had her master's for fucks sake. And it wasn't a push to see her being a good student in bed too.

Showing her all my toys and how I'll use them on her is going to be fun.

"Well, I asked you to come first. So be a good girl and let me make you."

"But I —" Margo started, cutting off with a sharp gasp as my teeth sank into her ear. I kissed down her neck again, revisiting the spot that was already blooming with color. I pressed a soft kiss and went to her other side to give her symmetrical love bites.

My hand on Margo's hip urged her faster and Margo followed suit, grinding her cunt against me as she chased release. But apparently, Margo wasn't good at keeping things just about her. She lifted the leg between mine up to press into me, a delicious and teasing amount of pressure that almost made me break. But even as Margo's hands tore at my bra, as her fingers found and teased my nipples, I kept my focus on her. On that growing heat between her thighs and the way her movements slowed as she got distracted by her impending climax.

"If we were at home," I whispered, letting go of her hip so Margo could frantically grind against my leg and I could play with her tits. "I'd make you get down on your knees and suck my strap-on before fucking you. Then you'd get to learn what I really like. A long, hard session where you have to tap out to get me to stop."

"Shit," Margo hissed. She stopped playing with my breast to wrap her arms under mine and dig her nails into my shoulder. With her face buried in my neck, she cried out her release. Her hips quivered against my leg before collapsing onto the bed.

With great restraint, I tempered my kisses. Slowing to full presses of my lips against her skin, occasionally twisting my tongue over goosebumps, drawing lines between them like they were constellations in the sky.

I kept an eye on Margo's face, the flutter of her eyes, as I traveled down. When I reached her hip bone and my fingers slid under the waistband of her underwear, Margo's eyes snapped open.

"No," she grumbled and grabbed my hands. "It's my turn to play."

Margo intertwined our fingers and pulled me up until we were at eye level. Then she wrapped her legs around my waist and twisted us around. My back hit the mattress and I burst into giggles.

It'd been a while since sex was light and giggly. In the last few years, sex was about scratching an itch. The person didn't matter so long as they were an active participant and we both got off in the end. But Margo was different. With her, I wasn't just some horny bitch, some means to an end, I was myself. And somehow I'd forgotten how valuable that was.

Margo resituated her legs so she was straddled over me and copied my movements from before. She kissed my cheek, a soft press, before her lips trailed down my neck with hungry and heated kisses accompanied by her tongue teasing me. She took her sweet time, like she was memorizing the feel of my skin, my taste. By the time she'd made it down to my collarbone, I was a squirming mess. My skin burned, my hips raised of their own accord, and my hands dug into Margo's hair trying to push her further down to my breasts.

"Nuh-uh," Margo tsked, pulling out of my hold and scooting further down until her mouth was hovering over my pussy. "It's my turn."

33

MARGO

There were no more thoughts in my head, just the need to find out what Shea tasted like. I needed to see her, see how wet she got getting me off. I needed that evidence to prove this was real and that Shea actually wanted me, wanted this.

Sliding my fingers into her waistband, I yanked her panties down before crawling off the bed and tossing them somewhere. With a tight grip on her thighs, I dragged Shea to the edge of the bed and sank to my knees. Shea's giggles from being manhandled died as I pulled her knees apart and I leaned closer to get a good look at her.

Shea was neatly trimmed, the dark brown of her natural color curled wildly, but was contained to the triangle of her mound. Her lips were smooth, the thick flesh swollen and dark, glistening in the dim light of the cabin.

There was a nagging thought in the back of my head that I should be worried about the untrimmed shape of my pussy. Since I wasn't anticipating going for a swim or getting eaten, I'd let things grow to their natural shape. My nerves could easily get eaten away by the comparison. But they weren't. I was too focused on the smell of Shea's musk and how badly I wanted to taste it.

"Woah, hold up," Shea said when my lips were halfway to her cunt. She pushed up on her forearms and continued, "Are you sure you wanna start there?"

"Very sure." As my breath landed on her sensitive flesh, Shea jerked away from me. Without thinking, I grabbed her by the knees and yanked her back in place, flinging one of her legs over my shoulder and holding her other leg open by the knee. I leaned in, tilting my face to kiss up her thigh.

"I don't think I'll be able to focus on anything else until I get a taste of you," I whispered into her skin, my lips trailing closer and closer to her center, drool pooling under my tongue.

When my lips first met hers, just a graze of a touch, Shea collapsed back onto the bed. The wood cried under the movement, and I got a heated joy out of the fact that we could make as much noise as we wanted, that the noise would represent how much we were enjoying each other.

"God, I wish I was a better person and had the will to tell you to stop," Shea said. One of her hands went to the nape of my neck, tangling her fingers into the mess of waves, twisting my hair around in a teasing motion.

"I think you're pretty fucking great," I grumbled. The idea that Shea thought she was anything less than amazing grated something inside me. And I felt determined to chase those thoughts of hers away.

With as gentle of a touch as I could manage, I traced the edges of her lips. After a couple of passes, and Shea's grip on my hair tightening, I pressed the flat of my tongue against her to make one rough pass. Then another. Then another. Until I was ready to work her lips open.

Using the tip of my tongue, I parted her lips. I took long swoops, tracing her entrance in a U shape, careful not to touch her clit yet. It was torturous to wait for a *real* taste of Shea's cunt, but the way she shook and screamed and grabbed at me brought me almost as close to orgasm as riding her thigh. I was unabashedly getting off on teasing her and I let her know by groaning into her cunt and letting my drool run down her ass.

"Fuck," Shea hissed. "If I didn't know you, Margo, I'd be calling bullshit on this being the first time you've eaten pussy."

I chuckled and Shea jerked against me, her whole body quivering. Watching her shake from such a little motion was satisfying, but...

"Am I going too far?"

This time, when Shea tugged at my hair, it was gentle, a light pull so I had to look up at her. And god, I was so focused on memorizing the shape and taste of Shea's pussy, that'd I'd forgotten to look up at *her*.

Shea's cheeks were a bright pink, there was a light sheen of sweat on her forehead, and her lips had distinct indents. Her chest rose in heavy waves, her nipples erect. She reminded me of an oil painting, she was that much of a vision.

"I wouldn't say too far," Shea answered with a chuckle. "But if you tease me any longer, I'm not responsible for what I might do."

"I'd like to see that." I pressed a kiss to Shea's cunt before wrapping my tongue around her clit. I ran my tongue around her clit twice before pulling back to say, "But not as badly as I want to feel you come all over my face."

I returned to her clit, sucking at the swollen bud. Then I slid two fingers into her, curling up to stroke against the swollen, spongy spot inside her. Shea's reaction was instantaneous. Her pussy squeezed against my fingers, spasming in tight pulses as a wave of heat radiated off her body. And the taste. The *taste* of her release was something I'd crave for the rest of my life. Musky and salty and so fucking perfect.

As her shivers started to subside, I slid my fingers out of her to lick them clean. She'd come so much, it dripped down my fingers, pooling in my palm. And I lapped it up eagerly.

"God, that's so fucking hot. Come here."

I was too absorbed in my meal to notice Shea had sat up until her hand wrapped around my neck and dragged me forward, our lips crashing together. Shea's hands dragged down my back, leaning into me until she could reach my ass and yank me up on top of her.

"You don't play fair," Shea murmured between hungry kisses. Her hands went under my panties and gripped my ass. Tomorrow morning, I'd likely find several little marks and I most certainly had a hickey or two on my neck. I'm not sure all those marks would count as playing fair, but I liked them far too much to complain.

Shea pulled at my ass until I was up on my knees, my tits pressed into her face. She nipped at my hard nipple, the sensation so sharp I jerked in her hold. But Shea held me tight. One of her arms snaked around my back, keeping me pressed against her, while her free hand pulled aside my underwear to lazily glide through my cunt.

"Did you get off eating me out?"

"Yes," I cried as Shea sucked at my nipple, swirling her tongue over the raised flesh.

"I know you did. Know how I can tell?" Shea asked before switching to my other breast. I made some noise that was supposed to be the word 'how'. It was hard to form coherent words when her fingers started tracing my cunt, occasionally dipping in just enough to make my knees wobble.

"I know because your pussy is fucking *drenched*, Margo." I think I hummed in agreement. But the noise quickly turned into a moan as Shea sank her fingers into me. "I was worried about getting you too worked up in case you ruined your panties. But that ship has sailed. You're going to have to ride back commando, babe. And you're gonna have to be okay with driving while I reach over to grab what's mine."

"Shea," I gasped. I had to grab onto her shoulders to keep myself upright. It was like my body was melting into putty at her touch. Soon I'd be nothing more than a puddle on the floor. A steaming hot puddle.

I buried my head into Shea's neck, letting my weight fall into her. She cupped my head, stroking my hair while her other hand worked my pussy to orgasm.

"I've got you," Shea whispered, teeth gliding over the shell of my ear. "Let me feel you come."

How was it that Shea knew dirty talk was my undoing? Was she making that assumption based on the fact that I was a bookworm or did she get off saying those things just as much as I got off hearing them?

I sank my teeth into Shea's neck, muffling my moans as I came on her fingers.

"That's it," Shea cooed, her fingers still stroking my G-spot and her palm pressed against my clit. "Give me some more."

"But … I … turns?" Words were hard when your orgasm stretched on and on, making your mind fuzzier and fuzzier.

"Hmmm, you're the one who wanted turns. And if we're talking turns based on minutes spent, it's not your turn yet."

I whined and Shea chuckled at me, nipping at my ear again.

"You ate me out so well for your first time, babe. That's got to be rewarded. And I already warned you I like to go until you tap out. So is that what you want? To tap out?"

"No."

34

SHEA

The fact that I was still orgasm happy the morning after was a sign of something I wasn't ready to assess.

But sitting back in the car with Margo felt a hell of a lot lighter now. I wasn't suppressing anything, I could lean over and kiss her whenever I wanted. It was nice.

And I knew it wouldn't last.

If we were going to keep going with whatever this was, we needed to set some sort of ground rules. And since I was the older one and the one with more closeted experience, I needed to be the one to bring it up.

It took two whole Taylor Swift eras, out of order, for me to get up the nerve. And honestly, *Paper Rings* might have had a heavy impact on building my confidence.

"Margo, I think —"

"We should talk about what our relationship is going to look like back in Snowfall," Margo said, crashing into the confidence I'd built like a freight train.

"That's probably smart," was all I managed to get out.

"I … I assume it's a little awkward for you since Bailey's your best friend, right?"

"Mhmm." It wasn't. I mean, it'll probably be awkward every once in a while. But that's assuming Margo sticks around long enough for that to happen. The real reason we would need to keep our relationship on the down low was —

"And I don't know if I'm ready to tell my parents I'm bi yet." Margo shifted in her seat, gnawing at her lower lip. As much as I wanted something lasting with her, I couldn't push her to come out for me. That'd be horribly selfish.

This was going to be like all my other relationships, fun but short.

I rested a hand on Margo's thigh and gave her a squeeze.

"I understand. I won't pressure you to come out. Ever. And if you decide to tell them, I'll be by your side when you do. No matter where our relationship stands. Friends or more." The words felt like swallowing thorns. I meant every one of them but I was already dreading the actuality of them. If Margo decided she didn't want me romantically, I'd be there for her as a friend even if that meant crying myself to sleep every night.

"Thank you." Margo's eyes were still on the road, but her voice was the kind of soft that felt special, tender.

"And I know it's hard for you to keep things a secret from your friends. And that hiding might feel like being back in the closet, which I imagine would bring up some unpleasant memories. So I ..." Margo's voice had started to quiver, her eyes glistening. She took a second to work out what she wanted to say and wiped away the tears. "I understand if that's not something you're willing to be a part of. So ... if you want to, I dunno, stop here and pretend nothing happened, I won't blame you. No hard feelings and all that."

"Uh, no." My response was immediate, so immediate it even shocked me. I mean, when had I gone from not wanting Margo because it'd be messy and complicated to wanting it so badly that I'd take what I could get?

Probably last night when I got concrete evidence that Margo was into me for more than a moment. Or maybe it was when she dubbed Bella's voice with a British accent. They were both pretty strong contenders to encourage my affection.

"No," I repeated, squeezing her thigh. "I told you I'd show you my toys, I'm not gonna back out of that."

Margo laughed, though it sounded tight. It made me worry she didn't believe me. And if she didn't believe I could handle it, we'd end up just being friends who knew what each other tasted like. And right now, that sounded worse than being a secret fling.

"Margo, I'm serious, we can keep this a secret. I won't out you, I promise.

The indent on Margo's lip deepened as she bit harder, brow furrowing.

"I'm not worried about you outing me. I'm worried that keeping a secret from everybody that's important to you will hurt. I don't ..." Margo's grip tightened on the steering wheel and she let out a long sigh. "I don't want you hurting."

"I'm not. I won't be." It was a white lie. Just a little, tiny white lie.

"Okay. But ... if it ever gets to be too much and you want to step back, you'll let me know, right? If this is hurting you, you'll say something, right?"

"Sure." There was a lump in my throat that I couldn't swallow, could barely breathe around. It was one thing for Margo to treat this as a fling, and not value it because it was short. But for her to care about my well-being over getting into this was something different. It made it feel bigger. Bigger than something that could be kept a secret.

"Okay. Cool. I guess we're dating then, right?" Margo's tenseness faded into jitters, her cheeks reddening as she said that we were dating. That was cute enough to distract me from the existential dread of the future.

"Yup, we're dating, babe. So, where're you gonna take me for our first date?" I leaned back into my seat and relaxed into the easy flirting and teasing. This was the part of a relationship I was good with, the jokes, the unserious conversations.

"What makes you think I'm taking you out? Shouldn't it be the other way around?" A smile was fighting at the corner of Margo's lips.

"And what makes you say *that*?" I challenged.

"Well, you're clearly the more dominant one in this situation. And you have this ... masc energy." Margo waved her hand wildly in my direction, not looking away from the road.

"Wooooaaahhhh. That's some heavy heteronormative thinking you've got there."

"Shut up," Margo grumbled, smacking my arm. "You're also older."

"And now you're talking about my age. Definitely not taking you out now." That got me another smack, this one accompanied by a nervous giggle that warmed my heart more than it should. It was just a laugh, it shouldn't give me butterflies. "Fine, I'll take you on a date. What're you doing tonight?"

"After this five-hour drive? Showering before I crash."

"Crash at my place," I told her, regretting it when her shoulders tensed in response. I stumbled over my words to take the offer back. "Sorry. You don't have to. I'm sure you want some space or whatever."

"No, no. Not space, just ... I've got a couple of things to do when we get back, you know? I mean, we're missing a whole day of work. There's gonna be a lot to do before we can ... fool around."

"Hmm." I sank into my seat and pulled out my phone. She had a good point. We had a lot to do at work with the tree lighting, at the very least I needed to call the tree decorator to give her an update on the precise dimensions of the tree. But we could do that together at my place.

"I can be there in ... maybe four hours after we get back. That okay?" Margo asked.

Four hours after we'd get back would be pretty late. Not many folks would be about to see her car pulling up to my place.

I swallowed down the unease. Margo wasn't ready. A little hiding was natural. I just figured us being a couple would be the only thing hidden. This sounds more like we wouldn't even be seen as friends.

"Yeah. Sure, that's fine."

35

MARGO

Olivia: I've gathered all the ornaments your mom was willing to donate and stored them in the town hall

Olivia: Y'all's attic is insanely well organized, I love it

Me: Yeah, Mom likes to decorate. I'm partially worried she'll waste all her retirement funds at craft shows

Zoey: And I've gotten Mason to teach me how to lasso

Zoey: We're one step closer to getting Clive to be a reindeer

Roxie: Zo, you're the only one who wants that

Me: It might be cool. Shea wanted to do something to stand out, make this year special. My only idea was to pick up an old tradition of hiding mistletoe around the Eve-Eve Fest

Rosie: Oh, I think I remember that. Why did we stop doing it?

Me: Ms. Taylor caught her then husband under one with somebody else

Roxie: Yikes

Ashley: We absolutely have to bring this tradition back

Rosie: No, ma'am, we're not inflicting emotional damage during the holidays

Ashley: She'd do it

Zoey: We don't need that tradition, we have Clive

Eli: I've gotten a few teachers from the elementary school to make ornaments this week. My students wanted to make some too, but they're … not all appropriate

Rosie: Oh dear

Rosie: Well I've gotten a few donations from folks in town. I'll drop them off at the town hall after my shift tomorrow

Me: That's all right, Eli, I can sort through them before handing them off to the decorate. Thanks everybody!

36

MARGO

When I slammed the door open to Wendy's shop, Tristan was curled up on the floor. holding his stomach.

"Wendy, did you actually poison him? Like for real?" I shouted, looking over to where my friend stood behind the counter. She rolled her eyes and walked around to kick at Tristan on. The man moaned, but otherwise let himself be rolled onto his back. His eyes fluttered open before narrowing on Wendy. Or maybe it would be more precise to say his gaze narrowed to what he could see at that angle.

"Pink underwear? Really?" Tristan managed to roll out of the way just before Wendy's foot stomped down on where his head had been. He scrambled out of the pizzeria and I sent up a thanks to whatever powers that be kept me from hiding a body tonight.

"What did you do to him?" I asked as Wendy went back to her station behind the register. I sat at one of the stools at the counter and leaned in to assess my friend. She was in her T-shirt dress, the green one I swear she's had since high school. Despite the chill of winter outside, it got blistering in the shop, especially in the kitchen next to the brick oven. But as far as clothes go, a dress was pretty easy to fluff out if Wendy had gotten rowdy. Though her hat and pigtails weren't askew, so it couldn't have been *that* bad.

"I'll tell you what happened with shit face, if you tell me where you got those," Wendy said, pointing at the distinct hickies on my neck. I'd been too focused on what was happening with Shea to remember to go home and get some cover-up before visiting Wendy. Honestly, it was a miracle I hadn't run into anyone returning the tow and truck earlier.

"That's from — you see at the tree farm there was a —" My stutters came to a halt because there was absolutely nothing that could have made these marks other than another person. Maybe an octopus, but to say I ran into one of those while in the mountains was a bit of a stretch.

"Um … we maybe entered a different stage of awkward." I looked around the shop, eyeing Jimmy in the corner booth. He frequented Pete's nearly every day, sometimes even twice a day. When Wendy's dad was still running the place, they'd shoot the shit all day long. But without Wendy's dad around, he seemed a little lost and tried to fill that hole with Wendy. I knew she saw him as an uncle figure, but we hadn't really talked about how she felt about him hanging around all the time.

"Jimmy, get out of here!" Wendy shouted. Jimmy looked up, pizza still stuffed in his mouth.

"But I —" he started to say through a mouthful before Wendy chucked a to-go box at him.

"Take it to go. I'm closing for lunch."

"But you never close for lunch. That'd be like ... like if crabs walked on land."

"Jimmy, they do."

"Agh, whatever. I'm going." Jimmy kept grumbling as he stuffed his pizza into the box and waddled off. After the door closed on him, he waved a fist towards the sky.

"Do you like that Jimmy hangs out here all the time?" I asked Wendy and she shrugged.

"It wouldn't be the same if he wasn't around. So I guess."

I opened my mouth to ask a follow-up question, like what the hell did they talk about when it was just the two of them, but Wendy spoke first.

"So you and Shea hooked up? How was it?" Wendy rested her elbows on the counter, head on her hands, and leaned towards me, eyebrows raising like a cartoon character.

"I'm not gonna tell you if you keep acting like a perv," I grumbled.

"Well too bad for you how good it was is written all over your face." My cheeks burned. "And your neck." I was likely going to combust in this seat and I hoped I took Wendy down with me. "I guess as long as it wasn't disappointing, you're good."

"Wait, what? Why would you say that?" I jerked up at the accusation that anything with Shea could be bad.

"Well, I mean, I know you've gotten to know each other lately, but like there's no way you could've known if she was selfish in bed. Or it could've been plain old bad and ruined the image of your childhood crush. Or she could have had her pubes shaved into a weird shape. Or —"

"Okay, shut up. None of that happened. God."

"Well, you weren't volunteering any information. What else was I supposed to think?" Wendy shrugged.

"But her pube hair?" Again Wendy just shrugged. "Ugh, whatever. We're dating now, I guess, but keeping it a secret. And I feel a little guilty telling you this because Shea doesn't have anyone to talk to and that's not fair. She probably wants a friend to freak out with too. But if she tells one of the girls, they'll all know. And if Bailey knows, then she'll figure out I'm bi and probably tell Mom. And Mom will tell Dad and then they'll sit me down for some awkward family meeting where Mom'll cry because she thought she'd done something wrong and Dad'll give me a disappointed look for making Mom cry. And —"

Wendy's hands slammed onto my shoulders and shook me until I shut up.

"You're spiraling."

"There's a lot of good reasons to spiral," I argued.

"Sure, but like, you just bagged your childhood crush. How many people can say that?"

"I guess that's pretty cool," I murmured, trying to shake off Wendy so I could wipe away the anxiety tears.

"You guess?" She shook me harder. "You *literally* have several markings. That's not just fucking, she claimed you. She wants you! Celebrate that!"

"I guess it's nice she likes me like that," I said, laughing through the tears. It felt cocky to say, but I didn't think Shea *just* liked me like that. I think she really liked me. Like maybe there could be more. But...

"But what about when I get a real job?"

"Oh my god," Wendy said, shaking me again before letting go. "You can't cross a bridge you can't see."

"What?" I asked, following after Wendy as she left the counter to go back into the kitchen.

"You can't figure out what you're gonna do when you don't know when or where your next job is. For all we know, you could replace Ms. Delaney. Lord knows she needs to retire," Wendy grumbled. She pulled out a pizza paddle and slid it into the brick oven pizza, not flinching at the wild heat that made visible waves. I leaned against the door and watched my friend continue to grumble as she pulled out a perfectly toasted pizza that she hadn't set a timer for.

"You just want me to stay in Snowfall for you," I teased once she'd set the pizza on a cooling rack. She immediately pointed the paddle at me and I backed up. But instead of arguing or snarking with me, Wendy sighed and set the paddle aside.

"I mean, it would be nice to have my best friend living in town," she murmured under her breath.

"Aw." I wrapped my arms around Wendy. "You miss me that much when I'm gone?"

"Well Abigail doesn't like leaving her house, so I'm kinda on my own."

"You've got Jimmy," I reminded her while patting her back.

"Jimmy's family, he won't help me steal shit from the downtown library."

"I wouldn't either!"

"Bullshit, you hate the downtown library. You'd be easy to convince."

I pinched Wendy's side and she nudged me away.

"You love me," I teased, following after Wendy as she went back to the front.

"Shut up!" Wendy groaned. I kept on teasing Wendy, enjoying the feeling of being at home with her and in Snowfall. I had big dreams of what I wanted to accomplish as a librarian, but maybe I could do that here. Not just because I wanted things to work out with Shea, but because I've missed Wendy too.

While Wendy went on a rant about how Abigail didn't participate in her pranks or shenanigans whereas she could push me into it them, I pulled out my phone to text Shea.

> **Me:** I know our situation is weird mostly because of me not being out and that means you can't to talk about us with your closest friends. That's not fair.

> **Me:** So you have my explicit consent to talk with someone you trust outside the girl group

37

SHEA

Just as I was about to slide into a depressive spell about not being able to gather my girls to talk about my impromptu night with Margo, she texted me explicit consent to talk to somebody. Not only was it so damn considerate of her to know I needed somebody to talk to, but the trust she was giving me to pick someone was massive. It was the kind of trust I wanted to cradle, swaddle it up and carry it in one of those front-facing baby holders.

Plus, it also implied she wasn't keeping us a secret because she was embarrassed of me. Which eased an anxiety before it had the chance to consume me.

So when I got to Steel Wheelz to talk to Denny, one weight was already off of my shoulders.

"Hey, Shae! How was your cabin sta— fuck. What lumber-jack did you abandon Margo for to give you that?" Dennis said, stopping mid-greeting to point at his neck. My hand instantly went to cover the hickey Margo left. I'd forgotten all about it on the drive over, too wrapped up in the satisfaction of see-ing my marks on her. They were *far* more noticeable than what she'd left. She was going to have a hell of a time explaining them if she runs into anyone before she can cover them up.

Pulling myself onto the counter, I did a quick look around the shop. "Nobody's here with you, right?"

"No. Does that mean you're going to act all weird again?"

"Yeah. And you still can't tell Olivia, all right?"

Dennis crossed his arms and leaned back against the wall. When he realized I wasn't going to elaborate, he sighed but nodded for me to continue.

"Right. So the girl I was talking about last time is Margo. And I'm not outing her, she gave me permission to talk to somebody who isn't close to Bailey because she's not ready to come out yet. And I didn't abandon her to fuck some lumber-jack. I fucked her."

Dennis straightened. He blinked. Then, without a word, he rounded the counter and went to the front door, flipping the sign to closed before turning back to me.

"What?"

"I know it's kinda crazy, but something just shifted in my head when I learned she was bi. I suddenly noticed how hot her ass is. And she was wearing those good girl outfits to work, working as my *fucking secretary*. So I understand what you meant about those clothes now."

Dennis grunted before returning to his stool behind the counter. He rested his elbows on the table to lean in and listen and I crossed my legs to get more comfortable.

"But you know, just cause I knew she was bi and was attracted to her, didn't really mean shit. And I wanted her to feel comfortable around me and being queer in the South. So that's why I took her to the Elmville pub."

"Where you became a jealous caveman seeing her flirt with someone else?"

"Yeah, sure. Whatever. After that, she was kind of pissed at me because she thought I was treating her like a kid and she gets treated like a kid a lot because everyone in town just sees her as Bailey's little sister."

Denny hummed, fully aware of what it was like for the folks in Snowfall to make assumptions about you and never change them.

"But then she helped me out when the kids got kidnapped by Mrs. Clause during the —"

"Wait, what?" Dennis interrupted.

"Oh, did that news not make it to you?"

"That kids were kidnapped by Mrs. Clause? No, I think I'd remember that."

"Well at the choir one group of kids followed somebody dressed as Mrs. Clause up to the attic. They were fine. It was clearly somebody trying to fuck with me planning the holiday events. Anyways, back to Margo."

"Anyways, she says. Kids are getting kidnapped and all she wants to talk about is some girl," Denny scoffed.

"Not some girl," I argued, nudging his arms with my foot. "After that event, where she totally saved my ass, we talked about why she'd gotten pissed at me and ... I dunno, the way she was vulnerable with me made me feel all soft and gooey."

"And then you got locked in the school, right? Oh my god, tell me you didn't fuck in the middle of the high school? Is that what that bitch Abe was talking about when he said compromising position?"

"No! We didn't fuck in the school. God. Abe just caught us cuddling. Probably with my hand in Margo's pants, I'm not sure. But before that, I'd asked why she hadn't come out to her parents since they took care of me and stuff. Which made her cry. So I tried to cheer her up by doing a sleepover in the school. But then, you know, she was wearing my clothes and we were in a blanket fort and I got all fuddled. So I suggested truth or dare to lighten things."

"Uh-huh, sure, you did. And you weren't just trying to copy me?" Dennis had spent a couple of hours with Olivia locked in the shed behind the community center because Clive sat in front of the door. This was back when their relationship was still a front for him fitting into the community. Apparently, things were just getting good when I went to check up on them.

"Shut up. Maybe. Anyways, she dared me to let her look at my Hinge profile. And she ended up like ogling one of my photos and we sorta wrestled for my phone. Then we just kinda started making out, like *really* making out. Margo was grinding on my thigh and everything."

"So you *did* fuck in the school?"

"No! My phone lit up with a text from some chick I've hooked up with a few times because I'd texted her earlier to distract myself from Margo."

"Oof."

"Exactly. So I just accepted we weren't gonna get anywhere and the kiss was just a fluke of the moment. But then we had to be in a car together for five hours straight. And every time we'd hung out, I got deeper into the idea that we could be something, you know? So during the ride, I just kept to myself. I put my headphones in and didn't yap or stare at her hands or do anything else that might get me deeper in the liking Margo hole."

"*You* didn't talk for five whole hours?" Denny asked in disbelief.

"I mean, not the whole five hours, but whatever. I was keeping to myself. Except then there was some rock slide and we had to stay in this poorly heated cabin, with only one room."

"And one bed?"

"Naturally. And the family that runs the farm had us over for dinner and the whole time, I was trying *not* to think about how I'll be sleeping in a bed with Margo. Then when we headed back to our room, Margo started giving me attitude because I was being kind of a prick. Words were said. Kisses were had. And then more than kisses. And now we're dating I guess? Well, not I guess, we're dating. But since she's not ready to come out, we're keeping it a secret."

"Oh, so that's what you want to talk about?"

I chewed on my bottom lip and pulled my knees up to wrap my arms around them.

"I dunno."

"You don't know if you want to talk about it or you don't know how you feel about being in a closeted relationship with your best friend's sister?"

"Well, it's not like it's gonna be a hard secret to keep."

"What do you mean?" Dennis asked, an eyebrow raised.

"Everybody's busy. I mean, I barely talk to Bailey anymore since she's all wrapped up with Greg and the others are starting to get quiet in the group chat as they get busy with family holiday shit. Nobody's gonna notice if I get a little quiet too. Plus Margo's only in Snowfall into she finds another librarian job, so …" I trailed off, not ready to think about the ending of this relationship when it just got started.

"Why doesn't she just work at the downtown library? I'm pretty sure Ms. Delaney is gonna kick the bucket any second."

"No, I couldn't ask her to consider that." I shook my head. "She wants to do big shit at a library. Like you need big city funding kind of shit. I couldn't ask her to give up those goals for me. I mean, there's no saying we'll even last that long. We could fizzle out before she finds another job. Hell, we could fizzle out before the holidays end."

Dennis leaned back again, arms crossed, and assessed me.

"You don't want it to fizzle out though, do you?"

"I mean," I started, shrugging. "It's been a while since I felt myself with a partner. So it'd be nice if it works out. But I can't count on it."

"Why not?" Dennis' words were like a shock to my nervous system.

"What do you mean?"

"I mean, why are you already expecting it to fail? You said she makes you feel like yourself, that's a pretty damn good quality in a partner. And I'm not gonna pretend like I understand the pressure to come out or to hide a relationship, but I'm guessing it's pretty damn significant she wants to be with you even when the chance of her being outed, through neither of y'all's fault, is really fucking high. So why're you brushing that off?"

"Well," I paused to shrug, "It's never worked out before. Why should it this time? I'm better off not expecting things."

"Because the last people you expected to love you didn't?" Dennis asked. And if his words before were a shock, this was a meteor crashing into my gut at full speed. I turned away from Denny and slid off the counter.

I needed a drink.

"Shea, hold up," Dennis called. Without me thinking, my feet had already taken me halfway to the door by the time he spoke up. "I just meant you shouldn't be afraid of something because of *that*. Not because of them."

"Ha!" The laugh felt dry in my mouth, but I needed it. Needed the laugh, needed to make this a joke. "I'm not afraid because of them. Hell, they're the one's who're afraid of me. Scared them out of town and everything."

Dennis chuckled and nodded his head.

"All right, just making sure. Take care of yourself, all right?"

"You too." We waved each other off and I went straight home for a drink.

38

MARGO

"Sorry that took so long," I shouted as I stepped into Shea's apartment. After I'd finished talking with Wendy, I'd snuck back into my house to clean and cover up before talking to my parents and running around town to collect the ornaments. Becky, the decorator and one of the old lady gang's granddaughters, needed all the ornaments we collected cataloged so that she could sketch out a design. So even though I'd told everyone to turn in their ornaments by Wednesday, I spent most of my evening getting a head start on that.

It had sucked spending several hours with an open spreadsheet and boxes of ornaments that were in need of a dusting, especially when I could have been spending that time with Shea. But whenever I thought of her face when she sees what the town put together for her, I got all buzzy and giggly.

After locking Shea's front door and tossing my bag on the couch, I looked around for Shea. The TV was running one of those Netflix original baking shows that probably wouldn't get another season and the coffee table was littered with pint glasses. But no Shea.

I snagged a few of the glasses and brought them into the kitchen to put them in the dishwasher. No Shea there either.

"Shea!" I called, starting to worry that she'd fallen asleep since I'd taken so long.

"In the shower!" Shea called back, her voice faint. I followed the sound of her voice down the hallway and opened the door to the bathroom.

Obviously, I knew Shea would be naked in the shower. What I hadn't known was what seeing her in the shower would do to me, skin warmed into a soft red, hair darkened and flat, water droplets falling over the curve of her breast and hips. She had the water on so hot the room was basically a sauna, the shower door clouded just enough to hide all the little details of Shea's body. Though not enough to hide the hickey I'd given her right at the nook of her neck and collarbone.

Shea winked at me through the glass before opening the door. She leaned out, water dripping all over, and looped one finger through my belt loop. Pulling me closer, she brought our lips together and I was rendered into a puddle of want. The kiss was hot and sloppy, Shea's wet skin pressed against my dry clothes. The opposition of our bodies left me eager for more.

Though if I was being honest, I'd wanted more all day.

I kissed her back with that starving feeling. I mean, it was only fair, she's the one who made me this way. But as I licked into her mouth, I got that strong cinnamon taste and the sharp burn of alcohol.

"Join me," Shea said, pulling back just enough to tilt her head to the shower.

My brain was buzzing, want and logic battling each other.

"Will you touch me if I join you?"

"Abso-fucking-lutely," she said, the response partly laughed and partly slurred.

"No. You've been drinking."

"Just a little bit," Shea pouted. She leaned back into me, pressing sloppy kisses against my neck, right where her hickies were covered up.

"Well maybe after we've had a nice long talk about how we want to handle consent while drinking."

"Ugh," Shea groaned. Her kisses stopped and she pressed her head into the crook of my neck, letting her weight fall into me. "You're no fun."

"That's not what you said last night," I reminded her, poking at her side. Shea chuckled, the sound soft and light-hearted.

"I like teasey Margo," she murmured, her face still buried in my neck. She was silent for a moment before whispering, in the tiniest voice I'd ever heard, "But you do want me, right?"

For a second, all I wanted to do was shove her hand in my pants to show her just how badly I wanted her. I mean, it had to be physically impossible to not get drenched with her hot and wet and pressed up against me like this. It was wild that she even doubted it.

But I pushed the horny thoughts aside and instead took her hand to press it against my heart. The organ was pounding against my chest like it was trying to break free. When Shea felt it, she pulled back to meet my gaze.

"Yeah, I want you," I whispered back to her. After a beat, Shea rested her forehead on mine and kissed me. This time the kiss was soft, not hungry but a reassuring touch, like she was making sure I was there and not an illusion.

"Okay. Okay," she murmured.

"Okay," I repeated. "Why don't you finish up with your shower and I'll get you something to eat?"

Shea slid her arms around my waist and pulled me closer. Head shaking against mine, she squeezed me tighter and I knew there was no hope for my clothes. But I also knew that whatever drove Shea to drink to this extent couldn't be brushed aside. Or more accurately, I shouldn't let her brush it aside even if the reason was me.

"Shea," I prompted. "Are you gonna get back in the shower?"

"Eh, I'm good." With her arms still around me, she shrugged.

I guess it wouldn't be taking care of your drunk girlfriend without a little stubbornness.

Not that she was my girlfriend yet. Or maybe ever. I don't think I deserved that title while forcing her to keep a secret from her best friend.

I should talk to Bailey. I *have* to talk to Bailey. At the very least to tell her I'm bi. We'd been texting a lot since I asked her for advice on making up with Shea. It'd be a good place to start. Even if just the thought of it made my stomach twist.

"Are you at least rinsed?" I asked, leaning around to check Shea's hair. The coconut smell was strong, but there were no bubbles in sight. With Shea still holding onto me, I waddled over to the shower and leaned in to turn it off. As the shower head drenched us both, Shea giggled, twisting in my arms to keep the water out of her face. Her movement made me lose balance and trip into the shower, barely managing to twist so my back hit the wall instead of my head.

"Hey, I got you in the shower after all." Shea chuckled, then leaned over to turn the nob, one arm still wrapped around me.

"Har, har." Carefully, I pulled us both out of the shower and grabbed a towel to dry off Shea. As I ruffled Shea's hair with the towel, her mouth dropped open and her hold on me slacked. I stepped out of her arms to run the towel down her body and legs before standing up to wrap it around her. When I was finished, I looked up to a pair of dazey and beautiful hazel eyes.

"You dried me off," she said. I nodded, because what else could I do? Of course, dried her off. She was drunk and tumbling and giggly. And honestly, if I had to look at her tits any longer without touching them, I might break.

"I don't think anyone's ever dried me off before. Normally folks are trying to do the opposite." Laughing, I looped my arm around Shea's and guided us to her bedroom. Before I could set her down on the bed, Shea leaned in closer, her breath tickling the fine hairs on my neck, and whispered, "Not that you don't get me plenty wet."

The way my body instantly heated up at the thought of Shea being wet for me under that towel should be embarrassing. But I could also feel drool pooling under my tongue at the thought of tasting that wetness, so all the embarrassment canceled itself out. That's how it worked, right?

I moved Shea to the side of her bed and let her go. Pointing to the mattress, I said, "Sit."

"Yes, ma'am." Shea sat, giving me a dopey smile that made butterflies riot in my stomach.

Not responding to her come on, I turned to her dresser and started rummaging around for comfortable clothes.

"No, Margo," Shea groaned before I heard a thud of her collapsing back onto her bed. "The toys are in the bedside table. *Obviously.*"

I tossed a pair of underwear at her face, then a shirt and joggers.

"I'm not looking at your toys right now, Shea."

A damp towel hit my back.

I turned around to glare at Shea. She'd gotten her underwear on but was standing shirtless, staring at me with a raised brow and a challenge in her eyes.

Rising to her challenge, I walked over to Shea. Then stepped closer and closer until she collapsed back onto the bed. Hands braced on either side of her, I leaned in to whisper into her ear.

"Do you really wanna show me your toys that bad?"

"*Fuck yes,*" she hissed, head dropping back to expose the long curve of her neck and the hickey I'd given her. It certainly was an ego trip to see my mark on her, to have her whining to fuck me.

"Then maybe you should have thought about that before drinking alone," I teased before grabbing the shirt I'd picked out and sliding it over her head. When her head poked out, she was pouting. I kissed her pursed lips while maneuvering her arms into the shirt.

"You're mean," she grumbled, shaking out of my arms to grab her pants. As she pulled those on she gave me a stink eye, except as her gaze lowered to my wet clothes, her eyes heated right back up. "You'll at least change into something of mine, right?"

It was probably a little presumptuous that I'd packed for a sleepover even though Shea hadn't specified that's what we were doing. But even though I had my own clothes available, I turned to strip out of what I was wearing and grabbed something from Shea's dresser. When I turned around, fully clothed, Shea groaned.

"God, that's fucking hot. What about morning sex? Or like middle of the night when I get sober sex?"

The idea of Shea getting up before me was laughable. It was probably the first thing I *really* learned about her when we started texting. She stayed up *very* late and woke up five minutes before she had to be anywhere. And while she didn't seem terribly drunk right now, I doubted she'd get up by her normal time.

"Hmm, if you can wake up without a hangover an hour before I head to work, then maybe." I tapped her nose and she fell backwards onto the bed, whining.

"You're so mean, Margo," she grumbled, shuffling around the bed until she was tucked in on the side against the wall.

"Mhmm, we'll see if you're still calling me mean when I come back with dinner."

39

MARGO

T hree minor arguments later, the biggest of which was what to put on while we ate, Shea and I were tucked into her bed eating grilled cheeses.

"His dad hates him," Shea said, her voice tiny as she waved an arm at the screen showing Buddy's dad tear down paper decorations.

"I don't think he hates him. He just doesn't understand him yet."

"Some times that means the same thing," Shea grumbled, sinking further into the bed so she was staring at the ceiling instead of the TV.

"But he does love him, he helps him save Christmas and everything."

"What?" Shea gave me a look like I was speaking nonsense.

"What do you mean what? How long has it been since you've seen Elf?"

"I've never seen it before."

"Seriously? But it's like a classic now?"

"Back when I had a family for Christmas, we didn't really *do* new movies. My parents liked those claymation ones."

"Oh." The sound fell out of my mouth and everything else sank into place. I always thought she was over her parents' abandonment, that maybe it affected her from time to time, but on the whole, she didn't think about it. I hadn't considered that the holidays would be a constant reminder of what she lost when she came out.

I thought about all the holiday things we'd done, the shifts in her attitude, the Pinterest board of homey Christmas trees. Shea wanted to reclaim the holidays but wasn't fully ready to confront the emotions surrounding them.

Just like me with coming out.

"I'm still a little hungry. I'm gonna see what else I can scrounge up in the kitchen." I pressed a kiss to Shea's forehead and crawled out of the bed.

"Do you want me to pause this?" Shea asked, gesturing to the TV before her hands started fumbling with the sheets to look for the remote. I grabbed our empty plates just in time to keep them from flying off the bed.

"That's all right, you keep watching." After pressing another kiss to her forehead, I left for the kitchen. There I put the dishes in the dishwasher before pulling out my phone. I got as far as pulling up Bailey's contact page before setting it down and wiping the kitchen counter clean. Then I swept the floor and found some more scattered dishes to put away.

Then I told myself I couldn't be a little bitch anymore and picked up my phone. And since I'd gotten my med reminder, I set my phone down again to take those.

Then I picked my phone back up and called Bailey.

"Hey, Margo! How's it going?" My sister's chipper voice came through the phone and I instantly panicked.

"Hi! I ... um I wanted to ..." I stumbled over the words, my voice pitching up.

"Everything okay?"

"Oh, yeah. I'm just ... at Shea's place. We're watching Elf. I made her grilled cheese and uh —" Before I had a chance to say anything else basic and stupid and clearly a cover for something, Bailey interrupted.

"You got her to watch a Christmas movie?"

"Shit." I said the word like it had 20 Is in the middle. "Is it that rare that she watches them?"

"Well ..." Bailey dragged at the word.

"Fuck," I sighed. "We kinda argued over what to watch, but she let me win with the 'it's Christmas' argument. I didn't think it'd be a big deal. I thought she'd like having a Christmas moment with ... a friend."

"Oh, I think you're right. Shea totally wants more Christmas moments. She's just got ... a speed bump on the way to enjoying it. I think sometimes she looks at the speed bump and thinks it's too big to get over. I appreciate you giving her some of that holiday spirit. I always try to get her to do some holiday things with me or join us for family stuff and she refuses. Guess having a new friend suggest it helps."

Friend is not the word I would use to describe my relationship with Shea. Friendly, sure. But we weren't friends. Friends didn't know how each other's cunts tasted at the very least.

"Actually, I wanted to —"

"Oh, I've cleared my schedule so I can go to the tree lighting! I'm getting so much FOMO seeing y'all plan the surprise decor. I even made a few ornaments of my own to add!"

"Procrastinating your own art project?" I asked and Bailey laughed without answering. So that was a yes.

"I wanna keep it a surprise from Shea, so mum's the word, all right?"

"Sure. I won't say a thing."

"And I'll probably crash at her place since I'll need to leave first thing in the morning and I wanna fit in as much hangout time as possible. Can you make sure the couch is relatively clean before you go tonight?"

"Ah, yeah. I can do that." Before I leave the morning of the tree lighting. Because Shea definitely isn't drunk enough to not remember wanting to show me her toy collection, so we were probably going to spend a significant amount of time this week in her bed.

"Thank you! Have fun watching the movie!" And then Bailey was gone.

Sighing, I headed back to Shea's room. I guess for a first attempt at telling Bailey I'm bi, I didn't do ... horribly. I mean, I didn't tell her, but I did establish I hang out with Shea. That was something.

"Shea, I didn't find anything to ..." I started as I turned into Shea's room, only to stop when I realized she was asleep. Her hair was an absolute mess, short curls splayed out on the pillow or sticking up in the air. It was a cute look, a vulnerable look.

As quietly as I could manage, I turned off the lights and TV and slipped into bed beside her. As soon as I got settled in, Shea wrapped an arm around my waist and snuggled into me.

40

SHEA

In under a second of my phone alarm blaring, I slammed it off. I held the offending device up to my face, squinting at the time. 5:00. Why the hell did I set my alarm for 5:00?

Beside me, Margo shuffled around in her sleep. She turned onto her side, an arm flopping over my stomach before she cuddled closer.

That's right. I got bored waiting for Margo yesterday and tired of my own thoughts, so I drank just a smidge too much. I tried to jump in the shower to sober up when Margo said she was heading over, but that didn't work out. Didn't keep me from shooting my shot though. And while it was totally fair that she didn't want to fuck me tipsy, the rejection still hurt. Hurt until she pressed my hand to her thundering heart and assured me she wanted me too.

In that moment, I realized I could actually fall in love with Margo.

And what did tipsy me do with that realization? Confirmed Margo would be down for morning sex and set an alarm.

Sober and blessedly without any hangover symptoms, thanks to Margo, I turned to the woman in question and debated if I wanted to fuck her right now. I mean, the answer was obviously yes. But it felt wrong to fuck her just because I realized how hard this relationship would be to let go of. There was a part of me that wanted to call it quits right now. Tell her that keeping our relationship a secret was already too much for me and we should just stay friends. The other part of me wanted to hold on to Margo so tight, I'd risk suffocating her. I wanted to hold her and slowly coax her into coming out. I wanted to wait for her as long as it took. I wanted to suggest she get a job in Snowfall and bribe her with endless orgasms.

And it couldn't hurt to start presenting those bribes now, right?

Careful not to wake Margo, I slid out of the sheets and crawled off the bed from the end. After grabbing everything I needed from the bedside table, I scurried into the bathroom to get ready. Lights on, I saw the abysmal state my hair was in. Half of it was straight from being pressed between the pillow and my face all night and the other half was a fuzzy mess. I did my best to smooth it all down with water, before *actually* getting ready.

Kicking my pants off, I slid my harness on and tightened the straps. The toy I wanted to use was technically strapless, but I liked the aesthetic of the thin black straps. And given the way

Margo stared at my Hinge picture, I thought she would appreciate it too.

Then I rewashed my toy, my heart thundering in my ears with each pass of the dildo. The process of preparing for sex always got me hot, the anticipation making my blood simmer. But the tenderness I was beginning to feel for Margo made things different, *more*. Not only was everything buzzing with a high intensity, but my body itched to touch her. It was like withdrawal, my hands shook knowing I was about to get a hit of Margo.

Toy clean, I put the shorter end inside me, the cold silicon pressing against my G-spot in a way that made me tense in anticipation for it to buzz to life. I grabbed the bottle of lube and shook it, warming the liquid before drizzling a small amount over the dildo and stroking it.

The phantom appendage thing was no joke. I was so fucking hot rubbing the plastic cock, knowing I was about to slide it into Margo. *Fuck,* just *fuck.*

I went back to my room, keeping quiet as I opened the door. As light from the hallway filtered in, Margo's eyes fluttered open. She smiled up at me reaching out a hand and making a grabby motion. Then her eyes went down to my cock and her eyes widened.

"You got up before me?" she whispered. I started over to her, one hand on my cock and the other holding up the remote and lube.

"You're the only person I'll set an alarm for, babe. You're the only one who's worth it." She's worth so fucking much and the only reason I wasn't running scared of those feelings was because I was out of my mind horny for this girl.

Margo hummed and once I'd gotten to the bed, leaned forward, mouth open and heading towards my dick.

"Oops, nope," I murmured, pulling my hips away so she couldn't suck the plastic. Margo looked at me, lips turned down, brow furrowed.

"But you said," she started but I knelt down by the bed and took her hand before she could keep going.

"I already put some lube on it. And not the tasty kind."

Margo's face started to redden, the color spreading across her cheeks and to her ears. And when I tossed the sheets aside and manhandled her legs to the side of the bed, the blush reached down her neck. I grabbed at the waistband of my sweats and Margo instantly lifted her ass to help me get them and her underwear off. Strike that. She'd been wearing my underwear too.

I was damn near panting for this woman.

Tossing her knees over my shoulders, I leaned into Margo's cunt and immediately ran my tongue over her lips and the swollen head of her clit that peeked out between them. Margo was swollen and wet and ready.

"Were you thinking about this?" I teased.

"You kept coming on to me last night. It was hard not to —"
I cut her off, swirling my tongue in rough circles over her clit. Margo's back arched off the bed, pressing her pussy into me. I dropped the things that I'd been holding on to on the bed and grabbed her ass, pulling my meal closer.

Not that it mattered much to me, but in the few hours Margo had been away yesterday, she'd shaven. I could imagine her sneaking into her house so no one could see the hickies I'd left and heading straight for the shower because she wanted to be ready for more, ready for me.

And *fuck* was she ready for me. After just a few passes of my tongue, Margo was already shaking. Her fingers dug into my hair, each tug urging me on. I pressed the flat of my tongue against her clit, testing out different rhythms and patterns until I found the one that had her crying out my name. Then I slid two fingers into her cunt and was instantly rewarded with the taste of her release.

"Fucking hell, you taste good," I murmured. As much as I wanted to get another taste, I was too impatient to fuck her for that. I slid my fingers out of her, tonging her pussy while I wiped her juices over my cock.

Once I was satisfied, I stood. Margo's eyes instantly went wide as she took me in up close. Her eyes lingered at the dip of my hip, where black straps crossed down to my crotch. I expected her to reach for my cock, to stroke it, guide me into her. But instead, her hands went up, reaching for my shoulders. Knees hitting the bed, I leaned towards her so she could grab me. She pulled me closer until our lips crashed together.

I'd been with other folks for their first time with a woman. Most of them were hesitant about kissing after going down on each other. But not Margo. No, she kissed me with a thorough hunger, like she was memorizing what we tasted like together, like she got off on tasting herself on me.

Unable to wait any longer, I pulled Margo's ass to the edge of the bed and guided her legs around me without breaking the kiss. But when the tip of the dildo pressed against her, we paused, foreheads pressed together as we both watched it slide into her.

"Fuck," we hissed in unison.

I pressed a quick kiss to Margo's lips before shuffling us further up the bed and moving her legs to my shoulders. As the toy sunk deeper into Margo and pressed against her G-sport, she pulsed, making the toy shift inside me. It was so fucking hot.

Another kiss and I started to rock into her. I kept my movements slow, just the friction of the toy and Margo's nails digging into my shoulders enough to get me close.

"Shea," Margo whined my name, her voice beautifully distressed.

"What, babe? You wanna come on my cock?" I asked, though I was barely holding on myself. My limbs were shaking, so close to an orgasm if I had just a little more stimulation.

One of Margo's hands let go of my shoulder and slid under my shirt. She cupped my right breast with a firm grip, her thumb grazing over my hardened nipple.

"You first," she murmured before pinching my nipple and pulling.

"Margo," I cried as my orgasm ripped through me. Luck was the only thing holding me up as the heat shook through my body. And Margo only made things worse, tightening her legs so she could grind into me, rocking the toy against my G-spot.

When my breath finally started to come in sweeps instead of pants, I opened my eyes to a smiling Margo, so pleased with herself to have made me come. I couldn't help but smile too.

Grabbing the remote off the bed, I pressed it into her hand that hung around my neck. She pulled it away, looking at it with squinted eyes over my shoulder. I reached around to point at one button, then the other.

"Top one is the power button, bottom one is the vibrations."

Margo's eyes widened again then she licked her lips.

With no warning or preamble, Margo brought the toy to life and hit the vibrations up to a three out of five.

My arms gave out, knees shaking, and I collapsed onto Margo. She giggled underneath me, her heels digging into my ass to keep grinding.

"You're mean," I hissed, resituating myself onto my forearms and started thrusting into her in earnest. Margo's giggles immediately shifted into moans and she turned her head to press kisses to my arm.

With each thrust, the tight heat in between my legs tensed and the only relief I could find, the only relief I wanted, was in Margo. In the smell of her hair. The taste of the sweat building on her neck. The shudder in her voice as she said my name. The dig of her nails on my back. It gave me so much more than sex with anybody else has.

"Come for me, Margo." I captured her lips, kissing her with every ounce of feeling that was building and twisting inside me. In turn, Margo turned the toy up one more notch.

We were all heavy pants as we came together, our hands somehow finding each other and tangling together. It was heat and soft and deliciously tingly.

Margo turned off the toy and tossed the remote to the side, showering my face with kisses. She loosened her legs just enough so that she could roll us over and straddle me. The kisses continued along with slow rolls of her hips. Her hands explored my body, slowing everything down like this was some sort of fever dream. I couldn't tell where my body ended and hers began. All I knew was that I was being adored, cherished.

This wasn't sex, it was intimacy.

And then, like it was all a dream, Margo's phone went off and it was time to enter the real world.

41

MARGO

Keeping a secret from Shea in this town was exhausting. By Thursday afternoon, I had to redirect 15 folks away from the realtor's office because they thought giving their ornaments directly to me was a better thing to do than following the instructions they were given.

Thankfully, Shea was too busy finding new ways to discretely touch me and sneak kisses to notice. And each time she did, a flock of butterflies went off in my stomach. Butterflies and ... bats? Whatever the nervous version of stomach flutters were.

Though bats are kinda cute, so not them. Maybe pigeons?

"Margo," Shea said as she walked up behind me. She squatted down next to my desk chair and looped her arm through my armrest. From afar, it probably looked like she took hold of the chair for balance. What she really was doing was untucking my sweater and rubbing her finger along my waist.

"Mhmm?" It was so hard to keep my voice even when she was touching me like that. Meanwhile, Shea was just casually pulling something up on her phone, completely unbothered by touching me.

"I haven't heard back from Becky these last few days. Do you know what's up?" Shea, still looking down at her phone, pinched the fat at my side and I squeaked, jumping in my seat and ramming my elbow on the other armrest. Shea started laughing and I smacked her shoulder.

"You all right over there?" Phillip called from the back half of the office. He was the only other person in and I was really wishing he'd just call it a day already. It's not like there was much to do this close to the holidays.

"We're good!" Shea shouted back, a devilish smile lifting her lips and flipping my heart. "Margo just thought she saw a spider. It was just her hair."

"I don't shed *that* much," I grumbled. After having taken a whooping two showers at Shea's place, her drain clogged. Shea claimed it was because of me, but I'd argue that I was just the final straw and not the whole hay bale.

"So, Becky?" Shea said, still giggling. Though she did grip my chair and spin me around so she could kiss my hurt elbow.

"Oh, yeah. I sent her your Pinterest board and some design notes. She'll be working on it tonight. During lunch, I'll step out and finish the catalog of the decorations for her."

"Oh. Cool. Thanks for handling all that. I'll come to help you catalog. I'm ready to go whenever —"

"No!"

Shea pulled back, brow furrowing at my outburst. God, why was lying to her so hard? Not a single suitable reason for her to not tag along came to mind.

"I mean it's just … the cataloging is boring. I'm sure you'd rather go hang out with Denny or one of your girls."

"I'm pretty sure we could find a way to make it interesting," Shea said, pushing up so she could whisper in my ear, her voice dropping.

"In a church?" I gasped and Shea just shrugged.

"I'm not religious. Except …" Shea paused, head tilting to look at the open office before she turned back to kiss my neck. "Except for when I'm worshiping you."

I was suddenly a firm believer in human combustion.

"Sure." I squeaked. Shea smiled, standing up and pressing a kiss to my head before returning to her desk. Once Shea was out of sight, I buried my head in my hands and internally screamed.

> **Me:** Can someone call Shea over for lunch? I said I was going over to the town hall to catalog decorations and she wants to come

> **Rosie:** oh dear, I can always invite her to the diner, but she might get bored if no one else is here with her

Roxie: Damn, I'm meeting a client in ten, so I'm out

Olivia: Oh, I've got it!

Olivia: I'll make Dennis call her for help at the shop

Me: That's perfect! Thank you!

42

SHEA

“Thanks for covering for me. Any issues while I was out?” Dennis asked as he stepped back into Steel Wheelz. He'd texted me that he needed someone to watch over the shop right before lunch, aka when I was about to fuck Margo in the baptismal pool or wherever she'd let me have her.

But outside the girls, Dennis was one of my closest friends, so I couldn't let him down when he asked me for help. Plus, his nana was the kind of elderly woman who didn't believe in limitations and was always getting herself stuck or in some other sort of trouble. It'd be a cold day in hell when I didn't help somebody take care of their family.

“No issues here. But everything all right with Ms. Summers?”

"Ah, yeah. She just ... she couldn't find her meds because she hadn't picked them up recently. So I had to go grab them, but since she'd waited too long to get them, it was a whole to do to get the prescription refilled." Dennis waved a hand around before rounding the counter and taking up his stool. I stayed propped against the wall next to him, chewing on my lip.

"What's up?" Dennis asked.

"I dunno. I think something's up with Margo." I didn't look at Dennis, just stared at the open shop and all its bike parts. Everything with Margo was warm and tender, except for a few moments when she got jittery and nervous. And if it happened when we almost got caught, I'd understand. But this happened at completely random times, like when I was just standing near her when somebody came into the office. I wasn't even near her desk and she got all jumpy.

"What makes you say that?" Dennis asked, turning around to face me.

"She's just been acting weird about the most random shit. Like we need to catalog the decorations that're stored in the town hall for the decorator and Margo was just gonna do it all on her own. I appreciate her helping me, but like, this is my thing. She doesn't need to take it over."

"She's just trying to take some pressure off your shoulders." Dennis shrugged.

"Sure, but lots of folks have been stopping by the office and she freaks out, like maybe she thinks us being in the same room will tip people off."

"Or she knows that any time you two are in a room to- gether, she's gonna be looking at you and thinking about whatever you got up to all this week. It's been weird not having you in the shop constantly, you know? You that smitten already?" Denny gave me a playful nudge and I stiffened.

Maybe that's what it was. I was digging into this relationship too deep and too quick. And Margo wasn't on the same level yet. Fuck, she might think it's gross that I'm so clingy. That's why she's been acting weird, she doesn't know how to tell me this is all too much too soon. Of course it's too much, she's been at my place all fucking week. She's had to lie to her parents every day because I didn't want to spend any time alone.

And that was all on top of the pressure she's probably feeling to come out since she's with me.

Fuck.

"I wouldn't worry too much about it," Dennis said. "I mean, it's probably just an adjustment period. Everybody has one."

"Me? Worried?" I scoffed, trying to laugh around the pain twisting its way through my heart. "You know me, I don't worry about shit."

"You say that, but you did come rushing over here when I said I needed help."

I knocked my foot into Dennis' and rounded the corner.

"I've gotta get back to work."

"Uh-huh. You mean you gotta get back to your girl?" Dennis teased and I threw up my middle finger as I walked out of the shop.

43

SHEA

Margo didn't come back to work after lunch. She didn't come over to my place after doing whatever it was she didn't want me to see. And now, on the day of the tree lighting, she was missing work to help Becky with the last of the decorating.

When I walked by the gazebo this morning, they'd gone so far as to put up a huge curtain around the tree. I tried to get a peak, but Phillip happened to walk by and dragged me into small talk all the way to the office.

I tried to give Margo space. Tried to force myself to not ask follow-up questions when she said she wasn't coming into work. Around an hour in, I lost that willpower.

> **Me:** What're you doing behind that tarp?

> **Margo:** Getting the last few decorations on the tree

Such a simple reply. Nothing suspicious about it at all. So why did it make my guts twist?

> **Me:** Do you need any help?

> **Margo:** Nope, we're good! I don't want to interrupt your work day

> **Me:** I've literally just been pretending to work for the past few weeks. I can take the rest of the day off

> **Margo:** No, no, it's fine. Plus you've still got a bunch of things to do for Eve-Eve Fest right?

> **Me:** Sure, but you've been working on that tree all day. Surely an extra pair of hands will help get it done quicker, right?

I didn't want to push, but it was also pretty fucking hard to think of a reason Margo was being so obstinate about me helping with a thing *I* signed up for that wasn't because of me.

I started typing and deleting, typing and deleting, several responses but nothing came out right. I didn't want her to think I was pissed, though I was getting pretty damn close. And I didn't want her to think I was being clingy either, though I don't think I slept at all last night since she wasn't there.

You know what? It'd be easier to have this conversation face to face. That way neither of us would have to guess about tone or what the other was thinking. I'll just march over to the gazebo and —

"Woah, Shea, where you going?" Phillip said, getting up as soon as I did and stepping in my way.

"I'm just going out for a bit. What's the matter?"

"Well, you can't leave. We're ... working?" The pitch of his voice made it sound like a question.

"You've been scrolling on your phone for the past hour. We're not working. And since we're not working, I'm leaving." I tried to step around Phillip, but he just sidestepped right back in my way. "Okay, dude, what the fuck?"

"Umm ... you can't leave." He even went so far as to hold his arms out to block my way.

"And you can't piss off your co-workers like this, so I guess we're both fucked." I turned on my heel and headed to the back door.

I was officially pissed. There's no reason why I shouldn't be a part of this stupid tree lighting. I picked out the damn tree, I signed up for this. And fuck, maybe I liked the idea of decorating a goddamn Christmas tree with Margo. Maybe I wanted that little homey moment with her while I had the chance. And fuck, I was so smitten for this girl.

"Shea, you can't just —" Phillip started, following me. Then his footsteps paused and he groaned. "She's trying to surprise you!"

"What?" I turned around to look at Phillip, his hands waving to the side in resignation.

"Margo. She's trying to do some type of surprise at the lighting. I dunno, I wasn't really listening. She just asked me to keep you in the office all day. So, you know, can you just go back to your desk and stay there?"

"What kind of surprise?" I asked, my brain rattling around trying to figure out what Margo could possibly be doing for me.

"I told you, I don't know. I don't really get involved in all that small town crap. But Margo was *really* adamant about you not leaving the office."

"Okay. I'll stay in the office," I grumbled before returning to my desk.

Knowing Margo was trying to surprise me definitely dissipated all my anger but it left me confused and out of sorts. And the only thing I could do about it was wait.

44

MARGO

I f Shea hated this tree design, I would throw up and move to the moon. Or maybe Mars. Or better yet, Pluto.

"Everyone's going to love it," Becky reassured me, putting a hand on my shoulder.

"I hope so," I whispered. I looked up at the Christmas tree so crowded with ornaments, that you could barely see the branches. The town had really come together for this.

It was a homey tree. A community tree. It was something that we all contributed to and it made my heart swell.

But I'm also pretty sure I pissed Shea off by going MIA all day and not letting her help with the tree. I could have royally fucked up our relationship by doing this. Or once she sees the tree, she might realize I'm a smitten mess for her and run for the hills.

The tarp keeping the tree from view parted and I jolted, sticking my arms out like I could hide the tree from view if it was Shea walking in.

But it wasn't Shea, it was Zoey.

"So good news, everybody is gathered, the food is out, and Shea is in the crowd, looking confused but not upset."

"And the bad news?" My gut clenched.

Zoey sighed and rested her head on my shoulder.

"I couldn't get Clive to come."

At first, my brain went into problem-solving mode. How could we find Clive and get him here? Where could we find a collar or something to keep him around? Did Zoey already get a red nose for him?

Then the words sunk in and I shoved Zoey off me.

"Zoey! I was really worried for a second there. I thought something important had gone wrong!"

"Clive is important!" Zoey pouted, crossing her arms and tossing her hair over her shoulder. "He's the town mascot."

"Sure, but like, he's a wild animal."

"For now," Zoey grumbled as she kicked at the ground.

"Zoey, are you planning on domesticating Clive?" From behind me, I heard Becky giggling.

"They're ready for you to go," Zoey said instead of answering my question and ducked back out into the courtyard.

"Well," Becky said, patting my shoulder again, "if they're all set, we should get out there too. No telling how rowdy they'll get if they have to wait any longer."

"By they, do you mean the crowd in general or your grandma and her friends?"

Becky made a hem-haw sound and shrugged.

"Right. Well, no time like the present, I guess."

I took one last breath that did nothing to steady my nerves and stepped out.

My eyes instantly scanned the crowd for Shea. She was over to the right sid, near the front, and surrounded by her girls, including Bailey. My sister was the first to spot me, in a oversized floral sweater and big fluffy earmuffs. She bounced and waved and all her friends made similar greetings. Except for Shea.

I couldn't see her face clearly, but Shea didn't look happy. I mean, she didn't look mad either, but having her see me and not immediately smile was a gut punch.

She definitely hated this. She definitely thought I was a bitch for taking over her project and leaving her in the dark. She was gonna break up with me before we were official because I had the audacity to try and surprise her.

Nope, I can't do this. I need to find somewhere to throw up.

"Nope!" a familiar voice shouted before an arm wrapped around me to stop my retreat. As I was being dragged to the stage, I realized it was Wendy forcing me forward.

"But this was a stupid idea," I whined quietly.

"No it wasn't."

"But Shea looks upset."

"No, she looks confused. Those are two different things."

"But —"

"Nope!" Wendy said again, giving me a little push towards the stage stairs. "You've handled weird New Yorkers doing wild shit in the library. You can handle surprising your girlfriend."

"We're not really —" I started to murmur back but was pushed even further, sending me stumbling up the steps. The crowd of townsfolk quieted and I shot a quick glare towards Wendy before heading up to the microphone.

"Hello, everyone."

"Hi, Margo!" was the immediate response from the crowd, particularly Bailey and that crew. Shea just cocked her head.

"Thanks." I paused, taking a deep breath and praying my face wasn't too red or that it was super obvious I was looking at Shea more than anyone else. "I hope y'all don't mind if I take a minute or two to say a few things before Becky pulls the curtain." The crowd made a few grumbles, but I pushed forward. "For some people, the holidays are about family. But for others, the holidays are about home. About finding your way back home. About finding the place, the people that feel like home. I'm lucky to say that my home is here, in this town. A town where community is so integral that there's always someone to step in and help, from excessive casseroles when you're not feeling well to stepping up to run several holiday events without notes to go off of."

I took a second to clear my throat and let my eyes unfocus so I didn't see Shea's reaction.

"So when Shea and I started discussing design ideas for this year's tree, she showed me a lot of homey designs. You know the types, mismatched ornaments, hand prints on clay, popsicle reindeer. The kind of designs that screamed home and family. And, well, Snowfall is Shea's family. So I called you all in to help. Between classroom crafts and your kind donations, we have filled this tree with over 300 ornaments. Becky has placed each one with all the love and care you would decorating your tree at home.

"But there is one thing missing from our tree that'd we'd like your help with." I paused to let the rumbles of confusion have their moment. "While we have graciously been provided with drinks and sweets from Tost-Ka and the Pub and pizza from Pete's, we also have popcorn to make a garland. So after you've had a chance to walk around the tree, please take some time to help string up the popcorn and enjoy the food and company."

I gestured to Becky and she undid the ties that held the middle of the tarp tent together, then started rolling one corner away. I scrambled down from the stage to get to the other side and do the same.

As the tarp parted and the crowd got its first look at the tree, I was a bundle of irritated nerves. I was so wrapped up in Shea's reaction, that I forgot to worry about the townsfolk's reaction. Because if they went through all the work of donating their things and time and hated it, I was at risk of ostracization.

But as soon as the view was clear, the ohs and ahs were immediate. People rushed around the stage and started pointing out ornaments that they recognized or donated. There were giggles and cheers and a warmth that could only be described as community.

And then there was the warmth of arms wrapping around me from behind, their face burying into my hair and the scent of coconut cookies washing over me. Shea.

Her hug tightened and she pressed the shortest of kisses to the back of my head.

"We need to get out of here," Shea murmured into my hair, her voice shaky.

"Wait, why?" I turned around in Shea's arms to see those eyes I dreamed of throughout all my life filled with tears. It was striking. I'd never seen Shea cry before.

"Because that was the nicest thing anyone has ever done for me and I really need to kiss you. And it's honestly really hard not to do that right now, but I respect you. So we've gotta go somewhere else."

"What about Bailey?" I was giggling now, caught in the euphoria of a successful event and making Shea so happy she cried.

"I love Bailey, she's my best friend. But she's never brought the whole town together to bring me something missing from my life." Shea squeezed me again and rested her forehead on mine. If anyone was paying us any mind, they might think there was something going on between us.

I didn't really care if they did.

Though that didn't mean I wanted to make out in front of the whole town.

Squeezing Shea back, I slipped out of her hold and took her hand. I led the way to the closest building. The downtown library.

"Are we making out in the library or are you going to show me all the cool shit libraries have?" Shea teased as we reached the entrance, whispering in my ear as she squeezed my hand.

"Are you making fun of me for being a nerdy librarian?" I opened the door and in a blur of movement, Shea had me up against the wall of the vestibule.

"No, it's hot. You're hot. Hot and so fucking —" Shea cut herself off by crashing her lips to mine. Like she was in physical pain not kissing me and couldn't take it any longer.

And the kiss. The kiss was searing. It was full and wet and consuming. Shea's hands cupped my face, tears falling from her cheeks to mine. I wrapped my arms around her back and pulled her closer, needing to feel her thundering heart, her warmth.

The door to our left clicked open and we jolted upright, still holding on to each other but frozen in place. Like maybe whoever was leaving the library was a T-Rex and the theory that they could only see you if you moved was true.

"Ah, that tracks," Ms. Delaney murmured, walking past us to open the main door. "Have a good evening, Ms. White, Ms. Hartley."

We stayed still as the door shut behind Ms. Delaney and then Shea turned to me, eyes wide, face paling. She was clearly panicking and I should assuage her but…

"She said, 'That tracks'," I said through giggles. Shea let out a long sigh and rested her forehead on mine.

"You're not scared she's gonna tell somebody?"

"'That tracks'," I repeated, crying because I was laughing so hard.

"Margo, I can't tell if you find this situation really funny or if this is some kind of panic response." Shea took my elbows and stepped back a little so she could get a good look at me.

"It's really funny," I said, trying my best not to laugh. Shea smiled and pulled me back into a hug.

"Good. We should probably get back to the event then. I'm satisfied for now, but you better be in my bed tonight." Shea dipped down for a light kiss before nipping my lower lip.

"Oh, no."

"No?" Shea pulled back, brows furrowed.

"Bailey's here."

"Okay, and?"

"And she's planning on spending the night at your place so y'all have time to hang before she leaves in the morning."

"God damn it, Bailey." Shea threw her head back and groaned. It might have been a little demented, but Shea wanting to spend time with me over Bailey made me feel special.

"What if ..." Shea started, moving towards the door with her hand in mine. "You sneak in once Bailey falls asleep?"

As we pushed open the door to the library, Shea squeezed my hand and let go.

I knew she did that for my sake. I knew she was being considerate of me. I knew it had nothing to do with how much she liked or wanted me.

It still stung though.

"There you guys are!" Wendy shouted as she jogged up to us. As soon as she was within a few feet, she stopped, hands on her knees, huffing

"What's up?" I rested a hand on her shoulder, rubbing little circles until she caught her breath.

"Fuck, people who say running is fun should be studied," she murmured before standing up. "But anyways your saboteur is back at it."

45

SHEA

This time, my saboteur not only caused a little bit of trouble, they also gave at least a couple dozen folks food poisoning.

By the time Margo and I had returned to the courtyard, the tables were mostly abandoned. Half the folks ran to the library restrooms and the other half ran home. There were abandoned plates, knocked over bowls of popcorn, and a few spots where somebody didn't make it to a trashcan in time.

The only blessing about the whole mess was that Mason volunteered to clean the ... grosser parts up. Apparently one of the benefits of being raised in a family with a bar is that he wasn't squeamish around barf. Which will serve him well, because Ashley spent the whole time we were cleaning in the bathroom, Rosie keeping her company and reporting back to Mason every few minutes.

And by the time everything was cleaned up, Bailey was following me around like she was a bodyguard. She was convinced that the saboteur would strike again the moment I was alone. So she wasn't going to leave me alone for even a second.

Which meant I couldn't talk Margo into sneaking into my place.

"Woah! Your place is crazy clean," Bailey said once we finally got back to my apartment.

"Yeah, Margo helped me out. I'm guessing you asked her to do that?" I nudged into Bailey and stepped further in. While I went to the kitchen, Bailey made herself at home on my couch.

"Yeah, she texted me to get everybody's numbers to pull off the decorating surprise. I was getting FOMO watching them plan, so when she called earlier this week while she was over, I asked her to clear the coach."

"She called you when she was over here?" Habitually, I reached for a bottle of whiskey. But my fingers froze around the handle. I didn't really need a drink to distract myself or keep me occupied tonight.

"Yeah, while you were watching Christmas movies."

That actually didn't narrow it down. Over the past couple of days, when Margo was over, there was always a Christmas movie playing in the background. No matter what we were doing.

It was kind of like immersion therapy. And it was working. I was actually starting to enjoy the holiday season. I was even considering getting a tree for my apartment. Especially after seeing the tree Margo designed. We could decorate it together. Make our own popcorn garland.

Instead of pouring myself a drink, I grabbed a couple of water bottles and chips and returned to the living room. Dumping everything on the coffee table, I sat down and pulled out my phone to order a tree.

"Do you think Margo's been acting strange?"

I started choking on nothing, the first thing coming to mind when Bailey brought up Margo was when she got down on her knees for me the other day. Which would probably sound *very* strange to Bailey.

"What do you mean?" I asked, trying to play things off like I needed to clear my throat.

"Well, Margo and I have never been super close, just because of different hobbies and stuff. But she's called me like every day this week. I think she wants to talk about something, but you know, I get with awkward silences."

"Mhmm." There were two wolves in me, one who desperately wanted to ask Bailey more about Margo and another who wanted to keep Margo safe from being outed.

Though she didn't care about Ms. Delaney finding out. And that gave me a lot more hope than it should. Especially paired with her talking with Bailey more.

"What do you think she wants to talk about?" I asked.

"I dunno," Bailey grumbled, sinking into the couch until her back was fully pressed against the seat. "And it feels kinda sucky that I don't know my sister well enough to know what she wants. And it's super sucky she's nervous to talk to me."

"I'm sure that's not a reflection on you. Sometimes things are nerve-wracking no matter who you're talking to."

"I know." Bailey reached over and squeezed my leg.

God, I couldn't wait for when I could talk to Bailey about Margo. To gush to her about her sister, about how much it meant that Margo got the town together to build the tree of my dreams.

And how that gesture made me think I'd be able to talk with Bailey about Margo sooner rather than later.

I returned Bailey's gesture with a squeeze of her knee. "I'm sure she'll be ready to tell you soon."

46

MARGO

Ashley has added you to a group chat with: Olivia, Zoey, Shea,
Bailey, Rosie, ...

Ashley: This fucker has gone too far. And with the Christmas festival coming up, we need a defense plan

Roxie: You know it's not called that

Ashley: God, the Eve-Eve Fest

Ashley: Margo, add Wendy to this chat. I like her

Rosie: How're you feeling this morning, sweetie?

Ashley: Much better, thank you. I'd just gotten over morning sickness, so that fucker is going to pay

Ashley: When and where can everyone meet? Mason wouldn't let me work even if I wanted to, so I'm free all day

Roxie: I'm free to meet whenever

Olivia: I'm good whenever too

Zoey: I need like ... 40 mins?

Ashley: Why is that a question?

Zoey: Well, I brought Stephen along to an auction and had him pick a car for us to work on together

Olivia: Aw

Rosie: Oh that's so sweet

Roxie: Yikes, he's not doing great is he?

Zoey: No, but he's trying, which is cute

Olivia: Aw, you're in love

Bailey: Sorry I wish I could've stuck around long enough to join this war council. I just got back to Charlotte

Ashley: Damn, you must've left early

Bailey: Yeah, but it was totally worth it! I'll be back in town next week. Just have to wrap up my gallery thing on Wednesday and then Greg and I'll be in Snowfall for a solid week

Rosie: We're still doing white elephant the day before Eve-Eve Fest, right Ashley?

Ashley: Yes! And Margo, you and Wendy are invited too. We're not doing weird shit white elephant, but useful, nice things under $25

Ashley: Also, does Margo usually sleep in this late?

Bailey: No, we were texting when I left. But she might be working on admin stuff for the Eve-Eve Fest

Ashley: Do you guys seriously not get tired typing that all out?

Shea: Sorry! Margo and I were busy going over Eve-Eve.

Me: Sorry, I got caught up with Shea going over Eve-Eve Fest plans. We should have things wrapped up by the time Zoey's done with her thing

Shea: Jinx

Me: That's not how jinx works

Wendy has been added to the group chat

Me: Wendy, we're war counseling in 30

Wendy: Fuck yeah! Where?

Rosie: We normally meet up at the diner, but I'm not working this morning, so we don't have to if that's out the way for anyone

Me: Diner works for us

Wendy: Me too

306 | K.E. MONTEITH

Olivia: See y'all soon!

Zoey: Don't hold off if I'm late

47

MARGO

This morning, as soon as Bailey texted me she was hitting the road, I booked it to Shea's place. We spent ... a number of hours in bed snuggling and not snuggling. By the time we realized the war council group text was happening, it was almost noon.

We scrambled around Shea's apartment, helping each other get dressed and cover up marks. It was nice getting ready with Shea. Homey. It was easy to imagine this being our lives. Living together, getting ready together, the touches and teases.

This could be my life if I just got a little bit braver.

"Wait!" Shea shouted as I parked us in front of Dear Diner and reached for my door handle. I twisted to face her and her lips were immediately on mine, for a deep but quick kiss.

"Just wanted one last kiss." She pressed another to my cheek before sliding out of the car. I laughed, following her into the diner and to the back corner booth.

With the exception of Zoey, we were the last ones to arrive and had to pull up extra chairs so all of us to crowd together. The table had been covered with a large sheet of paper, like table cloth size. And at the top, by the wall, was "fuck a homophobe" in crayon. But after the "fuck" was a little carrot and an added "up". For clarity, I assumed.

"What took y'all so long?" Wendy grumbled.

"We had to finish up some emails," I said before raising my eyebrows at her. Wendy rolled her eyes and I noticed Roxie beside her clock my covered-up hickey and shrug. I didn't know Roxie well, but I knew the rumors. She could probably spot a covered hickey miles away. But she also wasn't one to judge or be a bitch about it.

I took a beat with my emotions as Ashley went on about what they'd done so far to see if the panic would set in. I kind of assumed that Ms. Delaney clocking me as bi didn't freak me out because it was so funny. Roxie was different. She was Bailey and Shea's friend. She would have some emotional involvement in me and Shea's relationship.

But the panic didn't come. Maybe it was because it was a stretch to say Roxie clocked the hickey and assumed it was from Shea. Or maybe it was because I was finally getting comfortable with this group of girls, comfortable being back in Snowfall, and I could be myself easier.

"Whoever poisoned the food probably did it during Margo's speech," Ashley said.

"And I went through pictures from the event to rule out some people," Olivia said, holding up her phone with an Instagram picture from Becky. She'd apparently been filming my speech and the crowd's reactions. I'd been so busy *not* looking at Shea that I hadn't noticed how many people connected with my words, holding their hands over their hearts and smiling.

"Are we sure it was food poisoning though? And not just ... a kitchen accident?" Shea said.

"Are you implying my cookies did this?" Ashley asked with restrained anger.

"Or my pizza?" Wendy didn't bother restraining how offended she was.

"Well, no, but —"

"I ate before the speech," Rosie chimed in. "And I didn't get sick or anything. I asked around today and a lot of people tasted something chalky on the pizza but they just thought it was clumps of parmesan."

"Right. So it was a hundred percent intentional," Ashley said, then pointed a crayon to a list of names. "These are our list of suspects based on who isn't visible in the video and has a strong connection to Ms. Taylor."

"Tristan did not make the list, unfortunately," Wendy mumbled.

"Was he even there?" I questioned and she just shrugged.

"I didn't see him in anybody's pictures," Olivia added.

"And he has no motive to ruin these events," Ashley said, her voice sharp like maybe Wendy had already tried to pin the blame on Tristan.

"We didn't eliminate the old lady gang, though they were in some pictures. Given their general attitude, they have a strong motive and resources to get others to do things for them," Olivia said, eyes focused on the list of names.

"Those ladies are bitches but they don't come off as homophobic to me."

"I don't think we should rule them out because of that. There's no evidence that these crimes were hate-motivated."

"I think calling them crimes is a little much," Shea jumped in.

"Well, have they felt homophobic?" Ashley asked and Shea and I shook our heads. Ashley hummed like she didn't quite believe us.

"I don't want to think negatively of Ms. Taylor," Rosie started. "But it might be possible she's had someone from out of town do things for her."

Olivia pointed her crayon at Rosie, nodding, then added 'Ms. Taylor's errand bitch' to the list.

"I'd add that Abraham dude too. He gives me the creeps and I wouldn't be surprised if he did shit just so he has something to write about," Roxie said and Olivia added Abe's name to the list. A few other names were called out so that by the time Zoey joined us, there were at least 30 names listed.

"Shit, is the whole town a suspect?" Zoey asked, squeezing into the booth so she could sit next to Olivia.

"Obviously not. These are just the folks with reasonable motives," Olivia said, nudging her best friend with her elbow.

"Ah, guess that journalism degree is coming in handy again." That got Zoey another nudge, this time to the stomach.

"It is an awfully long list," Rosie murmured.

"Yeah, we'd be hard-pressed to question all these folks by Saturday. Especially since Ms. Taylor's Errand Bitch could be anyone," Roxie said.

"Fine, then our plan will be to focus on defense and catch them in the act," Ashley said. She pulled the paper around until a clear space was in front of her.

"How do you plan to defend an open event, Ash?" Shea asked.

"Well, we'll need someone guarding the food at the very least. Mason can do that. Are any of the folks on this list vendors?" Ashley gestured to the names, then started jotting down stations that would need to be guarded.

"Umm … Abe requested to take photos at the event. Chelsea is taking up Ms. Taylor's knock the pins over type booth. Ms. Douglas has a booth selling ornaments and Ms. Stevenson is doing fortune telling," I listed.

"God, why'd we let Ms. Stevenson do the fortune telling?" Shea asked, leaning into me.

"Because she does it every year to get free food from the other booths and if we were the one's to stop her, there'd be hell to pay."

"Fair."

"Okay, so we need to keep an eye on them and the food. What else?" Ashley asked. She'd worn the blue crayon she was using down to the paper and had to pause to rip some off.

"Maybe the tree? There are so many gorgeous ornaments on it, I'm a little worried some teenager might try something,"

Rosie said, her eyes fluttering to the counter where one of her brothers was stacking cups precariously.

"Tree," Ashley mumbled as she wrote the word down.

"Are y'all gonna do a kick-off speech?" Roxie asked.

"Do I have to?" Shea whined and all of us nodded. The kick-off speech to Eve-Eve Fest was another tradition. Everyone would gather around the tree and gazebo and Ms. Taylor would blather on about how much the town meant to her and we'd all hold up cups of coffee or hot chocolate and cheers her when she'd droned on for too long.

As the others moved on to discuss where they could all station up during speech time, Shea pinched my sweater and pulled me closer.

"Will you do the speech for me?" she asked, voice low.

"No, I think it's your turn." Why did such a simple act make me giggle? I was going to out myself because I was incapable of hiding my giddiness around her.

"Hmmm, I could take an extra turn at something else to make up for it."

Or I would out myself by turning bright red every time Shea whispered something to me.

"Shut up," I whispered between giggles, trying to subtly reach an arm around her and pinch her other side. Shea retaliated by leaning her whole weight into me until she collapsed into my lap and we both burst into giggles.

"For the ones that are gonna face the brunt of whatever this hooligan has planned, you two sure are fooling around a lot," Ashley said.

"I mean, there's not much we can do," Shea said, pulling herself back up. My lap was cold without her. "We don't know who's fucking shit up and why."

"Well, they obviously want to ruin things for you."

"Oh, do you have any exs around here that might be pissed at you?" Roxie asked, putting her elbows on the table and leaning forward.

"Nah, I don't think so."

"You haven't ghosted anybody on any apps, right? Some folks get pissed about that kind of thing."

"Ah," Shea said and my stomach clenched. "I had asked somebody if they wanted to hook up because I needed a distraction earlier in the month. They took forever to respond and by the time they did, I ... wanted something else. So I never texted them back."

Shea reached over for my knee and gave me a little squeeze. It was like my heart went from 100 miles an hour to 25. I was wanted more than that woman I saw text her. I was wanted for something more than a distraction. I was maybe what she needed a distraction from?

"I mean, if she took long to respond, she'd probably not the type to get pissed over ghosting, but still." Roxie shrugged, sitting back into the booth, hand on her chin.

"No, she's not the type. Really, it doesn't feel like any of these incidents are personal. There's not even any proof they're connected," Shea said.

"Three incidents in a row, involving you, is proof enough for me," Olivia said.

"Wait," Rosie crooned. "Who's the new person?"

"What?" Shea blanched, sitting up and scooting away from me.

"You said you didn't text the other person back because you wanted something else. It's a new partner, right?"

"Oh, well ... it's ..." Shea stumbled over her words, looking around at everyone *but* me as she tried to figure out what to say.

"Aw, yay! I'm so happy for you!" Rosie cheered, clapping. "Are you two close enough to spend Christmas with her family? Do you wanna bring her to the white elephant party?"

"That's fine with me," Ashley said, not taking her focus off the list and shrugging.

"Rose, you're just assuming —"

"No, I saw that hickey on you earlier this week. You can't hide anything from me." Rosie tsked, wagging a finger at Shea. It'd be funny if I wasn't frozen in panic. I think Roxie was snickering, so at least somebody was having fun with this.

A foot met my shin and I broke out of my daze to look at Wendy. Her eyes were shifting from Rosie to me, a clear question of what I wanted to do in this situation.

But the thing was, I didn't know what I wanted to do. Or at least it wasn't my biggest concern.

My biggest concern was how Shea would react. Shea respected me coming out on my own terms more than anything else. I didn't think for a second she'd give me away. But no matter how she diverted them, it was going to hurt to hear.

We should have talked about this instead of making out all morning.

"Okay, fine. There is somebody. But I …" Shea paused, looking up at the ceiling. "I don't wanna go too fast and spoil things, you know? I like her a lot but I haven't had the best track record, so slow is for the best."

I felt every pulse of my heart like it was a hammer to my chest. I expected her to play off that our relationship wasn't serious. What she just said was the complete opposite of that.

"I thought lesbians were known for moving in immediately. Why don't y'all do that?" Wendy snarked, wagging her eyebrows at me in a not so subtle hint. Shea threw her head back and laughed.

"Oh sweetie!" Rosie cried, leaning out of the booth to hug Shea. "I'm so happy for you!"

"Thanks, Rosie," Shea said with a chuckle, patting her friend's arm. Her gaze met mine, eyes softening.

God, I am so in love with this woman it hurts. I loved Shea. The version of Shea that reaches for a drink when she's lonely, the version of Shea that cackles when she laughs really hard, the version of Shea that would leave dozens of cups all over her apartment. I loved her and not the version of her I crushed on all those years ago.

And Wendy was right. I really did need to up my fucking Prozac to get this done.

48

SHEA

After Ashley had come up with what she considered a fool-proof plan to protect Eve-Eve Fest from hypothetical homophobes, I was left with this uneasy feeling.

I don't know if it was because of how adamant Ashley was that there was someone out to get me or how I inadvertently told Margo I was in this for keeps, but when we left the diner, I was feeling rattled. It was like my body was bracing for something, my bones stiff and muscles achey.

Normally when I felt this way, I'd fix myself a drink and it would all ease away. But Margo didn't like it when I drank. And if I was being honest with myself, I didn't like it either. It was sad that the only way I could avoid misery when no one else was around was through a drink.

"You're staying tonight, right?" I asked Margo. She was driving us back to my place, but I didn't know if she was just dropping me off or what.

"Oh." Margo's cheeks brightened and she tapped her fingers along the wheel. "I kinda assumed that I could. But if you need a night to yourself to decompress or whatever, I —"

"No. Please, stay. I don't wanna be alone." Instinctively, I grabbed onto Margo's arm, the sleeve of her sweater wrinkling under my grip. Not looking away from the road, Margo placed a hand over mine and squeezed.

"You won't be alone tonight."

I hated how that already didn't feel like enough. I wanted more than she could give and I could see how that would lead to an end. I could see myself quieting, afraid to ask for more. I could see Margo killing herself with guilt for making me hide things. I could see me begging for her to stay. I could see her coming out for my sake and not hers.

It was only by a few years, but I was the older one, the more mature one. I should stop things here, I should tell her to go home, spend the rest of the holidays with her family, and forget about me.

But when Margo parked outside my apartment, she gave me one look and *knew*. I don't know how much she knew, if all she could tell was that I needed some comfort, but she immediately reached out for me. Her hand cupped my jaw, thumb stroking my cheek, deep brown eyes searching mine. Tenderly, excruciatingly slowly, Margo slid her fingers to the nape of my neck and pulled me forward so our lips met.

Over the past week, Margo and I have had plenty of different types of kisses. Most of them were hungry. A few had been giggly, the type of giggly you got from drinks or a rush of dopamine.

The only way I could describe this kiss was tender. Our lips dragged across each other, our tongues grazed, but the touches were comforting.

I wanted more. I wanted to know how far that comfort could go, how it would blend into sex, if it would burn up into hunger or fuse into something else.

"Inside," I murmured against Margo's lips.

"Just a little longer." Margo twisted in the driver's seat, pushing up on her knees so she was above me, deepening the kiss. Her free hand reached for mine, pulling it to her chest to mimic our moment from my drunken shower night. It was a reassurance that she was there, that she wanted me. It was wild how such a little touch had such a big effect.

"Please," I begged. Margo pressed one last kiss to my lips before pulling away. She got out of the car and rounded the hood to open my door.

"How chivalrous," I teased, but when her hand reached out for mine, I froze. Margo took my hand, not even looking around the parking lot to make sure no one was around, and pulled me out of the car. I followed her in a daze all the way up to my apartment and into the bedroom.

Margo spun me around and with the gentlest of pushes, sat me down on the bed. After pressing a kiss to my forehead, Margo sunk to her knees. I opened my mouth to tell her not to, to tell her I wanted to do something more mutual. But the way Margo looked up at me, the way her eyes didn't stray from mine, kept me quiet. And for once the quiet wasn't unsettling. It was peaceful.

Margo sat on her knees and undid the laces of my boots. There was no rush to her movements. It was slow and careful. And when she pulled each boot off, she pressed a kiss to my knees before setting the shoes aside. Then my socks were pulled off and another kiss, this time to my ankle. And on she went, removing clothing and kissing the most intimate parts of my body until I was fully nude and she was fully clothed.

That contrast was too much for me.

Leaning forward, I pulled at the neck of Margo's sweater until our lips met. The kiss was like sitting in front of a fireplace after being outside in the freezing cold. It tingled all the way down to my bones. It thawed through the walls of jokes and avoidance. And instead of feeling vulnerable, I felt whole. Not because Margo completed me, but because she quieted the anxious buzz that I couldn't mute on my own, she made it so I could fully be me.

Standing, Margo leaned into me until my back hit the bed. Her knees went to either side of my thighs as her hands started to smooth over my skin. Even though it'd only been a few days, she didn't need to explore my body. Margo knew which touch would make me quake, which would make me sigh. And she hit every spot with such slow touches that by the time her hands had worked their way down and up my thighs, I was shaking.

"Margo." I said her name like she was a goddess that could grant me mercy. Maybe she was. She was certainly too good for me at the very least. Too good for me to greedily take the way I wanted to.

I started to lean up, my hands going to her waist to slide under her sweater, but Margo put a hand to my shoulder.

"Let me take care of you," she whispered against my lips. I didn't have it in me to argue. I needed her to take care of me after what I'd said in the diner, I needed to feel some similar type of emotion, devotion. But…

"I can't feel you like this." I tugged at the sweater and in less than a second, she pulled it over her head and tossed it aside. Again, she grabbed my hand and placed it over her heart. A quick but steady rhythm. Another thing she did to soothe me.

Margo let go of my hand, her fingers trailing over my stomach to reach something lower, but I kept my palm over her heart. And I felt it quicken as her fingers reached my pussy.

She took her time tracing my lips, her strokes matching the pace of her heart. Then she gave my clit the same treatment, slow circles that made my brain go fuzzy. My hips lifted, begging for her to finally touch me, to make me come. But it wasn't until I could work up some muddled pleas that Margo gave me what I needed.

I was so worked up, so hot and needy, that by the time Margo started to stroke my G-spot, it only took a few passes for me to tremble in her hold.

"I've got you, Shea. Let go."

My orgasm ripped from me, a violent shaking followed by warm waves of relief. The two sensations crashed together. And when everything calmed, when my breath slowed, and my thoughts could form words, I realized I'd been crying.

"Shit, sorry," I murmured, moving to wipe away the tears. But Margo's hand caught mine. She leaned down, kissing where tears pooled on my cheek then dragged her tongue up. She copied the movement on the other side. Then she pulled away.

I sat up, ready to complain about the absence of her body heat, until I saw her head to the bedside table. Then I was drooling like a fucking dog, ready and willing to do whatever she pulled out.

Except when she turned around, all she had in hand was some tissues.

Margo wiped my eyes and then cleaned us both up. I just laid there in a state of confusion. Like she'd cast some spell on me.

When Margo threw away the tissues and finally shed her pants, the spell wore off.

I sat up, ready to return the favor of a mind-bending orgasm. But when Margo straightened, she smiled at me, a light laugh falling from her lips. She came back to the bed and instead of getting into position, she pushed me back down and laid beside me.

"But —" I shifted onto my side to look at Margo and she put a finger to my lips.

"I'm satisfied."

"But you didn't —"

"I got what I wanted. Did you?"

I opened my mouth to answer with a quick yes. But something about the quiet way Margo asked gave me pause.

When I asked her to stay, I didn't want just sex. I wanted company, I wanted somebody to keep the loneliness away. But I also wanted Margo, I wanted proof that Margo was in this with me, that she didn't think of this as just a fling.

I took Margo's hand and pressed it against my heart. "Yeah, I did."

Margo smiled and gave me a quick kiss. Then she shuffled around until her back was to my chest, ass in my lap.

"I like being the little spoon," she muttered, grabbing my arm and wrapping it over her. Laughing, I pulled her in tighter, kissing her hair, before reaching over her for the remote and pressing it into her hands. She immediately put on another Christmas movie and snuggled closer to me.

It was such a simple thing, snuggling and watching a movie, but simple things with Margo held an appeal I'd never felt before. And I wished more than anything that the comfort she gave me wasn't accompanied by so much anxiety.

49

MARGO

"You're not helping," I whined at Wendy who just returned with a cinnamon bun the size of her head.

"I agreed to take off work and accompany you to the mall. Not help you." Wendy sat down and dug into her roll, not even offering me a bite in this trying time when I had to find my sort of girlfriend the perfect first Christmas gift. And a good white elephant gift for my sister and girlfriend's friends.

"I'm gonna tell Ashley you got some garbage chain cinnamon roll," I grumbled, not expecting the threat to hit. But Wendy snapped straight up, her face slightly pale.

"You wouldn't."

I couldn't hold my laughter in to keep the joke up and Wendy kicked me under the table.

"Seriously. That woman is scary. But like in a I wanna be like her when I grow up way."

"If you wanna be like her though, you might end up with Tristan."

Wendy gagged dramatically and pushed the remainder of her roll towards me. "I've lost my appetite."

I happily ate the rest and got up to toss the box. Wendy followed after me but took a sharp left out of the food court and I had to scramble to catch up with her.

"Where're you going?"

"Well if you're gonna take forever deciding what to get Shea, then I'm going to go ahead and get my white elephant gift."

"Oh. I guess that makes sense. What were you thinking of getting?"

"I'm not telling you," Wendy scoffed.

"Oh come on." I moved to nudge Wendy with my elbow, but she ducked into the closest shop to avoid it. I followed after her and was immediately blinded by obscene amounts of sparkle and glitter. "Claire's? Really?"

"This is the perfect place to get a white elephant gift."

"Mm-hmm. Remember Ashley said something useful." Wendy scoffed at me and went further into the store, clearly trying to keep her purchase a secret.

With Wendy occupied, I started wandering around the shop. Turning the displays, counting the surprising number of *Twilight* merch.

Then my eyes fell on the initial necklaces and I remember what Shea put down as her favorite song on Hinge. *Call It*

What You Want. After seeing it on Shea's profile, I'd listen to it at least a dozen times in a row thinking about Shea. It was a love song. A song about the tenderness, the comfort of being known.

I grabbed the M necklace and headed straight for the cash register.

"That's the wrong letter," Wendy said, peeking over my shoulder. I elbowed her in the stomach.

This was the perfect gift for Shea. Besides maybe coming out. But I was still working up to that.

50

SHEA

Christmas and new relationships were hard. Did I get Margo a gift or is it too soon for that? Was she going to get me a gift? Was the white elephant party my only opportunity to get her something without making her feel obligated to get me something in return?

When I told Dennis about this predicament, he said I should just give her a gift like a normal person. But when I reminded him that me giving her a gift could add to any pressure she's feeling to come out, he shut the fuck up.

The thing is, I don't think one little gift would pressure Margo that much. The problem was I'd gotten in too deep with her too fast, that now I wanted her to come out so fucking badly that I could barely think of anything else. I wanted it all with Margo. I'd been an idiot to think I'd be able to stand keeping this a secret for as long as Margo was in Snowfall. And knowing our time was limited, knowing how badly I wanted to keep her, I wanted to make the most out of this time. And we couldn't do that with her in the closet.

But we wouldn't be anything at all if I pushed her for more before she was ready.

So I was going to avoid any type of pressure or hints as hard as possible, including anything that implied I wanted a Christmas gift. Margo can never know how badly I want her to come out or else everything will get fucked up.

However, that determination did nothing to keep me from eyeing the gift she'd brought to the white elephant party. It was a larger box, maybe a foot wide and two feet tall, wrapped in paper with little bats wearing Santa hats. The bats made me think of vampires, which made me think of *Twilight*, which made me think of how we finally got to the last movie this week but made out through most of it, which made me think that gift was supposed to be for me. Maybe.

"I'm going to see if Ashley needs any help in the kitchen. You want anything, Bailey, Shea?" Greg said, snapping me out of my stupor. Bailey whispered something to Greg and, after he'd walked away, put a hand around my arm and shook me.

"What is up with you? You've been in a daze all evening."

"Oh, I'm just ..." I'm just super obsessed with your sister and am feeling irrationally territorial of her gift because it might be the only thing I get from her this season. "Nothing. Just tired from all the Eve-Eve Fest planning."

"Is that going well? No sign of sabotage?" Bailey scooted closer to me, her voice dropping to a whisper. All of a sudden it was like we were back in grade school, cuddled together and sharing secrets. I miss the times when we were always this close. And I wanted to enjoy this opportunity, to pretend like the distance hadn't worn on our friendship at all.

But the things I wanted to share weren't mine to share.

"No." I coughed to clear my throat, facing away from Bailey. "No signs of sabotage. But I'm still not totally convinced everything that's happened was intentional."

"But it could be. I mean, has anyone actually heard from Ms. Taylor since she was put on bed rest?"

"What? Are you suggest she died and is haunting me?"

Bailey sat up and gave me a little shrug.

"You never know," she grumbled. "But also, what if she faked being sick for attention and isn't getting as much as she wanted because you're taking care of things?"

"Bailey Jean Hartley," I gasped. "Did you just imply something bad about Ms. Taylor? You're supposed to be the one who thinks the best of everyone."

"Oh hush," Bailey grumbled.

"What did Bales get fulled named for?" Zoey asked, coming from the kitchen with a plate stacked high of cookies. Stephen followed behind her with a reasonable number of pizzas for the both of them.

"She took Ms. Taylor's name in vain."

"Eh." Zoey took up a spot on the loveseat to the left, Stephen sitting at her feet.

"I think we're all a little tired of Ms. Taylor's antics," Olivia added, coming in from the kitchen too, a plate in hand and Dennis beside her. Apparently, I'd missed the call for dinner.

As everybody else started filing in and taking seats, I moved to push up and get my own plate. But one was held out in front of me.

"I got ya," Margo said, sitting down beside me once I'd grabbed the plate.

With everyone settled in, partners by partners, singles by friends, everyone turned to Ashley.

"Oh my god, can't you eat your pizza first?" she grumbled even as she stood up to grab a bowl sitting on the coffee table. "Pass the bowl around, keep your number a secret. The person who gets one goes first and gets a chance to steal at the end. A singular item can only be stolen twice."

We all nodded in agreement and the bowl was passed around. When it reached me, I fished for the bottom-most piece of paper. I opened it up and read two. *Shit.* Two was the absolute worst number in this game.

I leaned over trying to peek at Bailey's number, but she caught me and held the scrap of paper to her chest.

"Shea, no cheating," Rosie chastised.

I leaned back into the couch, arms crossed. At least this way, I'd probably be able to pick Margo's gift first. Though it might be stolen from me.

"All right, who's first?" Ashley asked through a mouth of pizza.

"Me!" Bailey cheered, jerking to her feet so the whole couch shifted. "And I want the one with bats."

"No!" I jerked, instinctively grabbing Bailey's arm to keep her away from Margo's gift.

All heads turned to me with various levels of confusion.

"I mean ..." I stuttered over my words, trying to explain why Bailey couldn't have Margo's gift. I couldn't come up with a damn thing.

"Take it, Bales. That one's mine and I told Shea some of the things I was thinking of getting, so she wants it for herself," Margo said, leaning around me to look at her sister. One of her hands slid under my shirt to rub small circles into my back.

"Right. Sorry," I murmured. I let Bailey go and she giddily grabbed Margo's gift. I sat back, my insides tearing apart in rhythm to Bailey's opening of the present.

"Margo really likes those off the wall, you'd never think of but are actually super practical gifts," Bailey explained, looking over to Greg.

"Is that an insult?" Margo asked.

"Sounds like it. I'd fight her," Wendy answered.

"No," Bailey cut in. She reached around me to place a hand on Margo's knee, giving her a squeeze before returning to un-wrapping the box. "You have a gift. I feel like I always pick out the most boring thing or something so off the wall nobody ac-tually wants it."

"That's not true, Bailey girl," Greg said. His arm wrapped around Bailey's waist and pulled her closer.

"Oh my god, stop talking and open the present," Ashley grumbled. Beside her, Mason got up, went to the kitchen, and before Bailey could pull out what was in her box, had a cup of tea placed in Ashley's hands. For a minute, Ashley's brows un-furrowed and she gave Mason a soft and loving look.

"Margo, did you go over budget?" Bailey chastised, pulling out a little device the size of a bathroom trashcan.

"No. It's a mini one. For wash clothes."

A towel warmer. I'd gotten all worked up over a towel warmer. A gift she definitely bought for anybody in this group to enjoy. A gift that wasn't purchased with me in mind.

"I am going to ask you very nicely not to steal this from me, Shea," Bailey said, her voice going into a sing-song, teasey pitch.

"Nah, I thought she'd go with something else. The towel warmer is all yours."

I couldn't do this. I couldn't want her this badly and keep it a secret. I'll fuck up it at some point and out her. And if I didn't out her, I'd pressure her into coming out before she was ready and she'd eventually hate me for it.

Either way I was going to give Margo more stress than she needed which would lead to her not needing me.

"I'm next, but give me a second to grab a drink." I pushed to my feet and Zoey started giving Ashley crap for not shuffling properly. Margo grabbed my sleeve when I walked past her, an eyebrow raised in question. I just shrugged and shook her off.

I wasn't going to grab anything strong. I'd do that after telling Margo I couldn't do this anymore.

51

MARGO

When Shea got up for a drink, I knew something was wrong. As far as I could tell, Shea drank for a distraction, and there shouldn't be anything in this room she needed distracting from.

Except maybe the secret she was keeping from Bailey. From all her friends but Dennis.

But when she came back with just a small pour of wine, I thought it was fine. I thought maybe it was a well-portioned drink for the nerves. A little nerves wasn't indicative of anything being wrong. Nerves were normal.

Her ordering an Uber as the party was winding down was not.

I thought, surely she'll say something. She'll text me that we were leaving separately so no one would find out.

But there were no text messages. There were no looks or funny hand gestures.

In fact, she was avoiding looking at me at all cost.

"My rides almost here," Shea announced and was immediately swept into a round of hugs from all her friends. I took the opportunity to slip outside and wait out on the porch for her.

When Shea stepped out the front door and saw me, she immediately sighed and took a seat on the steps, gesturing for me to sit beside her.

I didn't sit. I didn't want the twisting in my stomach to be proven right.

"What's wrong?" My voice cracked on the question.

"I suck at hiding shit, Margo. I got all touchy about a fucking white elephant present because I wanted your gift. Imagine *that* was how you got outed? By some stupid bullshit like that?"

"Well ... you didn't out me. So —"

"It'll be something else though. I mean, all I wanna do is tell Bailey I finally found someone I — someone I really fucking care about." Shea still sat facing the front yard, not looking at me.

I needed her to look at me.

Taking the steps two at a time, I rushed around Shea and turned to face her, placing my hands on her knees. She looked up at me, eyes brimming with tears. It was like a hammer to my glass heart. I did this. I hurt her. I kept putting off coming out, knowing Bailey would be around for Christmas, knowing we'd all be together, and that it'd hurt Shea to have this secret.

"I'm sorry." I squeezed her knees a little harder, as if the strength of it could communicate the strength of my feelings.

"I'm sorry. I should've known this would be hard for you. I should've been more considerate."

"No." Shea shook her head. "No. I don't want you to be considerate of me. I want you to be considerate of yourself."

I didn't understand what she meant, so I kept pushing forward with the problem I did understand.

"I'm coming out. I —I've been trying to tell Bailey, but it just — the words get stuck in my throat."

Shea's hands covered mine and squeezed, whispering, "I know."

"I'll go in there right now and tell everybody." It was a desperate plea. But I could do it. I'd withstand any amount of anxiousness to keep Shea.

"Absolutely not." Shea's hands tightened on mine, keeping me in place. "I will not let you rush yourself for me."

"It's not just for you." What stage was bargaining? And how close did that put me to an ending?

"A couple of weeks ago you didn't think there was any point in coming out."

"Well somebody changed my mind. Reminded me I matter and deserve to be celebrated."

"Celebrated. Not rushed. And I — fuck, I want to rush you so fucking bad and that's horrible. That's a horrible thing to want."

"No, it's not. It's flattering."

"Sure, until you rushing to come out leads to strained relationships and you start to resent me."

"There's no way in hell that would happen." I almost laughed. If I hadn't resent Shea for being my first crush and making everyone else pale in comparison, then nothing else could make me feel that way.

"But it could. Pressuring you to come out sooner is unfair of me. And —"

"That's not what you're doing though," I argued. "All you did was get excited over a gift. I have —"

"I like you too fucking much, Margo. And I'm not a patient person. Fuck, if you'd come out before you started working at the office, I'd have offered you to move with me at this point. But that's not where you're at. That's not what you're ready for. And that's fair. You shouldn't jump into something just because I want to jump."

"I just need a little more time. I ... couldn't you wait just a bit longer?"

"If you know I'm waiting for you to come out, then that's pressuring you. I don't want you to be under constant pressure in this relationship. That's not fair to you. And honestly, the idea of me pressuring you makes me sick. I can't handle it. It's better for both of us if we quit while we're ahead."

"But what if —" A horn cut off my words. Shea pulled back just enough to look over my shoulder and waved at the driver.

"That's my ride. I'll ... I'll take care of everything with the fest tomorrow, so don't feel obligated to come. And ..." Shea paused like the words were caught in her throat. Then she leaned in and kissed my tear-soaked cheek. "Take care of yourself, Margo."

Shea got up and walked around me, but I didn't move. I stayed, standing, facing Ashley's porch, and listened to Shea get in the car and take off. I stood and stood until I felt my knees go numb, then I sat on the porch steps, right where Shea had been.

This was so stupid. Why did Shea get to decide what was best for me? Why did I have so much trouble telling people who loved me that I was bi? Why didn't I realize this was hurting Shea before now?

"Margo?" somebody called from the front door. I looked up over my shoulder to see Bailey. When she got a look at me, red face, shimmering eyes, she quickly closed the door and sat down beside me, arms wrapping me up. "What's wrong?"

"I ..." I could just tell Bailey now and get it over with. But then when Shea found out, she'd think she pushed me to do it and feel even worse. "I'll tell you later."

Bailey stiffened, but quickly nodded before letting go of me.

"Sure. Sure. Well, I just wanted to say thank you for helping out Shea. She doesn't do great with the holidays and she definitely volunteered for the events just to keep herself occupied."

"Heh. Yeah, it was my pleasure."

"No, seriously." Bailey slapped at my knee. "It means a lot to me knowing Shea had somebody in her corner. I've ... been slacking on my best friend duties since I got together with Greg and it's been making me feel pretty shitty."

"Don't feel bad. Shea loves you and she'd feel like shit if she heard you say that." Apparently, that was the theme of the night.

"That's true." Bailey laughed and leaned her head on my shoulder. "You two have gotten close, huh?"

"Yeah." The word caught in throat, my voice cracking. Bailey shifted beside me, clearly fighting the urge to ask what was wrong. And I cracked a little. "She's just stupid sometimes, you know? Making stupid, dumb, shitty decisions for others, trying to protect everyone else before herself. It's … stupid."

Bailey nodded against my shoulder but stayed quiet.

I don't know if it was all my time with Shea and her aversion to the quiet, but this silence felt like scratching at my bones. I opened my mouth to say something, but the door behind us opened.

"You ready to go, Bailey girl?" Greg asked, just his head poking out of the door.

"Give us another minute, okay?" Bailey said, flashing her boyfriend a sweet smile. Greg murmured an affirmative and went back inside. Bailey squeezed my hand before getting up, stretching as she stared up at the stars. "You know, Shea doesn't really know what it's like to have someone new look after her. I think for her, it feels like new shoes you have to break in. I just happened to be her friend before she started pushing new people away." Bailey paused, giving me a soft smile. "She does the same thing with all her girlfriends, you know? Never lets them get close and the one's that do get pushed away before they can hurt her the way her parents did. She doesn't know how to accept unconditional love anymore."

"They're fucking bitches," I said, an instinctive reaction at the mention of someone who'd hurt Shea.

"They really are." Bailey sighed and started back to the door. Halfway inside, she turned back and asked, "Want me to get Wendy for you?"

"Yes, please."

"You gonna stay with her again tonight?"

"Yup," I said, stretching the word out because I'd told Mom, and Mom probably told Bailey, that I was at Wendy's the last few nights.

"Okay, have fun. Just remember Mom wants to do brunch tomorrow before the fest."

52

MARGO

"I just don't understand why she did this all of a sudden," I cried, surrounded by a pile of tissues on Wendy's couch while she sat on the floor working on a puzzle on the coffee table.

"Uh-huh."

"Why didn't Shea say anything sooner? If she was feeling bad about hiding our relationship, she could have said something."

"Uh-huh."

I tossed a pillow at Wendy's head. "Are you even listening to me?"

"No," she grumbled, taking the pillow and tucking it behind her back. "You're both being idiots and it's boring to listen to."

"Wendy!" I smacked her shoulder and she smacked me right back

"Don't Wendy me! I'm just telling you the truth. Shea broke up with you because she couldn't handle being in a closeted relationship with her best friend's sister. She probably went in thinking y'all's relationship wouldn't be that serious. And then she started to catch feelings and realized this was more than she could handle. Sure, the solution would be fixed by you coming out, but Shea cares about you and doesn't want you to feel pressured about coming out before you're ready. It's simple and stupid."

"You're stupid," I grumbled, shuffling so I could sink into the couch like I was sinking into my misery.

"No, I'm right. And if you're that upset, you could have fought harder. It sounds like you just sat there and took it."

"I asked her to wait."

"The thing she said she couldn't do without feeling like she was pressuring you?"

"Okay, well what would you have done?"

"Validated her feelings and insisted we both take a night to think things through before talking again to find a solution." Wendy returned to her puzzle, placing another piece together. I wanted to flip the fucking table.

"Aren't you the same person that sabotaged your parents' retirement move so they had to stay a week longer?"

"I'm more mature now."

"That was three years ago!" I shouted and Wendy just shrugged. I leaned over and knocked at the coffee table, sending puzzle pieces flying.

The silence that followed was bone-chilling. Wendy was prone to lashing out and just being generally dramatic. And fucking up her puzzle would certainly trigger that.

"I am going to let that slide because I know you're upset right now," Wendy said through gritted teeth before turning to face me with a glare that would make grown men shit themselves. "But if you do that shit again, I'm smothering you in your sleep and you'll never get the chance to make up with Shea."

I immediately shirked back.

"Good. Now you have two options for getting back with Shea. Both require talking though, so you know, brace yourself for that and skip the coffee tomorrow." I grumbled in response and Wendy continued. "You can go help Shea with the fest even though she told you not to and tell her your feelings for her aren't outweighed by any unintentional pressure she might have or will give you. You tell her you appreciate her concerns and you validate them. You don't do whatever the hell you did tonight and let her go."

"She just … she just looked so miserable. I was hurting her by not —"

"Oh shut up. She was miserable because she thought she was gonna hurt you. If your positions were swapped, you would have done the same thing because you're also a dumbass."

I didn't reply. She was right, I just didn't want to admit it. At least not to her right now.

"*Or* you come out to your family at brunch tomorrow then capture the saboteur in some flashy display and declare your love for Shea in front of the whole town."

"Oh sure, that'll be super easy to pull off," I muttered.

"I'll help you catch the saboteur."

"Glad at least one of us is confident."

"Margo." I looked over to my friend, who had the most serious face on. "I swear on my parents' graves that I'll catch this bitch."

"Your parents aren't dead," I reminded her.

"I mean, they're in Florida, so they might as well be."

I threw my head back and laughed. And then kept laughing because Wendy was right, this whole thing was stupid. It was stupid and it could still be fixed. The world was not ending and I could be together with Shea again as soon as tomorrow if I got the balls to do what needed to be done.

"I really have to come out to my parents, don't I?"

"Yeah," Wendy snorted before turning back to her puzzle. "But what's the worst that could happen? They're not gonna kick you out."

"No. But they might just not care."

"Well, if they don't care, then Abigail and I will make up for it. I'll even make you the abomination that is Hawaiian pizza."

"Aw," I crooned, sitting up to hug Wendy.

"Oh shut up." She tried to shrug me off, but I held on tight. "Ugh, whatever. You've still got one other problem before you can relax."

"What? The saboteur?"

"No. Where you're gonna get another library job." Wendy crossed her arms and turned to look away from me, pouting.

"Oh, right." I let go of Wendy and sat up, tapping my chin like this was something I had to think about. "I guess if I can get Shea back, it'd be pretty important to her if I stay in Snow-fall." Wendy made some sort of grunt, so I kept going. "And Abigail could probably use somebody to check in on her introverted ass." Another grunt. "And let's be real, once Ms. Delaney retires, the library will just shut down because nobody has taught this community what a library is worth. I mean, could you imagine the chaos the old lady gang would cause if they knew the library had sewing machines *after* it shut down?"

Wendy was seething so hard, that she was visibly shaking. So I put her out of her misery.

"Plus if tonight's any example, I'm going to need my best friend's help to keep my head on straight when it's constantly spinning from anxiety."

"Damn right, you do." Wendy turned around, smacking my leg excitedly before pulling me into a short-lived hug. She pulled back and narrowed her eyes at me. "But which is the real reason you want to stay? It's Shea, isn't it?"

"I mean, a little. But I always wanted to be in a big city so I could use big city funds to make a difference. Being a part of the event planning, especially getting all those ornaments for the tree, made me realize I could make the difference I want here."

"And you were gonna tell me this when?" Wendy nudged my knee before abandoning me for her puzzle.

"I was gonna tell you as a reward for catching the saboteur, but I'm not sure that's gonna happen at this point."

"You better fucking watch yourself, Hartley."

53

SHEA

"Dennis," I whined into my phone as soon as the call clicked through. "Fireball tastes like shit."

"Fucking hell? Shea, why are you calling me at one in the morning to tell me the obvious?" Denny asked, his voice followed by the sound of shuffling and eventually a door clicking closed.

"Margo isn't in bed with me and I'm miserable."

"Well, you're gonna have to spend some nights apart. That'd happen no matter the relationship. Can I go back to bed without worrying for your safety? How much have you had to drink?"

"Only a sip. It's really gross. How have I never noticed how gross it is?"

"Because you drink it all the time."

"Mmm. I did. But Margo won't fuck me if I've been drinking, so I haven't had any in …" My brain was fuzzy and for the first time in a long time, it wasn't because of a drink. Everything was fuzzy because it hurt. I was also crazy tired. On top of changing my drinking habits by withholding sex, Margo had also changed my sleeping schedule because I liked the feeling of falling asleep together. "I haven't really had much to drink over the last two weeks."

"Well, that's one motivator. But hey, if it works, it works."

"It did. But I broke up with Margo, so funny drunk Shea will be back soon enough."

"Wait, what?" There was the sound of screeching wood and I imagined Denny sitting at the dining room table in his and Olivia's apartment. An apartment I helped them find. "Did you break up with her because she was withholding sex to keep you sober? Sure, it's a little fucked up, but I'm sure it was coming from a good place. I mean, everyone's been getting concerned about your drinking habits."

"Seriously?" I sat up on the couch so fast that I got dizzy from the blood rush. "Nobody said anything."

"All the girls thought it was just your normal and convinced me of the same. But Mason has some history with his uncle, you know? Made us all take a second look at when you were drinking more."

"Shit, I'm sorry. I just —"

"Don't apologize," Denny interrupted. "Just … I dunno, reach out to us before reaching for a drink."

I tried for a solid second not to laugh. I didn't even last that long before I started straight-up cackling.

"Okay, shut up. I know that was cheesy, but I mean it," Dennis grumbled.

"I know, I know," I said through laughter. "I appreciate it. I'll put sickie notes on all my bottles that say 'call a friend'."

"You're flask too."

"Sure. My flask too." I let the moment be for a minute, let the silence stretch, before saying, "Thank you though. For caring and looking after me."

"Of course," Denny gruffed. "Gotta make sure my best friend doesn't drink herself to an early grave."

"Aw, I'm your best friend? Eli hasn't beaten me out yet?"

"Nah, that won't happen. He's a good guy, but he keeps asking me to play D&D and I don't think that's something I wanna get into."

"I dunno, it might be fun. All his board game suggestions have been good so far."

"But we have to talk in voices, right? And do math?"

"Pretty sure the voices are optional."

"I dunno, man. Maybe. But if the drinking didn't break y'all up, what did?"

I took a big, dramatic breath and fell back onto the couch.

"I was gonna fuck things up for her."

"The fuck does that mean?"

"I just … I dunno, I didn't realize how quickly I'd be all in for Margo. But I can't do that when she's still in the closet. So I broke up with her before I became a passive-aggressive dick that pressures her to come out."

"I'm going to need a clearer explanation here, Shea. I'm just some straight dude."

"Well … it'd be a dick move to pressure her to come out before she was ready."

"Right."

"And being in the closet means our relationship would be limited."

"All right, I'm following so far."

"And I've already fallen hard enough for Margo to want those things. So instead of letting that want to brew into resentment or pushing her out of the closet, I had to let her go."

"Uh-huh. See that's where you're losing me. What's her opinion on coming out? Or like, why hasn't she done it yet? Because as long as I've known the Hartleys, they've had a rainbow flag in their yard year round."

"She was worried about them not caring."

"Huh?"

"Like, it'd still be really shitty if she built up the courage and everything to tell them and they just shrug it off."

"Okay, sure. I can see how that would suck. So when you told her you couldn't handle the closet dating anymore, what'd she say? Was she just unwilling to come out or what?"

"What do you mean what did she say? I can't do the closeted thing, that's where she's at right now, the end."

There was a long pause on the other end of the line before Dennis said, "You didn't talk about the possibility of her coming out?"

"No! That'd be pressuring her or like issuing an ultimatum. The whole point of breaking up with her now was so I didn't do that type of shit."

"Okay, sure. But there's a difference between saying I won't keep dating you unless you come out and we're getting to a place where I'm not comfortable hiding our relationship anymore, let's talk about if and how you want to come out."

"But that's — I couldn't do that. That's practically asking her to come out for me."

"I mean, sure. But it's more like setting a boundary you need to keep the relationship going. Then she has the choice of how to proceed."

What Dennis was saying made a lot of sense. I made the decision for Margo and didn't let her get any say in the matter. I thought I had to be the more mature one and do the tough thing. I thought I was saving us from a lot of inevitable heartbreak. But maybe I was just saving myself. I mean, let's be real, when was the last time I was in a relationship and *didn't* dip before things got serious? I didn't *do* the tough thing, I avoided *asking* her the tough thing.

"But if I asked her and she said no, I'd be wrecked. At least this way, I'll be able to pretend I'm a functioning human the next time I see her."

Dennis sighed and I couldn't tell over the phone if he was frustrated with how I was running from possible hurt or remembering when Olivia did the same to him.

"Dennis?" a sleepy Olivia called over the line. "Who're you talking to?"

"Just Shea, darling. Go back to bed."

"Did the saboteur do something?" Olivia gasped.

"No. God, y'all are too obsessed with this damn saboteur thing." There was some grumbling and shuffling before Dennis spoke into the phone again. "Look, I understand not wanting to open yourself up to that sort of hurt. And I sure as hell don't want you hurting like that. But ... what she did with the tree decorations, her speech ... I don't think the answer would've been no. Just think about that. Night."

"All right, night."

I tossed my phone aside and stared up at the ceiling. Dennis had a point.

And Margo had asked me to wait.

But it was one in the morning, so no matter what I decided to do, I couldn't do it now. So instead, I'll turn off my brain and turn on some holiday movie Margo had put in my queue.

54

MARGO

M om took her brunches very seriously. Especially when
we had company or it was the holidays. So with Greg
over and it being a couple of days until Christmas, she went all
out. The dining room table was covered in brunch foods, fruits
and breakfast pie and breakfast casserole and any other breakfast concoction she could find on Pinterest. And in between the
food were ornament-laden garlands and sprigs of holly. She
even tied paper snowflakes to the chandelier.

"Wow! So this is where you get your artistic talent, huh?"
Greg said to Bailey, whose lips went into a straight line as she
nodded sharply. Bailey and Mom had … artistic differences.
Bailey liked to experiment and Mom liked traditional. It made
for a number of arguments over decorating the family tree. It'd
gotten so bad one year, that Dad bought trees for our bedrooms

to decorate however we wanted without messing up Mom's living room vision.

"All right, sit down, sit down." Mom came out of the kitchen holding a tray of rolls, waving a hand at us to take our seats. Dad to one side, Mom to the other, Greg and Bailey across from lonely old me. Had I come out already, Shea would be sitting beside me.

Fuck, just say it. Say it now. There's no reason not to.

"Can I —"

"Hold on, Margo. Your mother wants to say something before we dig in."

"Yes, I'm just so happy everyone could be here for Christmas this year," Mom said, a hand to her heart. Of my 24 years of life and Bailey's 29, we have collectively missed 3 Christmases total. Bailey missed two because of travel issues when she'd gone out of state for some art shows and I missed last year because I'd gotten swamped with school and work. For all three of those missed Christmases, the other child was here. So it's hardly like we'd left her alone for years on end.

"Happy to be here, Ms. Hartley," Greg said, raising a glass to Mom. "Thank you for having me."

"Oh, of course. I'm so happy Bailey has found someone who adores her so."

"Mom," Bailey groaned, rolling her eyes. Mom just shoved a basket of rolls in her hands in response and we all started fixing our plates and passing around the food.

Once everything settled and plates were filled, I took a deep breath to try again.

"I just wanna share —"

"What's Shea doing this morning, Bailey? I should have thought to invite her over beforehand, but I know she's got her hands full with Eve-Eve Fest." Mom was looking at Bailey, like always. Even though I was the one who had been helping Shea all month long with these events.

"I dunno. Margo, when're you leaving to help with set up?" Bailey asked.

"I'm not." I stabbed at a large chunk of sausage in the casserole and chewed it like it was my mother forgetting about everything I'd done this month, *specifically* with Shea and the event she was talking about.

"Why not? You guys have been working together all month for this. Is something wrong? Is it the saboteur?" Bailey asked, her voice pitching up.

"What saboteur?" Dad asked.

"You know, the one who poisoned the pizza at the tree lighting," Mom explained. "It was in the Paper."

"They're totally gonna try to pull something today. You should really be there," Bailey continued.

"Shea told me not to go."

"What? Why would she do that? I'll text her. Something must be wrong." As Bailey pulled out her phone, Mom tsked at her. Bailey bit her lips and tried to give Mom a smile. "Just a quick text to make sure Shea's okay."

It felt like my brain was just screaming and running wild while my body was numb. This was all so stupid. What did I care if they brushed off my coming out? I had Wendy and Abigail. I might get Shea back. And if I get Shea back, I'll probably get Bailey and all of her friends.

Plus they couldn't brush it off if I did a dramatic reveal, right?

"Shea doesn't want me to go because she broke up with me."

It was like the moment was in freeze frame. Everyone was breathing and blinking, but otherwise frozen. Mom's fork scraped against her plate, eyes wide. Bailey's mouth was wide open in shock, Greg staring at her for a cue on how to respond.

The only one who wasn't in shock was Dad.

"I'm sorry to hear that, sweetheart. The holiday season is rough for her though, so you might be able to talk it out in a week or so if that's what you want."

"Bill!" Mom shouted and Dad looked up from his plate and around the table.

"What?"

"Did you know she was dating Shea?" Mom gestured at me, fork still in hand.

"Well, no. But I don't assume either of the girls would tell us about their partners until they're more serious."

"Did you tell Dad you were dating Shea, but not me?" Bailey cried. Greg instantly wrapped an arm around her shoulders and started rubbing circles.

"I didn't tell Dad. I didn't even know he knew I was bi."

"You're bi?" Mom and Bailey screeched.

I take every bad, dismissive thought about coming out I had back. This was actually really funny. I can't wait to tell Shea.

If she'll take me back.

"Congratulations, dear," Dad said, reaching over to squeeze my knee.

"Did you know?"

"Oh well ... no. It just makes sense."

"Seriously? Ms. Delaney said the same thing. Did you know about the socks?"

"What socks?" Dad said at the same time Mom said, "Ms. Delaney? The librarian? You told her before us?"

"No. She caught Shea and I making out."

"You were making out in the library?" Bailey said, looking over at Greg like he could explain the situation. When he gave her a little shrug, she turned back to me. "When?"

"Oh. I don't think I wanna answer that."

"Oh my god. You and Shea disappeared after the tree lighting before everybody got sick. You snuck off to make out?"

"Not specifically? I dunno, Shea dragged me off."

"Oh my god," Bailey repeated and my gut sank at the idea that this could hurt their friendship.

"Don't be mad at her," I rushed to say. "She didn't want to out me before I was ready. So she wasn't, like, keeping a secret from you. Just being respectful of me."

"Oh my god," Bailey repeated again. Greg shook her a little and I was beginning to think I broke my sister. Then, in perhaps the saddest voice I'd ever heard from her, she said, "You've been trying to tell me for like two weeks now."

"Yeah." Bailey started full-on crying, which made me cry. She pushed Greg's arm off and came over to my side of the table, wrapping me in a hug.

"I need to make a whole other meal. None of this has rainbow sprinkles," Mom said, looking at her huge spread in dismay.

"Dear, I don't think this is the moment for cooking," Dad said before tilting his head at me. Mom pushed away from the table to join Bailey hugging me.

"Should I …" Greg started but Bailey grumbled at him and he stayed seated.

"I am so sorry, dear. Shea is being a real … poop head," Mom said. "But I'm glad you've let us know about your lack of gender preferences in romantic partners. I love Shea, but I'm sure we could find you someone much better suited for you."

"Estelle," Dad warned and Mom let go of me to go playful smack Dad on the shoulder.

"I just want our girls to find good partners," Mom huffed before heading towards the kitchen murmuring something about sprinkles.

Dad looked over at me and Bailey, who was still burring herself in my hair, and stood. Plate in hand, he motioned to Greg and said, "Why don't we take our plates to the living room and find something to watch? Estelle is likely going to produce a rainbow cake in a few hours."

"I'm not making cake!" Mom shouted from the kitchen.

Greg looked to Bailey, clearly uncomfortable with the whole situation, before getting up to follow Dad. Once their steps faded away, Bailey pulled back to look at me, face puffy and red.

"I'm *so* sorry I've been such a sucky sister. I was so wrapped up with the holiday show and stuff with Greg, I haven't been paying attention to you or Shea. You tried to tell me so many times and I just —"

"Bailey, it's fine. The world couldn't stop just because I wanted to come out."

"But my world can," Bailey said, taking me by the shoulders and shaking me a little. "I mean, this is really fucking cool, right? My little sister can find the beauty in anybody. That's amazing!"

"I think you're putting a nicer spin on it than necessary," I said, chuckling.

"No, that's what loving someone is, finding their beauty and cherishing it." It was such a Bailey thing to say, all hippie and in touch with her emotions. So stupid.

It made me tear up.

"Margo," Bailey cried, hugging me again and rocking us side to side. "It's okay. It'll be okay. I love you. Mom and Dad love you. Shea will love you too! I just know it."

"You don't know that. I mean, she broke up with me, I'm pretty sure that's a good sign she doesn't love me."

"What? No way!"

"Bailey, she broke up with me."

"But that — it was because you weren't out yet, right? You're out now, so you two should be dating and falling in love and getting married."

"That'd be … really cool. But I think it really hurt her having to hide things. And she was really concerned about me feeling pressured to come out just because of her. So I don't know if just because I'm out now will —"

Bailey pulled back again, eyes narrowed and her grip on arms tightening.

"Hold up. Did she say she didn't want you to come out before you were ready or for her?"

In my life, I had only seen serious Bailey a handful of times. Most of those occasions had been when someone was being homophobic to Shea. Honestly, she might be the sole reason everyone in Snowfall is so queer-positive, or at least indifferent. Seeing serious Bailey would drive anybody who wouldn't comply out of town.

But this was the first time I'd seen her get protective over me. And sure, it was a little sad that this was the first time I was close enough to my sister for her to get this way. But also, we were close now. And she was being defensive of me over Shea.

"She mentioned both things. I think. I was kinda crying and trying to bargain with her the whole time. I didn't respond great."

Bailey's eyebrows pinched together. Then all of a sudden, she was up, dragging me out of my seat and to the door.

"We're going out!" she shouted over her shoulder as she fished her keys out of the bowl we used to dump everything. And while I imagined Mom or Dad or maybe even Greg had some sort of response, I didn't hear it because Bailey had us out the door and in her car in record time.

"It's like I told you last night," Bailey said once she'd gotten buckled. "Shea doesn't expect anyone to make changes for her. She won't ask or even accept it because the one change she asked her parents to make fucked her over so bad. So of course she wouldn't want you to do something big like come out just so you can have a comfortable relationship. She doesn't believe she's worth that sort of love."

"Okay ... so how do I prove she is?" I asked, wracking my brain for things that Shea would accept as proof that I love her no matter what.

"Well, I dunno what will work for you, but I definitely have to beat her stubborn ass for breaking my little sister's heart."

55

SHEA

The great thing about community events is that even though I was managing everything, everyone already knew what needed to be done. Most of the folks setting up for Eve-Eve Fest had done this dozens of times before.

Which should have meant that on the morning of the fest, everything would be smooth sailing, right? I mean, I did all the setup prep, I confirmed shipments, I double-checked receipts, I followed up with all the volunteers and staff, and at Ashley's insistence, I let her review the checklist Margo made and double-checked everything was done.

So when I got to the courtyard, I expected minimal chaos. What I got instead was seven missing tables, a broken popcorn machine, an iced-over gazebo, and reports that Clive had run off with his antlers full of lights.

No one bothered explaining that last bit to me, but as soon as they said Zoey was on it, I gave up understanding. The likelihood that she started whatever chaos that was happening with Clive was too high to bother with.

But ignoring the Clive issue still left me a shit ton to get done.

Thankfully, despite my assurances that I had everything under control, Ashley still sent Mason over to help first thing in the morning. He took on the popcorn machine, claiming it couldn't be more complicated than his espresso machine, and I went off to search for the tables. As for the gazebo stairs … we just had to pray they'd thaw as the day went on.

I checked all around the courtyard, in the school, the library, and the shed behind the courtyard. But every few minutes, I was pulled aside for something as equally ridiculous as Clive stealing lights. I was asked where cups were, what color tablecloth a vendor should use, and even where the bathrooms were.

A local asked me where the bathrooms were. That was the thing that finally made me believe in the whole saboteur scheme. At the very least, someone was trying to waste my time and fuck with my head.

And since I was a masochist, I guess, I decided to fuck myself up by searching the attic of the community center and start with the baptismal pool. The tables weren't there, obviously, but there were memories of Margo and Tootsie Rolls and decent wine.

I sat on the steps, hands over my eyes, and screamed.

Dennis was right. I saw a bad ending and immediately cut my losses.

She had asked me to wait. Why couldn't I have done that for her? I sure as hell liked her enough to wait, so why did it scare the shit out of me?

Because the first time I waited, it didn't pay off.

What kind of crime did I commit in a past life to deserve this sort of karma? It was unfair that they were the assholes and I was still paying for it. They'd rewired my brain to assume the worst in folks and I hadn't cared enough about anybody since to even *want* the best from them. Until Margo.

And boy did I screw that up. Even if she had liked me enough to want to work our relationship through, even if she did want to come out, there's no way she'd want to take me back now. What kind of an asshole wasn't willing to give someone a chance to speak or wait for them to sort out their feelings? I wouldn't date that kind of a bitch and I sure as fuck wouldn't want Margo to date her either.

"Fuck!" I shouted into the empty space, putting all my frustrations at myself and my parents into that single word.

And instead of the silence of an empty building, my profanity was met with a crash.

"The fuck?" I murmured to myself as I scrambled up to check it out. It wasn't beyond reason that somebody came into the community center to check for something or bother me. But it was weird that they'd be up in the attic.

And it was even weirder that they hadn't said anything.

Stepping out of the baptism door, I saw a flash of red heading back down to the main floor and a stack of ten tables in the room across from me. Whoever had just run out not only had the missing tables, but were also collecting more.

Fucking bastard.

I ran after the figure in red, tumbling down the stairs and racing through hallways only to trip up over a pile of lights dropped in the entryway. And by the time I'd untangled my feet and followed their path out of the church, they were lost in a sea of folks preparing for the fest.

I stood at the top of the steps, eyes narrowed to pick out the culprit. If I couldn't get Margo back or beat myself out of these bad habits, I was at least going to get some answers as to why this fucker had it out for me.

"There you are!" somebody shouted, but I was focused. I wasn't going to take my eyes off the crowd until I spotted Santa Waldo.

"Shea?" a different voice said, a voice I was intimately familiar with, a voice belonging to someone I very much could not handle talking to right now. "What's wrong?"

"What's wrong?" Bailey scoffed. I finally took my eyes off the crowd to look at her and Margo. Bailey had her arms crossed over a huge cardigan that was most likely thrifted, her eyes narrowed and stormy. Shit. Bailey didn't get like that a lot, something big must've happened.

"Wait, what's wrong with you?" I asked before looking back to the crowd.

"'What's wrong,' she says," Bailey scoffed again. "I have to beat you up, is what's wrong. You're doing that thing again where —"

"Shit, there," I interrupted when I spotted the saboteur heading to the back side of the gazebo. Without explaining the situation to Margo and Bailey, or questioning whatever the fuck they were talking about, I sprinted to the gazebo.

"What the hell?" Bailey shouted after me.

"Actually, can you go get the tables in the attic?" I shouted over my shoulder.

"No," Bailey yelled at the the same time Margo said, "On it."

"Don't do what she says. She needs to answer for her crimes."

"Breaking up with me is not a crime, Bailey. Besides, this is for the fest," Margo argued with her sister. My brain went fuzzy as Margo spoke, but I shook it off. I needed to catch this asshole so I can finish up this fucking festival and crawl back into bed for a nice long cry.

"Hey! Asshole," I shouted once I'd caught up with the saboteur, who was on their knees pulling something from under the gazebo. Up close, I recognized them as one of Ms. Taylor's nieces from out of town who only ever showed up during the festivals, probably because they'd been guilt-tripped into helping the family out.

Guess they got guilt-tripped into more than just helping carry shit this time.

"Shit," the woman murmured as she scrambled up and ran off.

"Shit," I repeated because I really didn't think they'd bother running after I saw them. But of course, it wasn't that easy.

I gave chase, dodging folks asking me for advice on booth placement and when they should bring out food. We zigzagged all across the courtyard, between booths and crowds, through garland curtains waiting to be hung, and barely dodging folks carrying kegs of, presumably, hot chocolate.

It was a regular old movie montage, except instead of looking cool and composed, I looked like a mad woman chasing around Mrs. Clause. I was yelling at her to stop, just generally cussing up a storm, and anytime we passed by something small and disposable like a paper cup or plastic ornament, I tossed it at them. Unfortunately, I never went through a softball phase and every item went sailing off into the crowd.

Then there was Clive. Rampaging through the courtyard, screaming and swinging his light covered antlers around. And behind him was Zoey and Stephen, each carrying a huge Ziplock bag of carrots. As Clive was heading right to a booth of poinsettias that Margo's friend had grown to sell, Zoey pulled out a carrot and tossed it in the opposite direction. Clive immediately changed directions for the food.

Which was great, Abigail would have cried if her flowers were ruined. But across from Abigail's table was the popcorn booth, where Mason was still working on the machine.

Clive's carrot landed right on the table and Clive dived head first into it, knocking the machine into Mason and ramming the table into the walkway so it blocked Mrs. Clause's way.

"Thanks, Clive," I told the deer as I caught up to the saboteur, Zoey stopping beside me, panting. I stole a carrot out of her bag and tossed it to Clive who happily ate it.

"Now, you," I said, turning to Ms. Taylor's niece. Zoey immediately straightened and moved to block the lady's way. Stephen and Dennis picked up on the vibes and followed suit.

Clive, however, just huffed before running off.

"God fucking damn it," the woman said, removing her Santa hat and tossing it to the ground. "This is too much fucking work. First, she has me basically kidnapping kids with candy, then it's running around stealing shit all day. All because she's pissed about something from over a decade ago. She's in the damn library trying to talk Ms. Delaney out of retiring. Chase her around for answers. I'm fucking done."

Taylor's niece stormed off and we were all left stunned by her outburst.

Guess that answered the question as to who was behind everything.

"Isn't there some Shakespeare quote about the simplest answer always being it?" Zoey said.

"Sherlock, pretty girl. You're thinking of Sherlock," Stephen said before pressing a kiss to the top of her head. The little display of affection stung. I could have had that if I wasn't a scared little bitch.

"So what do you wanna do, Shea? Want us to go beat up Ms. Taylor or what?"

"Zoey, no," Stephen whispered. He wrapped an arm around her waist and gripped at her sweater to keep her from immediately rushing to the library.

"She started this shit," Zoey argued. She kept going but the words fuzzed out as I caught sight of Margo. She was on the steps of the community center directing folks carrying out tables, a clipboard in hand. When the last person received their directions, she leaned her head back and sighed.

She must hate being here, having to clean up after my mess. *Again.*

If I was her, I would have dipped out as soon as Bailey was out of sight. But I guess at this point everyone knows she's been working with me on everything, so she'd look bad if the fest turned out shitty.

All the more reason to get things settled sooner rather than later.

"I'll talk to Ms. Taylor. Can y'all get this cleared up and then see if Margo needs help with anything?" I didn't wait for them to answer, just took off to the library, trying not to look at the Christmas tree Margo had worked so hard on.

God, I was a fucking idiot. Margo made the tree of my childhood dreams. She had everything set up for us to make a popcorn garland together like the town was one big happy family. She gave me back a piece of the holidays I had been missing.

And I doubted if she liked me enough to do the hard stuff.

"Shea!" Margo shouted. I turned to see her and a small group of our friends heading towards me.

"Uh, no, sorry, uh … busy!" I shouted back in a disconnected mess as I started jogging towards the library.

"Shea, stop being an idiot!" Bailey yelled.

"If we could just talk about —" Margo started only to be interrupted by the others.

"I wanna fight Taylor too!" Wendy shouted, followed by Zoey chiming in, "Me too!"

"I can handle it on my own!" I started all out running across the courtyard between the gazebo and the library, the pounding of my friends' feet following closely behind me. By the time I crashed into the entrance of the building, they were on me, crowding me so my back was at the inner door.

And of course, Margo was the one right in front of me. Her face was flushed from all the running, lips extra red from nervously biting them. A stray, frizzy curl stuck straight up like an antenna and I wanted nothing more than to smooth it down.

God, I wanted to touch her. I wanted to beg her to take me back and forgive me for being an idiot.

But even if I could work up the nerve to do that, now wasn't the time.

"Sorry, I just ..." I tried to swallow around the lump in my throat, but it did nothing to help even my voice. "I just wanna talk to Taylor on my own."

"You're running away," Bailey accused, reaching out a hand to shove my shoulder.

I didn't take my eyes off Margo.

"I'm sorry, I just ... let me handle this and then ..." Then what? Then let me make it up to you? Let me sneak you away?

Margo grabbed my hand and my brain ceased functioning, only able to play the AOL dial-up sound instead of any useful thoughts.

"Wait, what's this vibe?" Zoey asked, waving a hand at Margo and me.

"I came out to my family."

"Oh." My heart was in my stomach. Or maybe my throat. I don't know, it wasn't where it should be, that's for sure.

The one thing I did know was that I could *not* get excited over this. Just because she came out to them, didn't mean she wanted me back. She might have been forced out. Or fuck, she might've been upset about me being an ass and had to explain why she was crying.

God, I made her cry. I'm the worst.

"I mean, I'm —" I started to say before everything tilted and I was suddenly on the floor at Ms. Delaney's feet.

"I believe I've told you all before to be quiet in the library," she drawled. Ms. Taylor's head poked out from behind Delaney

"Humph. Hooligans, the lot of them. You should hold them here for being so disrespectful."

"You know I can't do that, Evelyn," Delaney said, voice flat as she looked at Taylor.

"Oh, fuck off! You've been causing trouble all month," Wendy shouted, edging closer to Taylor. Wide-eyed, Stephen grabbed onto Wendy's shirt and pulled her a safe distance away from Taylor. And when Zoey made a step forward, he grabbed onto her too.

"You're niece told us everything. Why have you been such a dick to Shea? You're a lot of things, but I never thought homophobic was one of them."

"I am not! One of my nephews is gay," Ms. Taylor argued.

"Oh please," Zoey shouted. "You're just lucky Ashley is on bed rest today. She'll have your ass in court."

"Zoey," Stephen cautioned.

While more, harsher words were exchanged, Margo held out a hand to help me up. I debated brushing her off and pushing myself up because of the emotional damage I'd take from holding her hand. But in the end, I really wanted to feel her touch.

Margo pulled me up and I settled between her and Bailey. When I moved to let go of her hand, Margo held on.

"It was not a hate crime!" Ms. Taylor shouted.

"If it looks like a duck and quakes like a duck," Wendy snarfed.

"No, I did it because they were going to bring back the mistletoe." Ms. Taylor threw a hand toward Margo and me. I turned to look at Margo to see if she was just as confused as I was.

"Evelyn, I only told you that they read about the mistletoe tradition for you to mentally prepare, not make a fool out of yourself."

"I'm not making a fool out of myself!" Taylor insisted. "I'm protecting our traditions from these — these —"

"Gays?" Zoey offered and Stephen physical pulled her out of the conversation.

"I mean, she is right," I said while Margo hummed in agreement. Zoey immediately waved her hands around at us, looking at Stephen with big eyes that said 'I'm right'.

"But also what mistletoe thing?" I asked, trying to get things back on track but having trouble while Margo was still holding my hand. "There hasn't been any mistletoe thing. I mean, I guess somebody could've sold mistletoe shit at the craft fair, but that's a hell of a thing to get upset about. And really, if you didn't want some plant at events, you could have —"

"Oh," Margo interrupted, turning to me with wide eyes. "That old tradition I found in the Papers. The one where mistletoe was hung around random spots and couples that found them got happily ever afters."

"Oh right. Yeah, we totally forgot about that."

"You what?" Ms. Taylor yelled, face going bright red.

"Yeah. We got distracted with ... other things," I said, my face reddening as I looked at the floor.

"Oh my god, are you two boning?" Zoey shouted.

"All right, we're going," Stephen said, dragging Zoey to the door where he'd already deposited Wendy.

"But this is —" Zoey started to say before the front door closed behind the three of them.

"I can't believe this. I've been at my wits end trying to figure out how to stop you when I couldn't find your mistletoe order. And ... and to think you just *forgot* about it!" Ms. Taylor's eyes blinked rapidly as tears began to well, her nose bright red. And then in a flash, she was gone, dashing back into the library.

"Evelyn!" Ms. Delaney shouted but didn't make a move to chase after her friend. Instead, she threw her head back and groaned, a thing I'd done dozens of times but felt odd to see an older woman do. "Well, at least she won't be causing any more trouble tonight. I assume you already scared off her niece, right?"

"Uh-huh."

"Then you're good to go. I'll handle Evelyn."

"No," I said, surprising everyone, including myself. "I'll talk to her."

"Are you sure?" Margo asked, pulling at my hand as I moved to follow Taylor.

"I'm with Margo," Bailey added. "She's caused a lot of trouble over nothing. She gave like half the town food poisoning."

"Oh, no. That wasn't Evelyn. That was that Hux boy. Margo talking about community made Evelyn cry, so I was able to talk her out of dumping glue in the popcorn.

"We absolutely *cannot* tell Wendy that." Margo said in a horrified whisper and we all hummed in agreement.

"It's just a chat. I feel bad for her. Y'all go see if anybody needs help with last minute set up. Particularly with the frozen gazebo steps." I squeezed Margo's hand and went through the main doors into the library.

Our library wasn't huge by any means, but when I looked around at all the shelves, I was worried it'd take me a while to find Taylor. But it turned out she was a sniffly crier. After grabbing a box of tissues from the front desk, I followed her cries to the romance section. I sat on the ground next to Ms. Taylor, a woman who legitimately used to terrify me as a child, and held out the tissues.

She snatched the box from my hands.

"What're you doing here? Don't you and your friends hate me," Ms. Taylor scoffed, voice cracking.

"Nah. Well, Ashley definitely hates you. But you can't really blame her, that betting board was a shit thing to do." The betting board in question was over when Ashley and Mason would get together and it was up for three whole years.

"Fat load of good that did me. I ended up with nothing. Just like everything else I do lately."

"Look, I'm sorry about the mistletoe thing. Ashley kind of egged us on about taking over for you and making a big deal of things. Margo found it and that's kinda it. Like, beyond Ashley having a, understandable, vendetta against you, Margo and

I were too busy keeping the events on to bother with that. Seriously, the amount of shit you plan for December is outrageous. I don't know how you do it on your own."

"Pft. You've done fine. No one cares that I'm not the one running things, so long as they get done. Ungrateful is what it is. I've been running things for nearly 30 years. That craft show was completely my doing. Mine. And it just went on without me. How long will it take for everybody to forget about me when I die? A year? A season?"

"Oh, so this is an existential crisis?" I said, leaning my head back against the bookshelf. Is this what it would have been like to have grandparents you actually talked to? Weird behavior spurred on by their fear of getting closer to death? "You know, I didn't get a chance to be close to my grandparents, so I don't have much experience in the what happens when I die conversations."

"Har har," Ms. Taylor huffed.

"But nobody is gonna forget you. I mean, for one, I assume your will has several demands including a parade and federal holiday."

"I've considered it," she murmured.

"Plus, it's not that nobody has forgotten about you and we moved on with our lives. We were literally told not to bother you by your family. How're you even here anyways? Your granddaughter made it sound like you were under lock and key."

"Tsk. Chelsea likes to exaggerate. She invited herself to my last doctor's appointment and asked about a bunch of nonsense. I'm fine."

"Sounds like she really cares about you." I nudged Ms. Taylor's knee with mine and she grumbled. It was kind of sad seeing her like this. And for that reason, and definitely not because I hadn't prepared for it, I made her an offer. "Why don't you do the speech for tonight? Like a big hurrah that you're in good health?"

"Well … I couldn't …" Taylor drawled, her eyes glazing over as she thought about the possibility of a surprise return. It was the exact kind of shit she loved.

"You'd be the talk of the town. We'll take care of all the management stuff and you get to bask in the glory. I mean, when's the last time you actually got to enjoy a festival?"

"If you put it that way …"

"Then you should hurry." I pulled my phone out to check the time, dismissing several text messages from the girls. "You've got 15 minutes till you go on."

"All right." Ms. Taylor stood, took a few steps, then looked back at me. "You're sure?"

"I'm sure. You deserve the applause, you work hard for this town."

Ms. Taylor was silent for so long, I thought she was going to argue with me. Maybe even admit that I'd done a shit ton of work this month, a lot of it unnecessary because she didn't share information on how things go or literally got in my way.

But in the end, that's not who Ms. Taylor was.

She gave me a curt nod and walked away without a word. Leaving me alone in the quiet library that reminded me of Margo.

Part of me wanted to be hopeful. She'd come out to her parents. She'd come out to Bailey. She held my hand. All those things pointed to her taking me back.

But then I thought about how I was such a dick last night. How she asked me to wait and I flat out denied her. How I let my fear speak over her feelings.

The lights of the library flickered and I took that as my sign to face the music. Good or bad, Margo deserved the chance to say her peace.

When I rounded the shelves, I saw Ms. Delaney at the front desk, frowning at a cup of something steaming.

"I think somebody's slipped rum into this," she murmured.

"Not me this time," I said, hands up. During high school, it was a bit of a tradition to see who could slip something into the hot chocolate or punch or whatever seasonal drink there was at the festival. What I didn't know back then was that they kept a spare barrel under the tables to replace the drink once the kids' had their fun.

"Hmm." Ms. Delaney sat against the desk, quietly looking through the glass doors towards the gazebo. "You did a nice thing there, Ms. White. Letting her do the speech. She's not gonna shut up it about for months."

"Ha. Well at least this way she's staying out of trouble." I shrugged, then gave her a tight nod before heading to the door.

"You know," she said and I turned back to look at her. "All the couples I've caught making out in this library have had happy marriages."

"Like the mistletoe tradition?" I said through a tense laugh.

"It has a better track record." She shrugged. "But I am a little partial to you and Margo staying together. If she has a reason to stay in town, she can take over the library and I can finally retire."

"Ha!" I threw my head back and laughed. "Sure. I'll see what I can do about that. Good night, Ms. Delaney."

"Good night, Ms. White. Happy holidays."

56

MARGO

When Ms. Taylor stepped up to the microphone in front of the gazebo, somehow managing to avoid all the unthawed steps, it was like a TV gasp was played in surround sound. Loud and exaggerated.

But in comparison to Ashley's reaction, the crowd seemed quite reasonable.

"What the absolute fuck?" she screamed, taking a few steps forward before Mason materialized and wrapped an arm around her stomach.

"Sorry, sweetheart. Not gonna let you pick fights today. It's Christmas."

"Exactly! It's Christmas and that bitch made life hell for Shea all month," Ashley argued. She tried to pry Mason's arm off of her, but he held tight.

"Right, but it's not our decision to get revenge or not. Shea said to let her do the welcome speech, so we're gonna let her do the welcome speech."

After Shea and Ms. Taylor had their chat, Ms. Taylor came out of the library with her head held high and started barking orders at us. All the other townsfolk followed along, but it wasn't until Shea texted us to go along with it that our group chipped in.

Since then though, we hadn't heard a peep from Shea. And across the 15 or so minutes it's been, I'd asked the girl group no less than 20 times if we should go check on her. Each time they shrugged or said they'd check with her and then sent me off to take care of something else.

"Bailey, do you think —" I started, turning to my sister as Ms. Taylor's speech began. But Bailey put a hand on my arm and pointed me towards the Christmas tree. Shea stood by the tree, kicking at the ground, hands in her pockets.

Without thinking, I ditched everybody and ran to her. I reached the tree, out of breath and unsure what to do with my hands. I wanted to hug her. I held her hand in the library, but that was ... that was probably just happenstance. It was a weird situation and she needed support. Not even my support, probably, just support. And if I reached out for her now and she brushed off the touch, I wouldn't be able to get the words I needed to say out.

"Shea, I'm sorry I didn't —"

"What?" she interrupted, hands flopping, still in her pockets. "Why're you sorry? I'm sorry. I didn't think you'd do the hard thing for me, so I bailed. I didn't even let you speak, I just —"

"But I should've fought for you! I should've been more assertive about wanting to come out. But I saw how hurt you were by everything and I —"

"I was just scared that if I asked you to come out, you'd realize I'm not worth that kind of trouble."

"Of course you are!" I grabbed Shea's arms and shook her a little. "You're more than worth coming out for. I —fuck, I'm sorry I didn't make that clear before. But you're worth the difficult and uncomfortable parts of life. *Keeping* you in my life is worth any kind of trouble."

Shea's eyes, which were red and puffy from crying, brightened and a smile pulled up her lips.

"Are we seriously arguing over who's insecurities are to blame for this?" Shea asked through a shaky laugh.

"Well, you started it." I was half laughing, half crying, still holding onto Shea's arms.

"Yeah. I'm sorry," Shea whispered before pulling me into a hug. The embrace was tight, Shea's hands shaking as she gripped my sweater to hold me closer. I moved my hands from her arms to wrap around her waist and poured just as much into the hug.

"So that means we're together again, right?" Shea murmured into my hair. I pulled back, or at least as much as Shea's hold would let me, and pulled Shea's gift out of my skirt pocket.

"This might answer your question," I told her. Shea raised an eyebrow but let go of me with a grumble and tore off the paper. My heart was in my ears the whole time Shea opened the gift and when the box lid fell to the ground and the necklace with my initial was revealed, my heart stopped altogether.

"*Call It What You Want,*" Shea whispered, tears forming at the corner of her eyes.

"Yeah. And I *want* to call you my girlfriend. If that's all right. And if that bad attempt at a joke wasn't a turn-off." My nervous giggles were immediately smothered by Shea's lips.

"This is fucking perfect, babe. Shit. I need to get you one too. What store do you think is open right now?" Shea looked over my head and around the town like the perfect shop would just pop up. Laughing, I took the box from Shea's hands and removed the necklace to put it on her. Once the clasp shut tight, Shea's finger wrapped around the M, centering it along her collarbone. The image settled my heart, a visual confirmation that Shea and I were together. It also set my heart on fire, I was practically drooling at the thought of kissing around the necklace, following it down and then lower.

"Don't look at me like that, babe. This is a family event."

"Like what?" I asked, trying to blink away the desire.

"Like you want this," Shea said with a chuckle before pulling me into a long, deep kiss. She licked into my mouth and I immediately opened for her, moaning at the sensation of our tongues touching. But before I could really enjoy it, she pulled back. "See?"

"Get a room!" somebody shouted a little ways off and I turned to see Zoey with her hands cupped around her mouth and the rest of our friends gawking at me and Shea. Shea took my hand, squeezed, then walked us over to join everybody.

"It's so cute," Bailey squealed, squeezing Rosie's hand and jumping up and down.

"Wait, since when have they been together?" Olivia asked.

"Since the tree incident, right?" Roxie said, looking over at Shea and I then tapping her neck. My face instantly heated and I looked down to the ground to avoid everyone's eyes.

"Does this mean you'll do Christmas with us now?" Bailey asked, hoping over to the other side of Shea.

"Uh." Shea turned to me, a question in her raised eyebrow.

"Mom will literally throw a fit if we're dating and you still decline her open invitation to come over for Christmas."

"She will," Bailey affirmed.

"Plus she's making a whole gay themed breakfast now. And since I came out for you, it's only fair you have to deal with that too." At that, Shea pinched my stomach but nodded.

"Sure. I guess it's time for my first Hartley Christmas."

57

SHEA

I don't know what I expected Christmas with the Hartleys to be like. Awkward probably. Like I was out of place or a third wheel.

But of course that wasn't the case.

As soon as I came over on Christmas Eve, I was handed a set of flannel pajamas and a Christmas romper to wear the next morning. There was cookie decorating and board games and holiday movies. And then on Christmas morning, Estelle forced us all to sit on the stairs in our matching PJs for a family picture before we each opened presents from "Santa".

It was a quintessential family Christmas, the happy ending of every holiday Hallmark movie, the type of Christmas I had been missing out on. And as we were settling down for the evening, me and Margo cuddled up on the couch, her dad in his armchair, her mom in the kitchen, and Bailey and Greg on the floor putting together a puzzle, I realized this could have been my holidays the whole time. This place had been open for me and I'd been too scared to take it just in case it would fall apart too.

Fuck, had I been stupid.

"You wanna put on another movie or something?" Margo asked, looking up from her book for the first time since the last movie was put on a few hours ago. I pulled Margo closer, resituating us so my back was on the arm of the couch and she was between my legs.

"Nah, I'm good with the quiet actually."

"Really?"

I looked around at the peaceful living room then back at Margo, smiling.

"Yeah, really."

Margo shuffled up and pressed a soft, quick kiss on my lips before settling back down.

"You know, Ms. Delaney pulled me aside after Eve-Eve Fest and offered me a job," Margo mentioned casually, like we were just making run-of-the-mill conversation.

"Mmm, she might've mentioned something about wanting you to take over." I toyed at the bottom hem of her flannel, nervousness and excitement bubbling over inside me. I knew Margo and I could make things work if she decided to move out of Snowfall, it'd be hard, but doable. That said, if she did decide to take Delaney up on that offer ...

"I told her I'd consider it if my girlfriend was still willing to let me move in with her." Again, her words were so casual, but this time Bailey processed them and dropped the puzzle piece she was holding to scramble over to the couch.

"What? Are you serious? You're moving in together?" she asked, wide-eyed.

"What?" Margo's mom repeated from the kitchen before coming out with two large bowls of popcorn.

"Hmm, that's nice, dear. Be sure to still come over for brunch sometimes, they mean a lot to your mother," her dad said without looking up from his tablet.

"Bill! Did you know about this?" Estelle asked before one of the popcorn bowls thunked onto the coffee table.

"Well, no. But the term U-haul lesbian is popular for a reason, right?"

"Dad!" Bailey shouted, turning to chastise her father while Margo and I burst into a puddle of giggles.

Once our laughter died and while the rest of the family argued over whether or not it was harmful or justified to call me a U-haul lesbian, Margo turned in my arms to look at me.

"So?" she asked, head tilted so a curl fell over her face. I tucked it away before sliding my hands into her hair and pulling her close so I could kiss her forehead.

"Yeah, I think I could be convinced."

"Convinced?" she repeated, eyebrows knitting together.

"Sure. I mean, if you're willing to pick up my cups, then I could be convinced."

Margo snorted before collapsing into my chest and squirming her arms under me for a hug.

"I'll happily pick up after all your cups and anything else," Margo murmured as she nuzzled into me.

"Best Christmas ever," I whispered back, placing another kiss on Margo's forehead and feeling truly at home for the first time in too many years. All thanks to the underfunded library system in NYC.

K.E. Monteith is an anxious hot mess that writes about people like her fall in love and get spicy. You'll usually find her talking about her dogs, complaining about chronic pain, or screaming about something DropOut related or her current hyper fixation.

Sign up for her newsletter for bonus scenes, giveaways, and more.

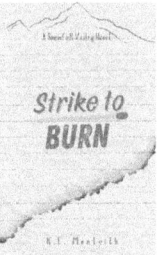

Milton Keynes UK
Ingram Content Group UK Ltd.
UKHW021454121124
2788UKWH00002B/3